The End of All Our Labors

Potassium Cockburn

The End of All Our Labors

Cover design by: Pski's Porch

ISBN-13: 978-0692506165
ISBN-10: 0692506160

for more books, visit Pski's Porch:
www.pskisporch.com

Printed in U.S.A.

- For Comfortina -

Eternity is a long time to continue Numbering, and the Eye a Wide and Comprehensive Artist: it will take a Million at a time, and Adde twenty Millions in a moment. To continue this is Addition and Multiplication to all Eternity is an Endless Work, and yet the Soul will never be cloydd nor Opprest with Numbers. In realitie they fill no room: but in the Mind are Spiritual. Lest therfore there should be an Endless Progression; all that the Soul can take in by Degrees, were it to Reckon by its own Powers to all Eternitie, it shall receiv in an Instant, and from the Beginning to the End attain all immediately. For indeed All from the Beginning to the End is the END, of all our Labors and Desires, of all our Powers faculties and Inclinations, of all our Thanksgivings and Enjoyments.

—*Thomas Traherne*

to be naked for a little while
in the very jaws of time
is all that I am asking
of this mad world.
Listen:
silence is playing like an orchestra.

—*Chris Wallace-Crabbe*

Chapter 1

I remember the explosion. I remember turning toward the Facility just before a great *whoomp* and blast of light and heat sent me flying. Then, nothing, until I woke up here. I have no idea where "here" is, and thought at first that Paulie had actually succeeded, that I was in a different multiverse, since everyone here wears a tight, shiny, black mask that covers their faces from eye to collar, with a small grill or speaker in the center that must allow them to breathe, and perhaps to speak, though none of them said anything, at first. Then one of them brought me a speakeasy, and spoke, clear American English, and told me things would go better for me if I "told what I knew." I should be grateful, I now have something to occupy my time, the glow of the speakeasy interface hovering above the metal table beside my cot, a gentle blue turquoise hologram of an ear waiting for my words to tickle it and set the colors rippling.

I should be grateful, but to whom? Paulie failed, obviously, I'm still on the same rotting planet we tried to leave behind, and now I'm in some sort of prison, guarded by men with imposing masks. Could they be medical devices, prostheses? The air is fine, stale, but I breathe freely enough. I count three guards, one is shorter, one is very broad in the hips, one has a slight limp, all have very severe military haircuts. They bring me food, bland and soft and of vaguely recognizable flavor, and lukewarm water, and they take me down the hall to a toilet when I ring the bell beside the door. Aside from the door to the toilet and the door to my cell, there is one other door, at the end of the hall, through which I assume the masked ones enter and exit. I have a bed, a chair, a table, no obvious conduits in or out of the room, I'm not even sure how they pump in air and regulate temperature, but regular it is. Oh, and my slippers. I have no clothes, but I do have a pair of cheap plastic slippers. They were the first thing I saw when I awoke, three, five, seven days ago, I can't tell. This is my life, then, the room, the masked guards, the toilet, this speakeasy. It glows an angry umber when I say "speakeasy," as though it hates reminders of its own existence. So, I suppose there is nothing more to do but to tell them what they want to know, the way they want me to, but I don't really know what they want, tell what I know, tell what I know, I know so many things. I assume they mean about the Facility, and why it's now a pile of slag. If my augments were operative, this would go much faster. I guess shutting down net access is just another wall of my cell. Then again, maybe it's better that I don't go so fast, that I can't just compose and archive to whatever address the speakeasy must dump into. I haven't used a speakeasy since I was running my college scripts. But the longer I take, the longer I live, I think that's the contract I'm operating under.

§

So what's to tell? I'm not sure if the world has gone off the rails, or if I have, or both. I know that I believed, years ago, that we were, all of us, on the edge of a precipice, that humanity was falling to ruin. I know that I was not alone in that belief, it was endemic, in the refugee camps and the favelas and the towers and everywhere in between. I remember, still a child, when the first camps were set up in Illinois and Ohio, when the first pandemics ripped through them, when we had to leave the city and go to another city in a train that smelled of sick, and then I remember seeing the first feeds on the net of bulldozers pushing bodies into a hole. This is what happened in our world, did the same thing happen here, wherever "here" is? Is this the kind of story my captors want? Or is it me, somehow, is there some secret knowledge encoded in my life, in these words, that I'm not even conscious of? Something they did to me at the Facility, or even before, something Gardiner lodged in all of us, or maybe he didn't even know what he was putting there. But I won't talk of that, I cannot, I signed a contract. Listen, speakeasy: I don't know where I am, or what I am supposed to say, but I have to keep saying it or I believe they will kill me. I don't know why I believe this, they haven't threatened me. They haven't said anything except "tell what I knew," and that, in a cell surrounded by men in masks, is threat enough.

§

Here's something, then: my mother. My mother was a force of nature, a squat, strong woman with a skull like a boulder and hair that clung to her head, a dark and certain moss. And then, my father: a tall, long-limbed man who moved like liquid, like oil, since he was so dark. And my grandparents, should I tell you about them? Would the knowledge my gran-papa tried to instill in me by cutting a chicken's neck to call Papa Legba help get me out of this room somehow? I doubt it. I tap tap tap on the walls, and no one taps back, I scratch myself, I talk to the speakeasy, and wait for a masked, mute guard to bring me food, or take me to the toilet. At least the toilet is in a different room. There are cameras there, of course, just like there are cameras here, watching me, just like every tap tap tap surely is recorded and analyzed. Hello! Hello! I can't see you, but I know you're there. I don't know what you want from me, which makes it very hard to give to you.

§

When the man with the limp came to bring me to the toilet, I asked him: "What do you want me to say to that thing," I pointed at the speakeasy, "and when I have told you what I know, what will happen?" He didn't even shrug, only waited for me to walk out the door of my cell. When I returned, he stopped in the doorway before bolting me in and spoke: "Someone will be here to answer your questions." These were the first words I'd heard spoken by another person in some while, and my mind had trouble processing them at first, a jumble of noises. Then I grew excited, despite myself. I have already resolved that they will kill me. Well, my little good angel has resolved thus, my *gros bon ange* is still strong and will probably fight until both big and little sail away together.

I've always been that way, a head ready to surrender in a body that never will. Does that entertain you, Mr. Speakeasy? I hadn't thought about my grandparent's faith in a long time, until I took the job and went to the Facility, and now I can think of little else, but I cannot articulate what it is I am remembering, flash and image, flash and sound. Being trapped in a tiny cell with a blue holographic ear for company does that too you, I suppose. Just as such confinement makes a brusque statement from a masked guard excite my mind like a child at Christmas, a lover watching the plane carrying his beloved taxi into the gate. Not that I would know much about that kind of love, of course, except that as an observer, I know more about it than almost anyone.

§

The man came, the man who would answer my questions, and he did and he didn't answer them, he is a slippery one, from his smile to his gleaming black shoes that squeaked on the floor of my cell. I will try to remember what he said, though of course it has been recorded already, but I have no access to the speakeasy controls, it is always on and always listening and that's that, no playback, no recall. But, what he told me, Mr. Deebs did, as that is his name, was to rest and then try to remember what we'd talked about. A kind of test of my memory, he said. See, I remembered that, your name and your instructions, do I get some pharma now? Ah, petulance, my little good angel is stirring. Very well, Mr Deebs, here is what I remember:

I was dozing, the half-sleep of prisoners, when I heard the door locks clacking. I knew it would be you, somehow, and not just another guard. Sorry, I knew it would be Mr. Deebs. Not to use "you," I understand. I think I understand, it was part of the list of rules, the memory test. Mr. Deebs was smiling, and he looked very like an albino crocodile, but was not himself an albino, just very, very white, with pale orange hair glistening on his head. The smile that would eat you, that was the crocodile part, but then he spoke, "may I come in?," as though it were my spacious new penthouse flat in Jefferson Towers he wanted to visit, and the crocodile changed into a maître d'. He sat on the chair, I on the bed, and we both drank tea that the guard behind Mr. Deebs was carrying in a can.

"Mr. Duval, how are you feeling?" his voice was soothing, low in register, but insistent.

"I feel like I am in prison."

"Yes, well, you are being held separate for now, for your own protection. I am Mr. Deebs," he nodded, and I felt myself nodding back. He sipped his tea, glancing around the room.

"We really should be able to do better than this, in terms of furnishings, but our, ah, resources are very taxed as late. What could I get you, what might make your stay more pleasant?"

"I would like to leave."

"I understand, but of course, you must know that the destruction of the former Tailwind Comm Bunker falls under the definition of terrorist activity, under the 2057 Homeland Security II protocol?"

"I didn't destroy it." I had some of my tea, then, I believe. I remember it was quite good, a hint of mint and some kind of soy milk.

"No? Well, that's the kind of information we can use, certainly! I assume you have some idea who did destroy it, and as part of the Gardiner Group, you must know a lot about how it was destroyed. We are very interested in how it was destroyed, you see. Seismometers a thousand miles away detected the blast, and when we arrived, we found an extremely large hole, some stray bits of rebar and the like, and you. How, exactly, did you people extract a square mile chunk of property—most of it underground, mind you—from the planet, and leave little more than a bit of trash and some angry earthworms?"

It was at this point I realized Paulie might have succeeded after all. And what that means, Mr. Deebs, I cannot tell you, even if I wanted to. I could form my mouth around the words, and they wouldn't come out. I know, I've tried. I told you as much, and you nodded, I expect you knew already about the Confidentiality block, and that you couldn't hack it without melting my brain, making it useless to everyone, complete ontological incoherence. So, you let me ask you some questions, bless your dark little heart.

"Where am I?" That seemed fair enough, I thought.

"Ah, of course, you are in the Paris Detention Camp, Paris, Missouri. Roughly 570 miles from Tailwind."

"And you think me a terrorist?"

"I don't know what to think of you, Mr. Duval, but it is my job to figure out how to think about you, and what you know, and what you think you know. Information extraction is very tricky business."

One of the guards came in at that point, and must have messaged Deebs something through his ments.

"Where is your mask, Mr. Deebs?"

"Ah, yes, well, too many faces spoil the broth, really, they will hinder your ability to remember accurately. Also, the masks the guards wear are now standard issue for all NAS troops, since the SGN launched nanovirus attacks last March. We had to screen your body for two weeks before we could be sure you weren't a virus seed." He smiled again, more crocodile this time, I think.

"The SinoGanra Nexus? I watched the feed, the Lahore virus, they blasted each other into dust, total annihilation, desertification of the Himalayas—" I stopped. Something awful occurred to me, something I couldn't quite place, but which was awful nonetheless.

"Afraid not. That might be preferable to what they've loosed on us, and on the world, actually. They can't control the L-class viruses anymore, lost control almost immediately. They are fairly easy to protect against, luckily, and easy to immunize, except they keep mutating, I'm told, though with each mutation, the effects become less harmful. Really annoying. Makes it very hard to entertain."

I realized he was trying to joke, but I felt a place in my head darkening, the things I was trying to realize were struggling against the Confidentiality block, my neurons shifting around it... lights swam before my eyes.

"Are you alright, Mr. Duval?"

"No, no, not really..."

When I woke you were gone. How did I do? Did I remember everything correctly? It's been three days now. Am I useless? Why won't you come back, please, Mr. Deebs, anyone, my brain is fracturing, I can feel it pulling apart, like tectonic plates, groaning and straining against each other.

§

I'm not going to follow your rules anymore, Deebs. No more trying to polish and clarify every detail, all that has passed. But I do need to tell what happened, in case these are the last words my dutiful little ear gets to parse, and I know it will just be stored in some jar of foam somewhere, with countless other testimonies—how many subjects have undergone this procedure again, Deebs? You claimed a 32% success rate, but how many subjects did you grind through before getting the that number? How many did you have to kill? And what do you consider "success"?

Focus, Manny. Here's what it is: Deebs came again, three days after the first visit. I know it was three days because he told me, and I was asleep most of those three days because they put pharma in my food. I know that because, again, he told me. He told me because there was no reason not to, we both know the Confidentiality block is failing, and that it will destroy large chunks of my brain matter as it fails, and sedatives can help slow the process a bit. According to Deebs, there is only one way to dissolve the block: an overlay to my existing augment that can overwrite the encryption of the block. When I joined Gardiner Group and the FD project, I got a new kind of ment, everyone did, nanobots injected through the hard port that rebuilt the existing, garden variety augments we all had. I had never heard of such a thing. Like most people, I had the trepan-and-drape ment operation 20 or so years ago: drill a small hole in the skull, pop the folded ment in the hole, then unfold and drape it onto the surface of the brain, voilà, augmented reality without having to wear those stupid lenses, which always made my eyes itch. And, like everyone else, I had a hard port on my neck for gaming and vids and the like, but after the Gardiner bots were done with my head, well, the hard port was all but obsolete. I know this because Deebs told me, and I don't know how he knew all this, but he knew it, and as he told me, I knew it too, and if it weren't for the sedatives, I'm sure I would have passed out and maybe had a stroke, since every piece of knowledge he gave me butted against the Confidentiality block, made it chitter angrily.

§

So, I have two choices, says Deebs: let them put me on an operating table and inject me with a nanoviral overlay that will rewrite the encryption, or die a shuddering mess, brain goo slopping out my ears. Wonderful. And how does the virus work, I asked, and Deebs got very excited, his fingers started clicking against each other. Apparently, to remove the encryption, I have to relive the experience the block is preventing me from recalling, and what do you know, Deebs has a way to plug into my hard port and record the whole thing. What luck.

I am going to eat this dry little cake they've given me now, I so wish I had a danish instead, and presumably enough sedative is contained therein that I won't wake until after the procedure, unless I don't wake at all. And if that happens, well, please know that I found much of life very curious, and much very sad. I don't believe anyone will ever read this, because I don't believe humanity will survive much longer. We have fouled this planet beyond repair, and we kill each other on a whim. I once hoped our fate would be otherwise, now I only hope it happens quickly. Good night.

Chapter 2

[Subject 336136 responding well to keriport application of decryption lattice. Begin recording]

Most people hate applying for employment contracts. I actually find it interesting, the whole process is a weird dance, and no one is very good at it, so part of my interest comes from watching people try to cover up their awkwardness. Every once in a while, you meet someone who really can do the dance, and that was what struck me about Ms. Bye. Her hair was middle-parted, in acquiescence to fashion, but still curly, in defiance of it, and she chewed the tip of her stylus and touched her nose occasionally and folded and refolded her ankles beneath the desk as she screened my résumé, her every movement choreographed, intentional. Even as her eyes flicked back and forth while viewing my work history, hovering somewhere over the flat black sheen of her desk, her halo stayed green and impassive. She was either exceptionally good at halo suppression or she wore some kind of colorizer, very expensive, but very useful for someone in a job like hers. I was thrown by the fact that she had, thus far, ignored the yellow envelope at the corner of her desk. One of the prime reasons I'd decided to apply at Gardiner Group was the fact that they asked for a hard copy of my résumé, something I hadn't seen in at least 10 years, and that Ms. Bye was using her ments and not looking in the dutifully prepared envelope of smart paper I'd prepared was very disappointing.

"Very good, very interesting..." she was leading the dance, of course, I had to follow, and now she was gripping my shoulder a bit more tightly, announcing her intention to perform a turn or dip in the next few seconds. She flicked her stylus in the direction of the desk and refocused her eyes on me.

"An exceptional record, Mr. Duval. Your credentials are spotless, your experience wide ranging, and your references sparkle, though all express some regret that you did not choose to stay with them. You are something of a rover, yes?" She crossed her legs at the knee and reclined slightly. A turn.

"I find that I need more of a challenge, so I move on, having fulfilled my obligations."

"Yes, a challenge, yes." Her eyes flicked again, perhaps someone was messaging her. She stood, picked up the envelope containing the hologram of my résumé, and put it in a small tray on a stand beside her desk. The tray dropped, the envelope vanished.

"I think you will find," she said, sitting back down, "that the Gardiner Group will provide you all the challenge you need. We are a very dynamic firm, about to engage on a project of great scale and importance. This project requires the very best team, and will demand a great deal from them." A small orange light blinked in the bottom corner of my vision. She had sent me something, but hadn't told me to open it yet. She was twirling me, I think.

"The overview I've sent you describes the require-ments of the position, and provides a mission state-ment. Of course, we can't go into great detail, a project of this scope requires tight security. Please, go home, read through our offer, then come back on Thursday, and I will answer any further questions you might have. Is 10 o'clock again good for you?" She glazed, searching her calendar. I did the same, though I knew my calendar was an empty field.

"Yes, 10 is fine."

"Very good," she rose and nodded, then swiped the door open. As I turned to leave, she called to me, her voice suddenly just louder than a hush. "And, Mr. Duval?"

I turned back and raised my eyebrows.

"It goes without saying: please do not divulge any of the contents of the package I've sent you. The confiden-tiality form you signed when applying for the position is actionable, and we are very serious about it."

"Of course." Then I *really* wanted to know what was in the files she'd sent.

§

I waited until I got home to open them, fighting the urge to view them on the monorail. The effort required to do so was physical, I had to clench my mind shut, I'm sure I was walking like I had to use the toilet, so I disembarked early, hoping an open air walk would help me focus. Some culchies hooted from the favela as I walked past and I nearly lost it, they must have seen the neuter thread in my halo. I really thought we'd grown beyond such primitive attitudes, but they were culchies, I felt bad for them more than anything. My grandparents were displaced, refugees after their home in Port-au-Prince was washed away in a mudslide, and they told me what a struggle it was then, how it was all the more difficult now. They'd come to New York when there still was a city, before the seawater and hurricanes pushed everyone inland, up-state, away. I think I can remember the store, the shop they ran, but I was only three when we had to evacuate and come to Albany. My memories of it and their stories about it are the same, I suppose. So, my memories are of the cleanest, busiest bodega and religious supply shop in all of Harlem, selling bottles of beer beside orisha dolls, bags of chips with enemy-be-gone gris gris.

My father was a typical first generation immigrant kid: hard working, but more interested in assimilating than in learning the old ways. I never met my mother's parents, they both died soon after reaching the US, leaving her to be raised by my Aunt, who'd been here for 20 years by the time her sister and brother-in-law appeared on her doorstep. That is likely why my mother assimilated more quickly than my father, and was, not doubt, part of what attracted him to her. In the close-knit Haitian immigrant community, the pressure to marry within the group was strong, and she was about as distinct from her peers as one could get while remaining part of the tribe. Manman dressed like an American kid, worked like a Haitian, and was stunningly, almost painfully beautiful, how could Papa resist?

Well, he didn't, she did, and the story of their courting

is mythical in scope. That they only managed one child, myself, and a neuter besides, surely struck them, and everyone they knew, as a terribly ineffectual denoument to their story, but if they felt that way, they never let it fall on me. They were as strict as every Haitian parent, as demanding and inflexible, and they celebrated all my successes and adherence to their rules admirably. They loved me, in short, and I understand how lucky I am in that regard. I do not wish they were still alive, for their deaths were both quick and relatively painless, and for that, too, I am grateful, but I do find myself crying, a little, when I sit in granmè's chair, or fiddle with Papa's old digifiles, the scrapbook of his patients—I still have his scanner, even, though of course no one uses them anymore, and I would be in enormous difficulty if I did try to diagnose someone with it, all kinds of flags would go off if I even turned it on myself. So I just touch it, and remember, and sit in granmè's chair where she did all her bidding from, before augments and ports, back in the days of gesture interface and keypads.

I hear there are people that collect old medical tek, black market stuff, of course, but I'd be too scared to even think about trying to find someone like that, and anyway, they're keepsakes, that's the point. When I recieved my Médecins thread, my halo shining golden, I felt Papa's presence, and I knew that while he would not have truly understood what had happened to old jobs, to doctors and nurses and aides, he would have shone too, even without a halo. I remember trying to tell him what a halo was, how all the different tags and threads you gathered, or that other entities saddled you with, were woven together above your head and glowed various colors, depending on your current socioemotional state. When I got my Médecins thread, pure gold for nearly two days; when I was blamed for the fire in the dispensary on my first work assignment, shit-colored, until I cleared my name. "It's just your meeple index," he laughed, and I tried to explain how much more complex a metric it was than that old curio, how much more interesting to watch it shimmer and change while you spoke with other people, when you missed a monorail, when the rain started and you had no umbrella. He was not tek averse, but he had no use for augments, and certainly not for a hard port, though he did pay for mine, I would never have gotten into a good school without one. It was good that he died before they outlawed so much of the old tek. So, I keep his scanner in the closet, along with a few other things that might get my Médecins thread revoked if they were discovered, and only take them out when I set my augment to incognito.

I was tempted to go incognito before opening the files Ms. Bye had sent, but too many incognitos in a short span of time is a flag, and if whatever she sent is really that sensitive, then it must have a built in flag or two as well. So. granmè's chair, a little bag of chardonnay, and now: what have you sent me, dear Ms. Bye?

Welcome to the Gardiner Group!
"We Will Be What We Will Be"

Greetings, prospective Gardiner Group Partner. Working with Gardiner Group is the second most rewarding thing an individual can do with their life. The first is for you to decide. Everyone who works with the Gardiner Group is considered a Partner, because we all decide What We Will Be together. Because We all decide together, We have a great responsibility to each other, to help one another become What We Will Be. Because We are responsible to one another, We must trust each other with many types of proprietary information. To proceed with this application, you must accept a Confidentiality Agreement, sortie 6.3.21. To accept, signal "Yes." To decline, signal "no."

You can alway tell the quality of an organization by the style deployed in their employment documents. This was top notch stuff, clear, paced to my heart rate, even the music was just right, light but intricate.

Thank you for acceding to Confidentiality Agreement, sortie 6.3.21. Breaking the terms of this agreement is actionable.

The rest of the batch was standard stuff, but again, very well produced. The overall number of Confidentiality Agreements, five, was intriguing, two was fairly standard, so they must be working on something very interesting indeed. I assumed there would be a pretty serious Agreement sealing the project and position descriptions, and indeed there was:

Thank you for your continued interest in the Gardiner Group. To access the Main Function/Employment Definition Map, please signal your acceptance of Confidentiality Agreement, sortie 26.111.35. To accept, signal "yes." To decline, signal "no."

Now, I like to think of myself as something of a job connoisseur. I've had 13 of them, and have applied for more than 100. I had never heard of sortie 26.111.35, and it took a little digging on the net to find a summary, and I still wasn't sure quite what it meant. If I signaled "yes," I was agreeing to let the Gardiner Group "define, alter, and encrypt any or all portions of experience" they felt was propietary, and that my proximity to their security signal was somehow important—I think, if I tried to cut the signal, Gardiner Group could arrest and try me in their own court, since the agreement effectively rendered me a limited citizen of the Group. Serious stuff for sure, and I could find nothing else on the net about it, other than the summary.

I suspended the document and fetched another wine bag. Someone, Ms. Bye, or another HR evil genius type, knew I would be tortured by this situation. My curiosity I got from my Manman, as well as my love of style and glamour, and this was a glamorous pitch indeed, frightening and all the more alluring because of the danger. I didn't have to renounce my NAS citizenship to agree to subject myself to certain of Gardiner Group's laws, and though I felt little nationalistic pride for NortAmeriStat, nor did I desire losing those benefits such citizenship conveyed. And the vague phrasing, the "define, alter, and encrypt" language, well, that could mean just about anything, and I'm sure that was the point. It was like a most delicious species of candy, and I couldn't resist one more bite, though I couldn't tell what exactly I was tasting.

Thank you for acceding to Confidentiality Agreement, sortie 26.111.35. Breaking the terms of this agreement is actionable.

Then my door light flashed orange. Always just when I'm getting to the good part. I suspended the document and set the door to "open" on my retina scan. It was 2331, so it must be Kirkus knocking. I checked the outside feed, and sure enough, Kirkus stood outside, shifting from foot to foot, one hand on his cart. I sighed and let the door slide open.

"Chooga, Manny, whatta want ya some two-bit?" 15 years ago, when I first moved to this block, I found Kirkus scrounging in a waste funnel, fingers dangerously close to the blades. I tried to help him learn to speak more professionally for a few weeks, but he had no port, let alone ments, and so I never could raise him very far above feral. Even the culchies looked down on him, though if they knew his savant for fixing old tek, they surely would have dragged him into the favela and tied him to a pole and made him work for scraps. I bought junk from him once a week or so, just so he had some cash to keep his hands out of the waste funnels.

"Hello, Kirkus," I said, nodding and opening my palms flat in greeting. The intimation that he should emulate this behavior eluded him.

"Chooga, lookie see," he spun his cart around so it sat between us and began digging through it. Kirkus was a fine test of my patience. He stopped digging and peered at something he held hidden in his hand, then thrust it at me: a small grey box, 7.5 cm or so long, 2.5 wide, metallic sheen, but likely plastic, no discernable buttons or opticals. "Yessir, big shiner. 200, say?"

"Big shiner? I don't understand, and 200 is quite a bit for a little rectangle of plastic."

He stepped back, rubbed his thumb on one side, then on the other side in the opposite direction, and pointed the box at the wall. When he pressed the top of the box, a shockingly bright light burst out and lit the wall, the floor, the whole corner of the hallway.

"Ah, that is very nice indeed," I said. He smiled and pressed again, returning the hall to half-shadow. "Power?" I asked. He pointed upward. "Solar? May I see?" I held the box in may hand. Solar paint, it seemed, and not a scratch on it. Where he found these things I'll never know. I nodded, transferring the cash from my account to the extruder in the living room. He smiled again, his gums red as ever, palmed the chits, and gave a little half-wave before scuttling down the hall.

I put the light in my pocket and returned to my chair to continue the Gardiner doc.

Thank you for acceding to Confidentiality Agreement,

sortie 26.111.35. Breaking the terms of this agreement is actionable. To continue viewing the Project and Position Descriptions, signal "yes." To decline, signal "no."

On my "yes" signal, the words dissolved and reformed into a head, male, architecturally handsome, with burnished grey hair, a rocky chin, glinting brown eyes atop a nose that made you look in whatever direction it pointed. He was smiling. The music changed to a simple, subtle raga.

Welcome, Mr. Duval.

Tailored content, very nice, excellent quality stuff. I felt myself relaxing into the chair.

My name is Ivan Gardiner. I will assume that your application for employment with Gardiner Group indicates preliminary research with regards to our organization, and my person. Hence, I will dispense with a more formal overview of our activities. The Project for which you have applied, Facility Dàtóng I, is an exciting opportunity for you to explore your vocation as a Médecins 3.2 in a stimulating environment, as part of a team devoted to Becoming What We Will Become in the fullest sense of the term....

The hiccup when my job title was fed into the boilerplate was barely noticeable, I'm sure only connoisseurs would notice. I let my POV drift around the head, felt my body growing more and more relaxed. One of the best employment scripts I'd ever run, certainly, even if the project and duties were still almost totally obscure by the end. All I knew for certain was that I would be paid very, very well; that I would have to undergo one more personal interview; that a further Confidentiality Agreement was necessary, one that involved "proprietary adjustments" to my ments; and that I would be asked to move to a different part of the country for the duration of the project. Of course, none of that really mattered. They could have offered me half the salary and said I would have to spend the next three years on the Moon, and I would have said yes. That's how good the script was. I signaled "yes" to the final screen and scheduled my final personal interview for the next day, after lunch, giving myself enough time to get all the way up to Cohoes. I exited the script both giddy and supremely tranquil, and also wide awake. I tried porting a vid, found it dull, and lay in my chair until I drifted off, replaying the details of the Gardiner doc in my mind, as all archival footage had been scrubbed as soon as I scheduled the interview.

Chapter 3

The Gardiner Building in Cohoes was fitted with a white marble skin, but otherwise was curiously indecorous. The white marble aesthetic usually meant all kinds of friezes and faux columns and gewgaws, so the sheer flatness of the thirty story tower drew attention through its restraint. It looked a bit like a runway, when one stood at the front and stared upwards. The skin shimmered away at ground level, and I found I was standing to the left of the three glass doors, a disconcerting position given I'd followed the directions exactly—even now, the arrow hovering above the sidewalk pointed not to a door, but to the wall. Something was miscalibrated, and now was not the best time for my ments to go wobbly. I found my way to the security kiosk, got scanned and had my map updated, wobbly arrow and all. Floor 30, the top.

I didn't see any other people in the lobby, just a few cleaner bots scrubbing along. It was delicious, really, the empty, gleaming space, further evidence of real style. The elevator read my destination and let me off on the 30th floor, and the arrow pointed me left. The floors were faux turf, the walls hung with a kind of microbeaded curtain, a darker green flecked with brown, and gentle forest sounds played along with suggestions of harp. I was tempted to take off my shoes and rub my feet in the carpet, but I resisted. The final arrow turned left, and I found myself staring at a dead end, or at least a door that wouldn't activate. I touched the curtain, and it shivered, but no door appeared. Oh dear. I felt my heart begin to race: I'd run the full update two months ago, and had two smaller patches since then, surely that was enough to work out the kinks. I turned off the map and worked my way backwards, stopping every so often to see if a door would activate, touching the wall now and again, gritting my teeth. Soon, I was back at the elevator, so I walked on, stopping, touching, and all at once I turned a corner and a door appeared, curtain evaporating. It read me, opened, and I went through.

Inside was a chair, nothing else, and the walls were skinned white marble, just like the outside. I sat in the chair and waited. This part was, I thought, a little less impressive than the rest, clichéd, even. Then the floor fell away. My chair sat, hovered, over a field, causing me to grip the arms tightly, even as I knew it was unreal. I'd seen animated skins before, but never one of such high quality. A door opened in the wall I faced, and a short, rather rotund man in a cream colored suit walked out across the clouds. Another chair hovered behind him, and when he stopped, 6 feet from where I sat, so did his chair, and he sat. His head was round and soft, like a baby's, hairless save for wispy yellow eyebrows. He wore tiny glasses with wire frames—I expect the wires ran into micro-ports behind one or both ears. His eyes were also tiny, piggish behind the glasses, and his lips were slightly puckered.

"Nifty, huh?" he said, jerking a hand toward the floor.

"Ah, yes, nifty, indeed, very realistic."

"It's not a skin," he continued, folding his hands together in his lap carelessly.

"Pardon? How so?" I asked.

"Yes, that is interesting, huh? Got you there, I think." He touched his ear and the floor was once again cut white marble. He smiled, which made his mouth even smaller, oddly enough.

"I'm not sure I understand." I was quite sure, actually.

"Oh I'm sorry, whoopsie, I forgot—" the name "Ivan Gardiner" popped into view above his head. No halo, I noticed, and no extra tags or dongles, just his name, in silver embossed script.

"You are Mr. Gardiner?" I asked.

"That's what it says, right?" He tilted his head upwards, looking at the bottom of the script.

"Yes, it certainly does, yes. Well, hello sir, I am—"

"I know, Mr. Duval, of course I know, of course. I watched you arrive, excellent job on the misdirect, by they way. Some people just get back on the elevator and leave. One man started crying and fell on the floor." He granted himself a small giggle. I was about to speak when it dawned on me: the map glitch was intentional, a test. I felt a warm flush in my cheeks. What a fine touch, I thought. I nodded, and waited for him to continue. He put his finger in his mouth and dug at a molar, then continued.

"The floor is not a skin, it's a small alteration we made to your augmentation, one that allows for other, even more neat effects, like full small room animation. It was part of what you signed off on with sortie 26.111.35. Very limited, of course, parlor trickery, simply intended to show you what we might accomplish, should you decide to join Project FD."

"FD?" My mind sat hollow, dumbfounded at the thought that they'd somehow overwritten parts of my ment wirelessly.

"Yes, the *Facility Dàtóng* project, due to start in two months time. The description on the application doc was pretty vague, huh, I getcha. FD we call it, quicker than saying the whole thing, true."

"True, yes."

"So, here's the sale: if you agree to our offer, we will fully upgrade your augmentation beyond anything the market can offer. Think about it: the floor effect," he jerked his hand and once again, we floated on chairs in the sky—"is accomplished by a patch so small it barely registered, did you notice? Of course you didn't, no one checks their data stream line by line. So small we could send it as a wireless, as part of a job script. Now, imagine what we can offer you if we use your hard port." It seemed like he was laughing quietly to himself, though he may have been choking. In any case, it was unsettling, intentionally so, a negotiation strategy.

"Wow," was all I could muster.

"Oh yes, wow for sure." The floor returned, and he touched his ear again. I saw a photo of a field somewhere, a dull brown field of corn, perhaps, or wheat, then the perspective zoomed in to a series of large concrete and metal buildings.

"And double wow: this is where you will, I mean would be, working, the FD itself. A fully self-sufficient research facility, that's just the top you see there, you'll see more later, if you choose, but it goes down almost, well, a very long way, the buildings on top are roughly 10% of the total floor space. An old molybdenum mine, retrofitted for scientific research, retrofitted again for nanofarming, and finally, purchased by yours truly." Pride radiated from his face, in concert with a light veil of sweat.

"Interesting." I was lost, and at least part of my body wanted to flee.

"Interesting?!" he blustered. "It's darn amazing, is what it is! Think of what we can do with a facility like that!"

"Well, yes, that is the question you see, I'm still not sure what exactly what you mean for me to do, what sort of work you intend for me to do. And, if you don't mind my asking, why do you not use your own face in the application docs?"

He frowned and scratched the top of his hand frantically, then noticed he was doing it and trapped both hands in his lap. "My what? Oh, the Wiz face. No reason, just being careful, not trying to scare anyone or give them reason to love me too quickly. A good rule, one you should learn: never let them love you too soon."

"Ah."

"And your job, of course, well, you are a well respected Médecins, you have a great faculty for evolving viral and genetic response codes, you take direction well, and you are neuter, so we can avoid some of the social snarling associated with people working together in close quarters in obscure settings. So, you see, you can help us in all kinds of ways, ways neither of us have even thought of, probably, huh? We can help each other be what we will be."

"But I don't now what that means?"

"That's fine, sheesh, don't worry so much! It's about discovery. Have you looked at the planet we inhabit recently, Mr. Duval?"

"Well, of course, every day." His manner was beginning to grate, even as I couldn't turn away. Love him too soon? Doubtful.

"Of course, every day, then every day you see people grinding each other into paste for the sake of a handful of corn, whole chunks of the earth turned to desert, jellyfish clotting the Atlantic, algae choking the Pacific, mercenary armies selling people as food—well, no, but yes, you see it every day, my apologies. So you know, this can't last. *We* can't last like this." He finished this speech, curiously, with another smile.

"No, I suppose not, though I try very hard not to despair—"

"Thattaboy! No reason to! I mean, huh, many reasons to, but not when we can be what we will be, when we can envision something more. The FD Project is exactly that: a means to envision and then test a new way, a new way of being in the world. New models, new modes, new actions and activities."

I shook my head. "It's still all just so vague..."

"It's really not. Look: you pack your bags, come back

here and allow us to upgrade your augmentation, go to the FD, and help a group of very smart, very skilled people work on new models for structuring sociocultural groups, models that will help us evolve past the mess we have now. Your job will involve helping the Médecins team evolve responses to any situation that might occur, ensure the overall health of the work group, and allow yourself to be what you will be. In return, for two year's contract, you will have the fiscal means to work on whatever you like thereafter, even if that means doing nothing but watching the sun rise and set each day. Now, is this position something you might be interested in?"

Again, part of me wanted to flee. My big good angel, the part with the flight instinct, whispered "leave, leave…" But the little good angel had all the reason, all the rationalizations, and was dazzled by the most fantastic application process I'd ever been part of. So glad my angels were always standing by, ready to wrestle.

"Yes, Mr. Gardiner, I assent to the terms of the employment contract and all associated agreements."

§

I remember next to nothing of the train ride home, of floating up to my room, of the carton of stew I fired up for dinner—though I can smell it, even now, foul stuff. The world drifted by like an ambient vid, until my messaging klaxon began to wail and I was present, too present, stew dripping down my shirt front like some culchie drunkard. It was Charon, my cabal leader, wondering why I hadn't ported into *Friend's World* yet. Yes, I played *Friend's World*, I'm somewhat embarrassed to admit, though I really shouldn't be ashamed of such middlebrow entertainments, after all, many a Captain of Industry could be found skulldugging their way through the *Friend's World* universe, and in fact I was quite good at it, hence Charon's insistent call. I answered the klaxon and Charon's friendface popped into vision, not childishly handsome, nor downscale freakish, though greenskinned and graced with ears furry and pointed. "What doing, Krabinay? We got a big safari tonight, dontcha know."

"Yes, yes, Charon, my apologies, I, ah, I have taken a new job and it is already quite demanding."

"Too demanding for the cabal?"

"Maybe so, yes." His question was not intended to be serious, I'd invested a great deal of time and not a little currency into maneuvering our cabal into a position of considerable influence on the Eastern circuit, and the idea that I would simply walk away because of a job was faintly ridiculous.

"No fucking way, reals?" Charon was older than I, but persisted in speaking like a youth.

"Yes, I'm afraid so. I have to relocate for a few years, and I don't believe I'll have a lot of time to participate, I don't want to give less than my full attention." His furry green brow scrunched tight, then lifted as he shrugged.

"Yeah well, you got to do your thing, I guess, sheesh, dingy fucking station, friend."

"I know, please forgive me, and send my apologies to the rest of the cabal."

"Will do. I'm gone."

"Good bye."

It was good that he'd prodded me out of my stupor, started me cutting the threads that bound me to the Albany corridor. I set to snapping others: truncated my lease and utility contracts, ordered a packer and moving ticket, messaged the rest of the cabal, and set my few belongings on the floor on a lift pad for the packers, carefully wrapping anything technically illicit in hard skins to be set in storage until the job was up. I hated moving, and had done so by myself only twice before: when I left to do my college scripts, and when I moved to this apartment. Moving always served to remind me just how isolated I was from the rest of the world, how the objects I lived through—antiques bequeathed by my parents, clothes selected via fashionbot, food and hygienics extruded as needed, porting accessories—all served to increase the isolation. My door opened to a hallway, which led to an elevator, which led to the train and mono station, so the only time I needed to walk down the street was when I chose to, which I did, from time to time, and these walks always left me miserable, ready for pharma. Kirkus was the only physically immanent person I had regular, extra-employment contact with. The only truly unusual aspect of this situation was that I felt my alienation. As far as I could tell, anyone who could do so had retreated from the squalor of the open air, the refugees and riots, the favelas foaming over with disease. We lived in towers, or, if we had enough money, in domed communities patrolled by mercs, and we lived on the net, on *Friend's World* and *NewsieBall* and in all the millions of Toralleys and screwdens. It was just as my father, and so many of his generation, had predicted, but no one could stop it, like watching a slow motion avalanche bearing down on a little village in the Alps from the top of another mountain. At least I tried to find jobs outside, I knew of too many people who'd gone full Hikikomori, working from home, playing from home... the only people having babies were the culchies, and all the culchies wanted was to get up in a tower, away.

I'd worked in a favela, just out of school, my first paid job, patching up wounds, trying to evolve counterviruses and biotics, cutting open waterlogged corpses to catalog causes of death. I never worked so hard, and I never got anything in return from the culchies except resentment, and some outright hostility from the ones with cheap augments, the ones who could see my neuter thread. I couldn't even blame them, they had no one to hate but each other. Every so often one of them would set up a kiosk and preach class warfare, play holograms that traced the funneling of aid money into the pockets of the already wealthy, the sheer opulence in which they already lived, the ongoing genocides and mass starvations, the whole carnival of souls plummeting into a precipice. And a small crowd might gather, for a night or two, and the preacher would set out a bowl for cash, and if the crowds were large enough, drones would hover, and the next night both preacher and crowd would be gone, and the night after that, the kiosk.

This is where my mind drifted, once I'd finished packing and settled into my chair. I couldn't sleep, and didn't want a pharma, as they so often left me groggy, and I needed to be sharp the next day. I thought of all the vids I'd meant to watch, all the sims ready to spill out once I ported, but something kept my attention focused on the drift of my mind from misery to curiosity to excitement and back again. I went over the detailed list of job responsibilities again, a list much more in depth than the blithe summary Gardiner had given, though essentially, categorically, the same as what he had offered—except for becoming what I would become, whatever that was supposed to mean. I took it for nothing more than sloganeering, but perhaps he really believed it, which was a bit frightening: few things are more dangerous than a zealot with a chameleonic ideology. That wasn't fair, I knew, I had no idea if he was a zealot, or if he even had an ideology, my characterization surely had more to do with my dreary cast of mind and the late hour. I finally switched on an ambient, just ments, no porting, and tried to ignore the chittering little voice in my head long enough to fall asleep. It must have worked, since the next thing I knew, my klaxon was sounding, and the sunlight had crept up through the blinds.

Chapter 4

The directions to the departure terminal led to a steel door set in the back wall of an outlying train station, Half Moon/Clinton. I thought for a moment that this was another of Gardiner's "tests," but a light came on in the center of the door and scanned my retina, and the door slid open. Inside was an alcove and another door. The door behind me shut, and a green light to my left did a full body scan, then I was in complete darkness for several seconds. A voice from somewhere above and behind me said, "Thank you. Please proceed," and a second door opened. I stepped through and the room beyond blossomed into a space the size of an airplane hanger, replete with several shuttles on the ground below and orange jumpsuited crews gathered here and there between them. "This way," came the disembodied voice again, and I saw my compass arrow now pointed down a set of metal stairs to my left. I followed it down and to the right, to a lime green quonset hut. I stopped at the open door of the hut and turned to look at the room behind me. The launch gate, or what I assumed was the launch gate, took up part of the ceiling and the far wall, so either there were two gates, or a single, very oddly bent one. Beneath the gate were three shuttles here, all the same size, all manifesting the Gardiner logo of intertwined "G"s, and most of the men in jumpsuits appeared to be leaning against hip stands, controlling various of the thousands of bots that scurried around via their augments. Two bots sat the top of the open door of the hut, vidding me, I suppose. It smelled of grease and fried circuitry and curried fish. I took a breath and followed my arrow through the door.

The curried fish smell rose from a long table in the center of the hut, spread with several tureens, plates, and bright neon cutlery. The walls at either side of the table were lined with stiff backed chairs, also various shades of neon, each with a pair of tan shoes stationed on the floor, facing the table. At the rear of the hut was a large screen, matte black and seamless. My arrow now flickered, then pointed to a yellow chair at the left of the table, after which a female voice requested I be seated. I suspect people are more likely to follow the commands of a disembodied voice than one issuing from a mouth, or even from a visible loudspeaker; I am, certainly, and I sat with my feet at either side of the shoes, careful not to touch them. "Good morning, Mr. Duval," said a voice I recognized as Ms. Bye, the HR rep who'd done my first in person interview. Her face flickered into presence in front of the black screen at the back.

"Good morning, Ms. Bye."

"I think so. Your journey was satisfactory?"

"Yes, certainly, and not long at all."

"Very good. The next journey will be a good deal longer, both in time and distance. To that end, I recommend you have breakfast."

I looked at the spread, which seemed tailored to my extrusion choices, every dish I favored, even little bowls of pain patate. My stomach tightened at the thought of eating, and of flying on one of the shuttles later. "Thank you, I ate before arriving."

Her brows pinched slightly with disapproval. "It's your choice. If you don't care to eat, then please replace your shoes with the ones provided you and follow your arrow to the next step of orientation."

I did as she requested, leaving my old shoes where the new ones had been, and walked out into the hanger. The shoes were the most comfortable I'd ever put on, much sturdier than they'd first appeared, while conforming gently to my feet.

The arrow led me past several of the crew, all of whom wore dark visors and ignored me completely, and up the stairs of the shuttle furthest from the hut. Inside was a white porting chair wired with cables several times the thickness of standard port cables. The cables disappeared through a bulkhead a few meters behind the chair. Ms. Bye's head appeared on a door set in the bulkhead and smiled. "How do the shoes suit you?" she asked.

"They're quite marvelous, thank you."

"Mr. Gardiner has a deep affection for footwear." She paused, glitching her script. "Please be seated in the porting chair, Mr. Duval, and we can get started. I assume you made arrangements for any traveling items you wished to bring?"

"Yes, I had them sent to the address provided."

"Very good. Now, I will provide you an itinerary, you may ask any questions you have, and then we will begin. Do you assent?"

"I do."

"Very good. First, we will connect the Gardiner Sim-Flex porting dongle. Once connected, we will begin the proprietary adjustment to your augmentation lattice. The procedure involves nanoscripting and reshaping your existing augmentation, as well as a certain amount of physical add-on. When we are finished, your augmentation will take up approximately 320% more surface area." Wow, from 5 to 15cm! I assumed that would be a great deal more processing power, though my understanding of augment engineering was embarrassingly weak. I knew they drilled a tiny hole in my skull, inserted a 5cm square, nanoscale membrane under the bone, then stimulated it to unfold on the surface of my brain. I had no clear idea how it made for augmented reality, for the map arrows and item tagging and halos all the other resources most of us took for granted. Those of us who could afford it, anyway.

"The procedure will take 2.5 hours, at which time we will land at the Facility Dàtóng, where I shall be waiting to assist you and show you to your living quarters. Please be advised that some disorientation may occur at the completion of the procedure. While the procedure is taking place, we will provide you status feeds detailing members of you research team. Do you have any question before we begin, Mr. Duval?"

"I do, yes: why is the hanger gate such an odd shape?"

"I assume you refer to our dual door/ceiling access panel. This panel does not, as you might assume, permit our shuttles egress. It opens to a larger space, of which the hanger is a smaller nodule. When the panel is fully retracted, it allows the hanger to function as part of a dampening ring for a particle accelerator."

"Particle accelerator? I had no idea people still used them."

"Mr. Gardiner has great interest in particle accelerators. He believes they have many uses others have overlooked."

"So, how do we—"

"The shuttle will taxi to an elevator, which will descend to runway level and exit. Do you have any other questions?"

"No, not right now, thank you."

"Very good. Have a safe journey, and I will see you when you arrive at Facility Dàtóng."

I felt a light pressure as the chair gripped my neck in order to steady my head, and then a bot snapped the cabling into my port. I thought I felt the shuttle begin to hum, but it might well have been my brain shuddering as nanobots streamed through my port and began rearranging the inside of my head, and a sudden urge of panic welled up, then fell away into a shining dark.

§

By the time the darkness returned, then slowly seeped away, I'd gained status and message access to the members of the team I would be part of, as well as to certain custodial members of other teams. The Custodian of Team Médecins was Meg Fiedler, an off-color choice that seemed well in keeping with Gardiner's taste for the eccentric. I'd never worked with her, or with any of the team members, but I knew her name, as did any Médecins who'd accessed the net in the last 10 years. She was as well known for her caustic running commentary on the distribution of medial resources as for her work in regenerative biomechanics, and for her strange insistence on the beneficial effects of electroneural deprivation, despite a lack of any corroborative research. She was generally regarded as a loony, albeit a necessary and enormously talented one. The member I assumed I'd be working most closely with, Candle Jeffers, was my age, and had held nearly as many jobs as I, though all of her work was in refugee camps. She'd been responsible for countering and containing the ciboria outbreak outside Vancouver, apparently. I'd always wondered whose work that was, some of the counterviral and addiction detox scripts introduced during that outbreak had become fundamental parts of my own toolkit.

The other two members, Cheta Hurtado and Barbara Gint, were both few years younger than I but were long on experience, Hurtado had served as field rep in a series of very bloody contact zones around the world, and Gint as a lab engineer and psych warden for the NAS bioaugmentation center in Detroit. I wondered what she would think about the nanosculpting all the employees had to go through, then realized if she was already on board, then I really did have little to fear.

I tried to extrapolate the size of the project from the size of the Médecins team, but my mind simply wouldn't go that direction, I was having alterations done, and could only vid the feed. There were many other Custodians, however, and thus many other teams, which did give me some idea of the scope of the project. The only other names I recognized were Gary and LouAnn Manpeiler, co-Custodians of something called Team Endo, who had been fairly well known netstars after their arrest a decade ago for fraud. Their real offense was leading a cult of orgasm worshipers near Portland whose membership grew to include the grown children of several prominent politickers and captains of industry, and their arrest only helped them to franchise their cult worldwide. Their popularity had peaked some years ago, and the peculiarity of their inclusion had more to do with their faded profile than their message; if the purpose of the project was to develop models for social cohesion, then the point of view of polyamorous free sex advocates surely would prove useful. Or at least, very entertaining.

§

An afterimage of Gary Manpeiler's face hovered on the wall as I opened my eyes, green and red traces, fading gradually into the pain that radiated out from my gums and teeth. I'd never been much of a drinker, two or three bags of wine and I was done, but I was fairly sure this is what a terrible hangover felt like. A bot arm extended a bottle of water toward my mouth and I tried to raise my head to sip, failed when bursts of color exploded across my eyes, and let out a small, feral whimper. After a few seconds, a gentle but insistent voice requested I try again to drink, and this time I managed.

"Welcome to Facility Dàtóng, Mr. Duval." Ms. Bye's head hovered once more on the white wall.

"Agh, huh, I m-m-" My lips refused to respond to the signals I was sending them.

"Please relax. You are now disconnected from Gardiner SimFlex. As I mentioned before you boarded the shuttle, you will experience a certain amount of disorientation as your nervous system and neural net acclimate to our proprietary augmentations. Drinking the prepared solution will assist in this process. The average time for re-orientation is 23 minutes, at which point you will be given a short assessment. Please sit still and drink the solution, which contains short acting pain mollifiers and Proprietary Augmentation Assistance."

I took another sip of the proffered bottle, then another, and sat back. The pharma came on fast, and I felt my body at a remove, as though I were looking over the shoulder of someone in great pain. I had no idea what Proprietary Augmentation Assistance involved, though I did recall from one of the Confidentiality Agreements that "Proprietary" was an info tag meant to trigger the encryption field they'd just keyed into my ments—any time a member of Gardiner group tagged something "Proprietary," I would be unable to access any information about whatever it was, once the job was over and I was off-site. Like so much of the employment architecture they used, it was a standard industry feature boosted beyond anything I'd seen or heard utilized elsewhere. I sipped more of the solution and visualized the nanobots in my blood dissolving into nutrient.

I noticed a small timer in the corner of my vision, ticking up toward 21, 22, then 23 minutes. Though my eyes were closed, light faded in slowly, and I saw I was sitting in a lush field of grass and clover. A message appeared in the air roughly 10 meters from my chair: "Please walk here." Before I could doubt what my body was doing, I was standing, teetering slightly, then walking toward the message. The words vanished as my hand touched them, as did the grass and clover and field, gradually, fading away as an indoor scene faded in. I was now in some kind of old gymnasium, padded floors and gymnastics equipment and folded bleachers lining the walls. A small, carefully groomed man with North African cheekbones and nose appeared a few meters in front of me, and led me through a series of exercises that I wold never be able to perform in the physical world: pommel horse, parallel bars, then 20 minutes on a treadmill, running full speed. It was the running, and not the more unusual exercises, that made me suddenly self conscious of my virtual body, and I fell and hit my nose. Blood flowed down my lip, salty and hot and thick, and the lights went down and out. I opened my eyes, still sitting in the chair, trying to understand what I had seen: virtual reality of greater holistic definition than the best ported vid or game, but fed, somehow, wirelessly, through my ments. Fear and delight swooned together, a single entity.

"You seem to be ready for mobility, Mr. Duval." I turned my head slowly and saw Ms. Bye, clad in a grey jumpsuit with the Gardiner logo on her breast. Something was different about her, a new hairstyle, or facial sculpting, or—

then I saw it, she had no halo.

"Yes, I think—that was amazing," I replied, swinging my legs off the chair and planting my feet.

"Very good, I thought you would be impressed. That script obviates me of the need to ask how your flight was." Her mouth twitched, and I realized she was making a joke, so I smiled. She waved her hand and a door opened in the shuttle wall. The air outside flooded in, hot and gritty.

"After you," she gestured.

The stairs led down to a short strip of concrete, and beyond lay the complex of buildings Gardiner had shown me in the pitch vid. Sitting 10m beyond the shuttle was a four seat transport, a shiny new reproduction of an ancient model, and in the front seat, a stone wall of a man with military posture and hair that looked like it would draw blood. As I descended, his sneer was audible.

"Mr. Duval, this is Colonel Mbete."

The man shook his head and rubbed his hands together. "No Colonel. Just Mbete."

"Very good, as you wish, Mbete. This is Mr. Duval, one of our Médecins." I nodded, and he squinted in reply. "Pleasure to meet you," he said suddenly. I wondered how much of his awkwardness was due to my own lack of a halo. I was struggling myself, as it grew clear how much we depended on them for social communication. I knew one of the Confidentiality Agreements had mentioned we would be operating on a local network, but I hadn't realized how much halos depended on a steady feed from the full net.

"You will get used to it, I promise," Ms. Bye said, as we sat in the transport behind Mbete, who swiveled his chair to face us.

"To what, I'm sorry?"

"To the absence of halos."

"Not bloody likely," Mbete offered.

Ms. Bye bristled slightly. "We are, above all a flexible species, don't you agree? Halo technology is, after all, only 17 years old. We survived quite well without them before that."

Mbete huffed and turned his chair back to face the front. We arrived at a large metal door, 7 or 8 meters in height, set in the concrete wall of one of the smaller buildings.

"Why are they turned off? The halos, I mean?" I asked Ms. Bye as we exited the transport.

"Per Confidentiality Agreement, sortie 26.111.35, we will be operating within a local net for the duration of the project. As defined in the Agreement, the 'local net' includes access points to the full net for research information only, so as not to bias the results of the project. Regular news feeds will be provided, as will access to an entertainment archive."

"Ah. So, halos might sully the project, in a way," I summarized, and she nodded, waving her hand to signal the door.

"We are lab animals," Mbete said, stepping through the door.

"That is one way to look at it, yes," Bye answered.

Beyond the door was an ancient elevator platform,

large enough to hold several transports. We descended past several more large metal doors, settling at floor seven. The doors slid open and we stepped into a long hallway of smaller doors, each marked with a name. Mine was on the third door on the left.

§

After Bye gave me a tour of my very spartan quarters—no extruder, as all meals would be provided by the nanofarms and meat lab and then eaten communally; no pharma drawer, as all meds would be distrubuted by the Médecins; a wall unit with three jumpsuits, green (though not the garish lime green of the quonset hut at orientation, thankfully); one chair, one old style sink and toilet, a table and a bed—she said I would soon feel very tired and should rest, because our first full staff meeting and dinner would occur at 1900. She showed me the door entry swipe, then left to show Mbete to his own quarters. I lay back on the bed, which was shockingly comfortable, given how bleakly utilitarian it looked, and wondered what kind of situation I'd gotten myself into. Mbete was right, we were something like lab animals, but that was always the point, the job definition had made that clear. Why was he here, if he felt the work was beneath him? Every position I'd ever held made me feel that way, I'd always thought it part of the nature of work, that it was an ongoing experiment over which I could exert some power, without ever really knowing the full nature of the forces conducting the experiment. Or if there were "forces," for that matter—organizations operate under a logic that is intentional and constructed in that it shifts responsibility for intention and construction away from individuals. That was why we were here, I'd assumed, to try and construct new ways of organizing people that gave them more responsibility, made them fell less like lab animals. Well, that's what I thought we should work towards anyway, I knew there would be many other models in play, many other ways of being. I grew excited again, thinking about what lay ahead, and thought I should grab a pharma to calm me down and put me to sleep, realized there were none available, and woke three hours later to a gentle chime calling me to dinner.

Chapter 5

The arrow directing me to the dining hall was different from the standard map pointer, it was in the shape of an actual arrow, and a primitive one at that, with fletching, a stone head bound to a shaft, and it had depth, dimensionality, not the flat orange symbol I was used to. It also pulsated slightly in the direction it pointed, a rather hypnotic effect that so entranced me I bumped into my neighbor, emerging from his own room.

"Chooga, right?" he said, staring at his own arrow, which had, oddly, fused with mine, so that we now shared a single icon.

"What? I mean, yes, it's fascinating, and now we appear to have meshed displays."

"Yeah, supatek, kinky. Can't wait to unfold my new ments a bit, you know? Take'em for a spin?" His grin threatened to overwhelm his narrow face, on which was impaled a shock of sandy hair. Behind a tangle of bangs, his eyes were large, speckled, and soft brown, and had the perpetual twinge of an animal expecting a lash.

"Hey neighbor, I'm Paulie," he said, opening his palm. I lay mine atop his and gripped it lightly.

"Manoushka Duval. Manny, for short."

"Manoushka? Isn't that usually a girl's name?"

"Yes, sometimes, it was for men and women years ago, my parents were old fashioned." I knew these were the kinds of facts he might unwind from my halo, but I had none. He seemed comfortable enough operating without one—how long since I'd shaken hands!—so I determined to follow him, as much as was possible. His jumpsuit was a kind of tweed pattern, brown on grey.

"Paulie LeVant, at your servissimo," he bowed, and started off down the hall.

I learned a great deal about Paulie LeVant in the 10 minutes it took us to reach the dining hall, since he talked for nine of them, entirely about himself. As he spoke, I remembered reading about him years ago, a child prodigy, accepted to MIT Node 3 before reaching puberty, made notorious for destroying a whole leg of the MIT data body during an unapproved experiment, then poached by HutCo, and finally quitting two months into his contract with them to "do my own shit," whatever that meant. I assumed he would still be in jail after breaking his contract with HutCo, but there he was, walking beside me. He said his group was Team Tek, that the Custodian was Clive Dunwoody, and that Clive hated Paulie with all his heart.

I also discovered that Paulie tended to focus maniacally on whatever he was doing, in this case, talking at me. He ignored the 20 or so other people who gradually joined us on the walk to the dining hall, chatting with one another, comparing jumpsuits, watching as their arrows all combined into a single icon. The dining hall was enormous but just as spartan as my living quarters. It could easily have held a thousand persons, rather than the few hundred who were milling about or sitting at the bare, flimsy tables lined end-to-end in the front third of the room. One smaller table sat alone near the wall to the left of the entrance doors, and three double doors lined the wall furthest away. A glut of duct work and cabling ran across the ceiling, some of it clearly brand new, some ancient. The arrow had vanished, but a small indicator in the southeastern corner of my vision indicated I should find a green chair, matching my jumpsuit.

The rest of my team was already seated, save Barbara Gint, who I was told hadn't arrived yet. Jeffers and Hurtado were guarded yet pleasant, and like me, seemed to be struggling to suppress their giddiness. Fiedler, on the other hand, seemed morose, and perhaps somewhat drunk, staring hazily around the room, fingering a gaudy silver-and-turquoise necklace that clashed with her jumpsuit. I surveyed the room, finding Mbete, in a sky blue jumpsuit, and LouAnn Manpeiler, whose jumpsuit was, I thought rather tastelessly, a garish pink. Suddenly, the walls sparkled at five second intervals, and everyone dropped into their chairs.

The sparkle effect turned steady, climbing the walls and spreading across the floor. A subtle shift in the shape of the room took place, making it feel as though we sat inside a glittering egg. Ivan Gardiner emerged from the pattern, flanked by Ms. Bye, both wearing grey jumpsuits.

"The interesting thing, the really interesting thing about this place, is the mix of old and new, the juxtaposition." He stopped, smiled, then kept wandering between the tables, talking toward some distant point. Ms. Bye stood near the place she'd entered the room, stiff, unreadable.

The sparkle effect vanished, and several people gasped as a montage vid began, swallowing the room and spilling out rapid fire images: neanderthals sniffing a burnt stump, proto-humans scratching cave walls with red ochre, a clutch of tiny, dark men and women huddled on a crudely thatched reed boat...

"Our species, I think, is always both old and new this way, brand new tek on top of the ancient, new ideas wrapped, layer after layer, around the primitive, the essentially human. I mean, huh, what is augmentation but an extension of language, a way to share symbolic knowledge more quickly than speaking or writing, but still offered and interpreted the same way, the way our brains were built for? Porting tek added a new, more direct means to access our nervous system, but did it render our senses obsolete, as so many naysayers predicted? Of course not, the only way we can understand and produce port vid is because we are bodies with eyes and ears and noses and tongues and skin, moving through time and space, and our minds are comprised of the experience of this motion. It's pretty neat, this place—" the scene shifted from proto-human montage to gliding shots of, presumably, the inside of Facility Dàtóng—"built in the middle of the last century, left to wild dogs and geese after the quakes of 2042, purchased by Gardiner group 10 years ago, and now, look what we have: 3.2 hectares of space; a 7 million liter reservoir of drinking water, and access to an aquifer with at least 25 million more liters; three nanofarms and meat labs, each capable of producing enough food for 10,000 people..." he paused, and the imagery slowed, then shifted back to the sparkle pattern. "We have, you have, the most advanced bioaugmentation in the known universe," he snickered a bit, waving his hand at the sparkling walls, "but what we don't have are extruders, or halos, any of the modern conveniences we all rely on. We have a vast archive of entertainments, and the means to make more, but we have no access to the endless, distracting feed of the net. We have a skilled Team Médecins, but no private pharma dispensation. We have experts and visionaries from a variety of threads, but no regulation hindering them from enacting their visions, from following their expertise, their interests, their passions wherever they might lead.

"We have, in short, huh, a really neat mix of old and new, and an opportunity to start from a baseline, to figure out what we need to do, as a species, to survive, because, whoopsie, doesn't look like we're going to make it, the way we've been going." The scene shifted again to a rapid montage, men in red robes thrusting knives into the gut of another, a woman being raped, a man being raped, a child with bloody stumps for limbs, a line of muskets firing, death camps, machetes hacking into flesh, piles of charred corpses. "But I don't need to tell you all about that. You know where we stand. And you all, I believe, have some ideas about how to fix things, how to make us, our species, our world, healthy again. At least I hope you do, because we are about to spend the next two years in a very old, very sturdy bunker, trying to figure it out."

He gave a little wave in the direction of the seated teams, then faded back into the sparkling effect. Ms. Bye's image grew larger, and much sharper, and a list of items began to scroll beneath her face as she spoke. "Very good, you heard the man, let's get to work. We understand we're in an incubation period here, so let's start with a daily and weekly schedule: you will have access to one of 23 news feeds from the net twice a day, at 0800 and again at 1600, for 15 minutes. Do not, under any circumstances, ask for other access to the net, it will not be granted. The meal schedule has been forwarded, teams will eat together, until further changes are mandated. Each team's standard duty list has also been forwarded, you should recognize it from the employment process. After the three day incubation period is complete, we will begin Phase One normal schedule, forwarded to you now. We will follow Phase One normal schedule until changes to the schedule are mandated. Please refer to the forwarded documents for definition." And with that, Ms. Bye and the sparkling walls faded away together.

No one moved for a few seconds, and then it felt as though the room exhaled. Voices rose and fell in swells, and one set of swinging doors opened to allow orange-jumpsuited men and women to enter, wheeling trays of the same kind of neon plates and cutlery I'd seen in the shuttle hanger. They handed stacks of plates to the people at the head of each table, who then passed them along.

"Wow, pretty dingy, yeah?" Candle Jeffers offered from her seat beside me, while taking a plate and passing me the stack. She had short, reddish brown hair, a wide nose, and a permanently bemused expression.

"Dingy?" The box of cutlery came the other direction,

and I chose a set and passed them to her.

"Yeah, greasy, middling, tacky, fufu, you know, lacking in style."

"Well, I, what part do you mean, the plates?"

She laughed. "No, those they're dingy too. I mean that whole rigmarole, the visiony thing he was trying to spoon us, hell, sparkly walls? Felt like I was vidding gramama's *Juice Tale Theater*."

"I suppose so," I said, "but then I'm old fashioned. I loved *Juice Tale Theater* when I was growing up." One of the men in orange placed a tureen of something that smelled wonderful between us, and Jeffers plopped several spoonfuls onto each of our plates.

"It was dingy, she's right," Hurtado joined, "but come on, get past it, what he's saying is pretty much on task, and I mean, I don't know, maybe we really can come up with a kind of model, some way to help put the world back on track." I watched Hurtado eating and wondered at the size of his hands.

"On track to what, my little sheep?" Fiedler interjected, pushing the food around her plate. "We have enough science to make living palatable, but people keep getting in the way, breeding and eating and demanding so many inconvenient things, what is our little experiment supposed to prove?"

"Well, for example," he continued, chewing with relish on his stew, "like you said, we have the science. We could reseed some of these deserts, mass produce purification viruses, we know what needs doing, so we just need a snap, a point of contact that makes everyone realize—"

"Everyone on the planet," Fiedler said.

"Well, yeah, or at least the ones in charge."

"Don't you know by now, my god, you worked in how many refugee camps, don't you get it? No one is in charge. There are people with guns and bombs and viral agents, and there are people with enough money to pay all those people, and that's it. No one is in charge, and no one with resources wants to hear about any plan, unless it means they get more wealth, or power, or men to line the walls of their castles. We're just wandering down the final cul-de-sac, back into the ooze. Except now the ooze is toxic." She got up, took her plate to the end of the table and dropped it into a wheeled bin.

"Ok," Jeffers said, after we watched Fiedler leave the room, "so, tell me again, why is she here?"

"Fiedler? Ha, ballast?" Hurtado offered.

"Huh?"

"He means her cynicism is there to keep us from getting too grounded, from being too enthusiastic about what we're doing," I said.

"Well, hell," she replied, "I'm not enthusiastic, I'm desperate."

§

After dinner, I lay again on my bunk and went over the documents Bye had forwarded. The incubation period schedule was simple: news feed, breakfast, informal team meetings and demos, lunch, informal team meetings and demos, news feed, dinner, inter-team socialization. A more or less typical orientation schedule. Team

Médecins would use the meeting time to set up the dispensary and viral algorithms, chart the results of everyone's health screening, inventory our pharma and blend matrices, that sort of thing. Then, Phase One would begin, following a similar schedule, except that afternoon meetings were supposed to focus on planning Social Organization Maps, SOMs, which each team would then, after weeks of planning, demo to the rest of the project. Also, each team was required to provide one Entertainment and Edification session at the end of the week where their SOM occurred. After all the teams had offered both one demo and one entertainment, we would move on to Phase Two. What Phase Two consisted of was, apparently, entirely dependent on whatever happened in Phase One, and the Gardiner Custodial Team—Gardiner, Bye, and three other people I didn't recognize—reserved the right to nullify "any decision or activity that endangers employees physically, mentally, or emotionally." It was all very orderly and all very vague, as was consistent with Gardiner's method. At least, I hoped it was a method.

A hand icon appeared and began throbbing, signaling that someone was "knocking" at my door. I closed the document and signaled the door open.

"Chooga, Mannie, you checking on 'the plan'?" Paulie made little bracket motions with his hands.

"Uh, yes, actually, I was going over the document Bye forwarded us." I sat on the bed and gestured toward the chair. He ignored the chair and stood, tapping his foot.

"Yeah, my third time seeing the big splash, but it's good, I just focus on the visuals now, did you know you can change camera angles independent of the script? I can send you the plug." I saw the data reception light flash twice.

"Thanks, yes, I will try it. What do you mean, your third time?"

"Oh, well, I been here now three weeks already, saw the rough cut, helped them script a little bit of the segues and such, Beaudoin is one hot supatek ment developer, that team is sharp. And your friend there, Gint, she was in there too, doing mad med tweaks to the bio back end—"

"I don't know who these people are, I'm sorry." I also got lost in his tweenspeak, why were so many tekheads developmentally stunted that way?

"Sorry, right: Elaine Beaudoin, former ERC Head of Information or some such, is in charge of Gardiner bio-augment development, for this project. Her and Salenas both, really, though Beaudoin is the brain tools, Salenas does the scripting—sorry, Juan Carlos Salenas, way more shadowy and way more scary, in my opinion, than Beaudoin. But yeah, Gint, she's on your team, she does the bio part of the bioaugmentation, didn't you get that?"

"No, I was told she wasn't here yet."

"Huh, no, she's here, or she was, when I got here. Or I heard she was, anyway, didn't meet her." He suddenly plopped in the chair. "The music is starting, better get back to bed," he said, without actually rising to go.

"The music?" I realized I could hear a faint tinkling of strings and piano.

"Yeah, they run a vid that'll knock you right out, of course you can shut it off if you want, but I have trouble sleeping anyway, always did, from babytime on, so—" He closed his eyes.

"But, back in your quarters," I said, rather sharply.

"Oh yeah, shit, sorry, the music gets me every time." He sprung up, grinning, and hopped to the door. "See ya mañana, Manyannie." He giggled and shot through the door as the music grew in volume.

I swore to dissuade him from calling me Manyannie, if it occurred to him to do so again. The music was rather hypnotic, and I read the specs of the the vid that would accompany it: ambient color washes tuned to neural activity, the usual script for a sleep aid, but I guessed the Gardiner ments would make it much more effective. I was right.

Chapter 6

The wake up vid was slightly more charged than the sleep aid vid, but just as soothing. I accepted the morning news feed, and watched as the world continued to crumble: PonDafrique declared the Burkina Faso Basin null, Lake Volta was effectively gone, refugees were streaming down the coast, overwhelming the camps full of refugees already there from the south. It was another pinch point, more oceanscapes full of corpses presumed imminent. NAS talks with Chilean Federation not going well, the Hague still offering show trials, with a sacrificial lamb or two from Harris/Blackwood being prosecuted for Crimes Against Humanity in the Red Gulf fiasco... a typical day at the end of the 21st century. I cut the feed once the sports started. It was remarkable how ready people were to succumb to distraction, watching endless Cup Qualifiers and World Series, Parkour Survival, *Friend's World* leaderboards, just as I had, just as I would be were I not here, unable to jump on and work my avatar through some derivations. The more the world burned, the more fiddle salesman appeared, and everyone who could afford to buy one, or twenty, did.

Breakfast washed away much of the depression caused by the news feed. I'd had rare occasion to try freshly grown meat and vegetables, and I understood why they were such a delicacy, even though immersing myself in the sensation of chewing was tantamount to the same kind of world-weary distraction I'd just bemoaned. But it tasted so good, peppers and onions, real egg substitute, soy cheese—the relentless unidimensionality of extruded food only came clear when one had the opportunity to eat really well grown stuff. I had a neighbor who grew beans in his apartment years ago, and he let me try them, and they were awful, like clumps of thread and dirt. What was on my plate now was masterful.

"Good stuff, right?" Hurtado asked, mouth full.

"Yes, it's really wonderful." Jeffers and Fiedler had both finished and were sipping tea, going over specs.

"The Farm Team is supatek, the best around. Can't imagine how he got them out of prison."

"Sorry?"

"Hendrickson, their Custodian, he and a few of his team ran the Brainerd Militia."

"Really, well, yes, that is interesting." The Brainerd Militia were a group of Agrarian extremists who'd fought Mondelēz International to a standstill for nearly three years, before Mondelēz got a court order to cloud their compound with methoxyflurane.

"Another lost ideologue, gathered to FD like strays to a shelter," Fiedler offered. She sent me a list of all FD employees who had registered as level five pharma users. It was a very long list.

"What's this?" I asked.

"Those are the people who will, very soon, start begging you for pharma." Jeffers, surveying the same list, gave a whistle.

"Wowza," Hurtado offered.

"Right. And, we can't give them any until they've been pharma free for six weeks. Here's a script for shifting responsibility back to the Team Custodial."

"Who wrote the script?" It was perfunctory, but would do the job of releasing us from uncomfortable conversations.

"Team Custodial," she replied.

I should have guessed, from the style of the script, but I wasn't used to Full Custodials taking the buck that way, as typically one arrived at Full Custodial status by mastering the art of shifting responsibility away from one's self. That's why they no longer called themselves managers, or officers, as they did before the big conglomerations of mid-century, when the North American continent became the NAS. This was more of Gardiner's blend of old and new, perhaps.

§

The incubation period blew by, more like a singles retreat than work, in many ways. My team developed a general profile of employee health, and had the lab ready for virus work. We also learned that we liked one another well enough, even Fiedler, which was crucial given the length and close working conditions of the project. I met employees from every other team: Custodial, Military, Tek, Farm, DataPsych, Endo, and the Runners. The hierarchy for Phase One was simple: every team had a Custodian member, who made up the Custodial Conclave, and the Conclave would decide whatever needed deciding. And, of course, Team Custodial oversaw everything, and could nullify Conclave decisions.

At our last meeting before Phase One, Barbara Gint finally appeared. She was, physically, an inverted reflection of Fiedler: where Fiedler was dark and striking and worked hard to look like a bohemian vid star, Gint was plain, with short, nearly shaved blonde hair, small, greenish eyes, and a hunched, thin body. If it was true that Gint had been part of the augmentation development team, she deserved to feel resentful for not being our team Custodian, but she seemed utterly unaffected, pleasant to all in a distracted way.

"I'm done with last calibration sequence here, what's left?" she asked, lifting her brows at Fiedler.

"I think that's it, Hurtado?"

"Done."

"Jeffers?"

"Done."

"Duval?"

"All done."

"Well. We finished ahead of schedule. If this were a normal project, you'd all get bonuses. Tough luck," Fiedler said, settling onto a stool, rubbing her eyes, fiddling with her silver-and-turquoise necklace. It was a nervous habit, and I wondered if she had several of the same kind, in case her endless fiddling broke the chain.

We looked at each other, unsure exactly what to do next. The lab was tuned and ready to go, and no demos were scheduled prior to the evening news feed.

"So, let's talk about the SOM," Hurtado said.

Fiedler shook her head. "Ok, fine, go ahead."

"Ok, so, I know we're not up first," he said, and everyone nodded. That was Team Tek's privilege, perhaps because they knew how to put it up the fastest. Our demo was third, three weeks away. "So, should we wait to see what Tek or Farm does, since we don't even have a template? I mean, hell, where do we even start with this?"

"If I may," Gint suggested, "we should start with a script detailing what we do know, and then develop some questions." Again, everyone nodded. Gint passed a blank script around, titled " Team Médecins SOM." Items began to appear:

- Social Organization Map. Per Gardiner Group glossary, "a plan for organizing large group interaction, including but not limited to: sociocultural, economic, artistic, sexual and procreative, industrial, dramaturgical, communicative, spiritual, biological, and morphogenetic relationships."
- Script Style: Live action, montage, static, augmented live, augmented static, interactive, audience response.
- Goals: Create map that shows the way to the greatest social cohesion and harmony.

"Wait a minute, now," Jeffers said stopping the script. "That style list, it's kinda limited, geez, with these new ments, we could do something supadupatek, right?" We all followed her gaze to Gint.

"Yes, I did the bio portion of the new augmentations,

and yes, we can do some very interesting things with them. However, I am not a scripter, and neither are any of you. If you want something more glitzy, you need to ask Team Tek for help, and I assume they will want something in return,."

"Ok, then—" Gint waved her hand and cut Jeffers off.

"And, and, the kind of script you saw your first day here takes a lot of man hours to create, a lot of archive dragging, pasting, collating."

Jeffers sighed. "So, we should just do another dingy, vanilla thing, is what you're saying."

"Yes, at first, at least."

"Ok, but what about 'goals', too?" Hurtado chimed in. "Who says cohesion and harmony are the most important things? I'm thinking about the world outside, and it is way hella far from cohesive or harmonious, how do we impose out idea of harmony on, say, a Kali cult?"

"That's a good point, yes, though a Kali cult is an extreme example," I began.

"It's not, not at all, it's extreme for in here, sure, I don't expect a murderous blood feast from this gathering of best and brightest, but the idea is to apply it outside, or at least make it relevant, right?"

"He's right," Jeffers added. "We need to have goals to apply within the Facility that will then apply on a larger scale outside."

"The whole thing is insane," Fiedler barked. "You can't grow social cohesion in a test tube, we're just hiding out in a tower, except the tower is upside down."

"Let's try this," said Gint. "We'll start with a map that

we can apply here, in FD, and then begin extrapolating. Make the need to extrapolate one of the goals, that it be applicable on a larger scale."

We mused on this for a moment, then Gint revised the script:

- Goals: Create Map that encourages greatest social cohesion and harmony among employees of FD, with the caveat that social cohesion and harmony are predicated on the Map being effectively scalable to much large groups of persons outside FD.

"So, whatever plan we come up with, real world effectiveness is part of the goal definition." Gint added.

"Got it. Ok, dingy as hell, but that's Custodian speak, you got it down," Jeffers added.

"Once again," I said, once the script was saved, "why cohesion and harmony? Don't we need to define those, and why we think they are valuable?"

"Alright, what other virtues might we aim for, Duval?" Fiedler asked. I was sure she had a few ideas herself, on that score.

"Well, a certain amount of stress is important for creativity, yes? And stress comes from disharmony, if not from a lack of cohesion. And, I worry cohesion could very easily become a means to stifle critique."

"Critique? What are you now, a fundie?" Hurtado laughed.

"I know, I know, most critique is laughable, but if we are trying to make the best system—"

"But a workable system," Fiedler interjected.

"Yes, a workable system too, then don't we need to include some working means of grievance? I know we snicker at the archived NAS scripts, how they fooled themselves into thinking they had self-government, but truly, they did have a great deal more, ah, self-determination, I think, in terms of—"

"No, he's right, we need to work at this like we are creating a world we actually want to live in," Gint said.

"I know you aren't going to like this, but I think the NAS still has a much better system than the rest of the world," Jeffers said, cringing slightly as she said it. Hurtado shook his head, Fiedler sneered.

"If you are a shareholder, a very substantial shareholder, then yes, you are correct," Fielder told her.

"Even if not, we all still get a vote."

"Oh my god, come on," Hurtado cried.

"Really, I mean, when Red Gulf happened, NAS rebuilt central Texas according to Community Conclave specs—"

"A Conclave of shills, you know that," Hurtado said, shaking his head.

"Maybe, most of them, but what came out of it was not terrible, the Locator Camps there were clean, well run, well organized—"

"Maybe we should base our SOM on them, then."

"Enough," Fiedler barked, "we only have a few weeks to put this together, and pulling at our staples won't get anything done. I want everyone to come up with a set of characteristics we should attend to when building our little utopia. We can distill them at the first meeting, and then make decisions, before starting on the presentation script." Hurtado, Jeffers, and I all rose from our stools. Gint remained standing. "And one more thing: I've had 11 requests already for pharma. Anyone else?"

I'd had three, Hurtado seven, Jeffers one, Gint none as yet.

"The script is holding, I have no idea what Custodial is telling them after the referral, but keep an ear to the rail, it could be tricky for a while." She nodded, rose, and gestured for us to precede her out the door.

I walked out beside Gint. "Your work in Gary was really exceptional," she said, looking down as she walked.

"Oh, well, thank you, it was really nothing, just running the algorithms."

She smiled. "And, reconstructing the basal frame on the fly after your team broke it, and then sneaking it through when the Conclave rejected the solution."

I reddened. How could she know that? It wasn't on my profile, certainly. I thought I'd buried that deep.

"My partner at the time was on the Conclave. She was one of the 'yes' votes, and when they lost, I did a little digging."

"I see."

"Just wanted you to know I respected your work, and your willingness to do what is necessary." She touched my arm lightly, and turned left, down a different residency hall from mine.

Respected my work, yes, but also wanted me to know she could "dig" and find out things. Fine, I was never very good at subterfuge, it's better when everything is clear and open, anyway. In fact, that principle should be the first characteristic on my script proposal for tomorrow: open lines of communications, no encryptions or break-walls or infodamming. Everyone knows everything.

I'd been back in my quarters less than two minutes when the next message came through, asking about pharma. I forwarded the script, then forwarded it again to the next four messages, all about pharma. I didn't really understand the restriction—well, I did, in theory, Gardiner wanted us to work at a remove from the society he wanted to rescue, and pharma was symbolic of that. Instead of a cocktail of chemicals tuned to one's body, including those intended to alter brain chemistry, we would be in charge of distributing necessities like insulin and stribild, but anyone wanting sedation or other sorts of mood escalation had to apply directly to the Conclave. That is what the script we were given said, and so far, no one had asked me for anything physically necessary, because we'd already profiled the population and begun distributing those drugs. What people were messaging about were the drugs to help them relax, or get along with people, or not want to get along quite so well with people. I had no idea how many of them received dispensation from the Conclave, since Fiedler was in charge of dispensing Conclave-approved pharma requests. I would have to ask her, when she was in a good mood. Perhaps after she'd been medicating herself a bit, which she did, more or less openly, by drinking Arack from dinner to sleep time. I wonder where she got it, if there was a still in her quarters, or a 20 million liter reservoir somewhere that only Custodians were privy to.

As I sat and waited for the evening news feed, I considered my own medication routine. I tried to stay away from pharma, since the first doses I'd ever had contained testosterone and paxil, neither of which I needed or desired. This was in the bad old days when certain very influential people thought neuter was a condition, and a treatable one, at that. That was 20 years ago, and I still avoided it. I took a daily dietary supplement, and I took Xarelto for many years, until I earned enough money for fibrillation corrective treatment. I drank white wine. I took a sedative once in a blue moon, when I looked outside and very much wanted to die. Other than that, I just never developed a taste for pharma. I was, to judge from the number of request messages I'd received, an outlier in this regard.

And yet, I was happy, if that word meant anything anymore. I was 43 years old, skilled at my work, and found great reward in it, in working as part of a team to solve problems and, I hoped, ease the burden of people whose burden was very great indeed. I could, conceivably, do this work for 30 more years, then file a life cessation request, as the idea of not working did not appeal to me at all, though I would have enough savings at the end of this job to fritter away my last years on entertainments, if the world still existed at that point. Like everyone, I had serious doubts in that regard, and like many people, I knew I would last a month or two before the desire to rid myself of this cheap suit would overwhelm me, and then I would have to wait for a year or more for my cessation request to be granted, or else do it myself, and have every hint of my existence purged from net and archive. I was privileged enough to have a plan, and was self-contained enough to follow it. I'd been following it since I was 12 years old.

It struck me: the most important characteristic I could offer our team's script was self-determination, which is really what open lines of communication and free flow of information pointed towards, and self-determination, in terms of developing a plan for one's life, meant being self-contained, not relying too much on the approval of others, negotiating when your plan did not mesh with the team's, and above all, feeling a responsibility to other persons and their own sense of self, helping us all develop our goals in concert. It seemed like a contradiction, that instead self-contained should suggest being self-interested, but narcissism is not the same as being self-contained. Like the poet said, "No man is an island entire of itself; every man is a piece of the continent, a part of the main." I *am* involved with humanity, inexorably, and living solely for my own gain closes one part of myself off from the other, which then bleeds all over the place, and everyone else knows it. At the same time, my responsibility to my fellow human beings demands I not always agree with them. Still, no one is more dependent on other people than the selfish person, and so no one is more owned by others.

I tried to cobble all these thoughts together into something like a script item as the news feed began. The lead bullet was a bioweapon escaping from somewhere in the SGN, and Beijing was pleading ignorance as Lahore reported mass deaths, while experts warned it could surpass the Red Gulf incident in scope. An NAS salvage mission in Old Miami claimed to have found a EuRusCo Eco-Barrage deployment system for clogging de-salination plants. Tenniver Wilkes won an Oscar for the vid, *All In Good Time*. Stunning that people still care, I thought, as my door icon blinked Paulie's knock code.

"Did you see? Hella bad, that virus in Pakistan, Sino-Ganra is such a basket of snakes, no one believes it was an accident." He sat in the chair, which he'd done ever since I told him his pacing made me anxious.

"It could have been, Red Gulf was."

"Oh come on down, serious? Red Gulf was totally engineered by the NAS to get heads in a row, you want to engineer a merger between nation states, you better have an enemy! No way some Havana virus masher could've engineered that, no way, not even by accident."

"I was there, I saw it unfold, I helped counter-engineer it. It mutated fast, no doubt, but without any human authorial profile, not even close. Some kid in his garage just hit the wrong button."

"If you say so," he laughed, rocking back and forth. Paulie was a veritable font of conspiracy theories, and I could never quite tell how seriously he took them.

"Anyway, what kinda show your team gonna put on?"

"You mean the SOM?"

"Yeah, circus maximus, what are the medheads gonna do?"

"I don't even know yet, we're just at the planning stage." I found my water bottle and took a sip. "What about you?"

"It's a secret."

"Oh come on, you asked me," I said, shaking the bottle at him.

"Nah, I'm kidding, it's no secret, it's just stupid, I can't get chooga about it, I'm a little embarrassed, I guess." He looked at his fingers.

"So, what is it?"

"Old tek dreams from, I guess, 50 years ago or something, the cyberfuture, nanoviruses that collect all the data of a life, then bank it in a quantacore, you know, live forever, paradise for the qubits, and a while lotta trust in bots to run the machines, blah blah blah."

"Not a fan of the noömorphs, huh?"

"Come on, they've been talking that gunk for a century. We got bigger problems."

"Yes, we do."

We sat for a few minutes in silence, swapped a few archival vid trails for later, then he went back to his room. I spooled an ancient, 2d vid about cops and robbers and let it play. The sleep script hadn't worked; in fact, it made me jittery, so I'd reverted to my old habit of 2d vids, keyed to my brain activity, with a long burn fade out so I wouldn't pop awake. I drifted off telling myself that building a new world from scratch was, without doubt, tilting at windmills, as everyone who wanted to make a new world was a product of the old one. We could alter habits, perhaps, but there was no way to reduce a person to tabula rasa and then re-form them, and certainly doing so on a grand scale was absurd. Whatever we ended up building, it would be from recycled materials.

Chapter 7

The day before the first SOM reveal, someone broke into the dispensary, presumably looking for pharma. The dispenser was keyed to Team Médecins retinal prints, so the thief couldn't get access, and the scanner recorded the thwarted thieves' print, so it was a fairly stupid, desperate, rather surprising thing for someone in the employ of Gardiner Industries to do. More surprising was that Fiedler didn't show up for the Custodial Inquiry.

"Does Ms. Fielder often not respond to communications?" Ms. Bye asked, clearly irritated. She was already at the lab when the team arrived, seated at a conference table beside a tall, scabrous man with slicked-back grey hair and some kind of metal sheathing on his left index and middle fingers, who she introduced as Josip Lem, head of FD Security.

"No, she's always right on it," Hurtado answered.

"I'll go check on her," Lem said, leaving the lab.

"We have identified the offender, and have placed them in custody. Now we need you," she nodded at Jeffers, "to administer them a contiguous rehabilitation script."

"Alright, where? To their quarters?"

"Yes, I'll send you the relevant documents. Now, everyone, Mr. Gardiner would like to join us." Gardiner's image shimmered to life beside Bye. It was still jarring, watching perfect 3d forms appear in front of me, without porting.

"Hello, everyone," he said, giving his strange little half-wave. He seemed to be looking at a point down and to the left of Hurtado, so something in the feed he was receiving was off. It was comforting, a frayed thread in the hem of a heavenly garment.

The team mumbled greetings.

"Well, nifty, we have our first scofflaw! How exciting. I really wish we didn't have to exclude self-administered pharma, I know it's perfectly safe and everything, I'm not some weirdo, but really we want to get back to a baseline here, or as close as we can get, and really—what do you think? You all have worked in populations where addiction was a serious problem, right?"

After a few furtive glances at each other, Jeffers took the point, as addiction treatment was one of her specializations. "Yes, though I think I should point out the kinds of addictions we are used to treating are for illegal, and often very toxic, substances, not pharma. There is no—" she stopped.

"No what? No evidence that pharma is addictive?"

"Correct," Jeffers said, looking at Hurtado.

"I know, I know, and I agree, but what do we make, then, of this offender, trying to steal while knowing they would get caught?"

"It does sound like addict behavior, sure, yeah," Jeffers replied.

"Ok then, let's give the offender a good going over, full genetic topography, you do a full case study as part of the rehab script, right?"

"Yes," Jeffers said.

"Yeah, take a good look, see if there is something we can identify, study, figure out if maybe pharma is addictive to some people. Cause, I mean, wow, what else?"

We all nodded. The sheer number of requests we'd all received for dispensation made it baldly clear that something in pharma was addictive, at least psychologically. It was such an elemental part of people's lives, the response was quite predictable. Hence the script directing requests to the Custodians, I assume.

"I don't know about you, but I'm excited about this!" Gardiner clapped his hands. "We're standing over a rabbit hole, ready to jump in!" Even Bye gave him a puzzled look. "So, let's get to it, how are things progressing with your Social Org Map?"

"Oh, good, yes, great, we'll be ready," Hurtado stammered, unsure who should speak in Fiedler's absence.

"Neat, all right, keep up the good work," he said, and faded away. Bye looked around the room, about to speak, then stopped, staring at the wall. "Right," she said, then turned to Jeffers: "Document sent." Without another word, she turned and left the lab.

"Wonder who messaged her," Hurtado said.

"I don't wanna know," Jeffers replied, stuffing her medbag to leave.

"I do," I said.

"So who was the idiot?" Hurtado asked her. She stood still for a few moments, scanning the document.

"One of the Runners, don't recognize the name. Kiko Xhosa?"

We both shook our heads.

"Anyway, that's our offender, and that's where I'm headed, three flights down."

"Figures it'd be a Runner," Hurtado said, after Jeffers had left and we'd started a diagnostic on water samples.

"What do you mean?"

"Lots of them are former prisoners, or favies, you know, people who aren't born with access to pharma, so that's why they get hooked on it. Their body chemistry is never quite in tune."

I felt like calling him a classist shitbag, but held my tongue. I had sussed his bigotries days ago, and simply avoided them. The little good angel holding its tongue held the fist of the big good angel in check.

"What happened to Fiedler, do you think" I changed the subject.

"No idea, chooga, she's a strange one—she wears those epimagnets, for shit's sake. How can someone educated as her still fall for that mess?"

"I've wondered that myself. Though it takes all kinds, and we need all kinds here for the project to run. Seems like everyone I've met here has some eccentricity," I added. He knew I'd read his profile before arriving here, and knew all about what happened in Bangkok. And Milan. And Boise.

"Yeah, shit on the project. I bought the Gardiner name, and whoa yeah, the money, but seriously, what the hell is this? We're going to stay here two years and produce exactly nada. While the world burns."

"I think we're here trying to save it," I said, quietly.

"Ok, well, even if that was our, um, purpose here in

the great Gardiner Love Pit, after two years, what world will be left? You saw the feed, people going grey goo all over Pakistan, which means the end of SGN, which means who knows what, nukes, quantum disruptors—"

"You know there's no such thing."

"Don't I? What, you believe everything on your feed?"

"No, but the science behind quantum disruption is unusable. And useless, when you can achieve the same thing with a nanovirus."

"But not as fast, and never mind, what other kind of hell demonic world killers you think are lurking in warehouses and silos, waiting for some pissed off favie to get a hold of it?"

"I have no idea. I do know, that if I dwell only on those things, and not on solutions, those things start to excite me, and such excitement is a perversion." I reset the diagnostic key and walked over to the viracoder. I'd been running early warning algorithms, based on the population profile, when I had free time.

"A perversion," Hurtado spit, "says the sexless one." That stopped me.

"I have a gender, and a sex, and neither are a perversion. Any more than a taste for Cannibal Front vids is a perversion. What is perverse is succumbing to the—."

"I got it," he barked, looking at me sharply. Maybe he hadn't known I read his file. Why wouldn't I? It was correct employment prep, basic stuff. It struck me then I might have to go back and read his profile more carefully. Maybe I should read all my teammate's profiles again, and make sure they'd all read mine. Secrecy made for inefficiency.

"I'm done, I'm gone," Hurtado said, his usual departure slogan. I nodded.

"I'm going to stay and run a few more of these algorithms," I said. He stopped at the door and turned back towards me.

"So, I'm sorry about the, the uh, remark about the—"

"That's ok. I understand," I answered. Funny how easily a slur slips out, but it hard to say intentionally.

I finished the algorithms and closed the lab. Lunch was in twenty minutes, then my scheduled exercise session. After that, our team and three others had "ment orientation," meaning guided exploration of what the new augments could do. I, and every other employee, I'm sure, had already tried to tinker with new features, but it seems like they were keeping most of them blocked, to be rolled out gradually. Hard to argue with the logic.

My message icon blared suddenly. It was Bye. "Go ahead," I said, opening the channel.

"I need you to come to Custodial. We have a new offer for you."

"A new—now? What's going on?"

"Ms. Fiedler is dead. We have a new offer for you."

I followed the arrow to the elevator that would take me up to Custodial. Dead? Was she the pharma thief? No, that was ridiculous, she could have just dispensed whatever she wanted to herself, and besides, she seemed to favor alcohol. As the elevator descended, I noticed I was grinding my teeth. I'd known people who died on project, but those were at dangerous sites, not bunkers buried in the side of mountains.

The arrow pointed me to an open door. Ms. Bye and Mr. Lem waited inside at a large, white table. Lem was showing Bye something on the surface, pointing with his metallic index finger.

"Ah, Mr. Duval. One moment please, I will summon the rest of the Custodial Team." She waved her hand, and sat back. After a few seconds, Gardiner shimmered into view, along with a short, dark, stocky man with a huge nose, and a slender woman, very pale, with a look of permanent resignation.

"Hello!" Gardiner waved. I almost waved back, but thought better of it He might think I was making fun of him.

"Hello," I replied.

"This is Mr. Salenas, and this is Ms. Beaudoin," Gardiner said, "and you know Ms. Bye, and you met Mr. Lem?"

"I did, yes," I agreed, nodding at Lem, who grimaced in reply.

"Well, this is the gang, your Team Custodian!" He clapped his hands. "And, as you know, an important charge of our team is meeting with the individual team's Custodial Reps, on the Custodial Conclave." I found myself staring at a small spot on Gardiner's jumpsuit, yellow, a food stain, perhaps, and waited a few beats too long to reply.

"Oh, well, yes, the org structure is pretty clear, indeed," I stumbled. Bye winced audibly.

"Good, good, well, a really interesting opportunity has come up, and, well, we'd like to make you an offer." He sent a document, and I opened it. They wanted me to be Team Médecins' Custodian.

"Well, now, I am greatly flattered, but—"

"But what happened to your previous Custodian? Of course, of course. Mr. Lem?"

"She is deceased." He said blankly. I waited, but that was all he was going to say.

"I see. Ah," I stammered, "m-may I ask what happened? The conditions of her passing may well weigh on my decision, of course."

"Of course, of course, well, it seems Ms. Fiedler was very involved in, ah, a sexy thing, oh, you tell him, Bye."

Bye winced again. "Ms. Fiedler was electrocuted, she was engaged in consensual electrobondage with another employee, and there was a malfunction and power surge."

"They were drinking, and knocked over a glass," Lem added.

"Very much an unforeseeable accident, as you see," Gardiner said, leaning over to look at the display Lem was still tinkering with.

"Yes, terrible, tragic, really, given her adamant belief in—"

"So, good, you will accept the offer, then? Nothing sexually deviant you foresee occurring in your future?" Was that an insult? Or was he trying to empathize with me via a lame joke?

I thought about Gint, the only other member of the team who I thought might want the position, and who I trusted to take it. Jeffers had made clear she wanted no part of administrative work, and Hurtado would be a nightmare.

"What about Bar—what about Ms. Gint?"

"Of course, of course, what a team player! But no, Ms. Gint has other duties that preclude her taking the position. But just making sure, I getcha. So, what'll it be?"

I didn't see a better choice. "Absolutely, thank you for the opportunity. I assent to the new contract."

Gardiner smiled. "You see? This guy gets it, he really gets it, just wants to help us all be what we will be. Nice!" He put his hand out as though he wanted to shake mine. I wasn't sure how to respond, since I couldn't touch an avatar, so I nodded and shook my hand in the air about two feet away from his, surely looking just as uncomfortable as I felt.

Salenas frowned, Ms. Beaudoin smiled at me, then all three faded out.

"Orientation scripts have been forwarded," Bye said, and returned to studying the display on the table. Lem looked at me briefly, then also went back to the display. It seemed we were done, and now I was a Custodian.

The first item on the orientation script directed me to proceed immediately to the Rostrum, a room on the next floor up. I followed the arrow, trying to review the contract I'd assented to while walking, which made for slow progress. I didn't like assenting without at least a day to review, but I was against a wall. It seemed a standard mid-project replacement contract, and my new duties were not terribly taxing: do weekly assessments of team members, attend the Conclave, and track all deliverables, primarily the SOM. The arrow stopped, having led me to an 8 by 8 meter door, incongruously white in the grey concrete hallway, and pointed up to a retinal scanner beside it. I submitted to the scan and waited for the door to slide open.

On the other side of the door was a wall that curved gently into hallways on both the left and right. I followed the arrow right, down a hallway that sloped away and grew dark, until I reached a door that flashed "Rostrum: Entry Permitted," and opened onto a vast vidstage. Gardiner, Salenas, and Beaudoin stood together near the back of the room, making the silent, jerky gestures typical of people involved in intense ment conversations. They stopped as I entered the room and sent me an invitation to join them. I paused for a moment to look at the vidstage, at its walls and ceiling webbed with filament, at the fist-sized bots scurrying everywhere along it. The invitation flashed again, and I accepted, and watched the scene fade into an ancient town square, Greek or Roman, perhaps, devoid of people but flanked with brightly colored stone buildings, a fountain of satyrs spritzing just beyond where the Custodians stood.

"Custodian Duval! Welcome to *behind the curtain...*" he giggled, then swept his hand toward the square.

"Yes, very impressive indeed."

"Oh, this is nothing, we have so much more in the works, really interesting stuff—" he paused, then nodded to whomever had messaged him. "But later, later. For now, I just wanted to show you our stage, and officially welcome you to the Conclave." He made a little bow, and smiled. I saw that he was sweating, or that sweat had been skinned on him for some reason.

"Thank you, I hope to do good work," I said, and

looked around at the scene. The detail was remarkable, even a little too sharp. I began to wonder if the Proprietary Process had been adequately tested before they shot nanobots into my skull.

"I'm sure you will," he said, and the scene surrounding us began to shimmer and fade, and we were back in the vidstage. "Now, if you'll excuse me, Ms. Beaudoin will give you a brief tour." He and Salenas turned and walked out a red door, stage right.

"How are you settling in?" Beaudoin messaged. I wondered why she wasn't simply speaking to me, since she stood barely 4 m away. She had the careful, guarded look of someone who treasured privacy.

"Fine, thank you, though I've only been on the job for about 20 minutes."

"Ha ha, I meant in the project as a whole."

"Yes, sorry, that was a bad attempt at humor. I'm settling in quite well, though I am still a little unsteady after the events of this morning." I attached a picture of myself looking woozy.

"Understandable. Well, as Mr. Gardiner said, this is our vidstage, much more supatek than your industry standard, but then it has to be for our purposes. The mesh—" a wave of highlight swept around the room, in case I had missed it, "is both 20 times smaller in diameter and 20 times stronger than normal vid mesh, and so our bots can be heavier, packed with more tools."

"Yes," I said, trying not to sound bored.

"When an avatar appears to you via ment, the mesh is recording and projecting that image directly onto your visual cortex."

"Yes, I do know how it works. Well, how it worked for porting, I assumed it was the same process."

She sighed. "You're right, this is boring. Let me just show you." A table blinked on between us. A vase with a red rose, and a dish of what looked like ice cream, sat atop it.

"Now, please, smell the rose," she said. I hesitated, olfactory tek had been tried several times over the years, but always flopped badly. I bent over and sniffed, and felt a wash of rose scent, sweet and powerful, in my nose. I saw my granmè clipping roses on her balcony.

"Wow," was all I could muster.

"Yes. Now, please, have some ice cream." If not for the example of the rose I'd just experienced, I would have laughed out loud. Without a haptic suit, there was no way to simulate lifting a spoon, even if I was ported. I reached a finger toward the spoon, and felt my mouth drop open as I felt pressure. I lifted it—it wasn't quite right, it was too smooth, and the tactility seemed ahead of the motion, somehow, so I felt its surface on my hand just before I touched the bowl to it. But it felt there, immanent, no doubt about it. I plunged the spoon into the ice cream and thrust it into my mouth, letting out a small sob as I felt a cold, wet, sweet sensation on my tongue. Though it melted far too quickly, vanishing long before it reached my throat, I took another spoonful, then another. When I opened my eyes, Beaudoin was smiling.

"How?" I stammered.

"Well, I'm not a tek maven, by any means, but I know

the olfactory sensation is just a hyperimproved version of what Toulouse rolled out in '87, and the gustatory is keyed to a combination of the pneumogastric nerve complex, the olfactory system, and the memory system. What it tastes like to you is at least in part based on how you remember it tasting, in other words."

"So if I never had vanilla ice cream," I began.

"It would taste like vanilla in your nose and on your tongue, but your memory might process it as yogurt or kit-butter, and there would be some dissonance. We're working on that part."

"That really is amazing."

We chatted for a while, pleasantly, and I left wishing I knew more about her status, wishing that she had a halo, essentially, so I would know better if her friendship was something I might pursue. I was surprised at how quickly I'd grown used to the absence of halos, but when I noticed, the shock was visceral. Perhaps there was some connection between the lack of halos and instance of pharma faux-addiction, I thought, as I rode the elevator down to the dining hall. It was worth running some scripts, certainly. And now that I was Custodian, I could even make someone else do it. I stopped in front of the dining hall doors, feeling suddenly filthy for thinking such a thing, not 24 hours after Fiedler died. The document from Bye mentioned that they would announce her passing after lunch, and that I was not to mention it until then. It made sense: an official word to all employees to staunch the flood of rumors before it starts. That it made sense didn't make me feel any better, or less devious, party to secret knowledge. I remembered, again, my granmès' roses, and how I'd clipped several and hid them in a jar in a closet, so I could smell them, and how quickly I crumbled when she asked my mother if she'd cut any of them. I was not endowed with a duplicitous nature, and wondered how much would be expected of me, as a Custodian. For the first time in many years, I wished I'd paid more attention when my grandparents tried to teach me about the *loa*—superstitions they may be, but I felt could use a few archetypes to help guide me through this next thicket.

Chapter 8

Despite the official announcement detailing Fiedler's death—and very detailed it was, including the identity of her unfortunate partner, one of the Soldiery—the murmurs did indeed soon blossom into rumors. Instead of having to explain to Hurtado, Jeffers, and Gint why I was now our team Custodian, which I still didn't quite understand, I spent most of the afternoon listening to Jeffers and Hurtado swap conspiracy theories. And recording them, as per the document Bye had sent earlier.

"Think about it: someone breaks into the dispensary, tries to break into the dispensary, and Fiedler dies. Got to be some connection there," Hurtado offered.

"I don't believe that stuff, usually, conspiracies are for people with no imagination, my gran used to say," Jeffers offered, "but I just spent an hour working up a rehab script for Xhosa, and she was being a weasel."

"What do you mean?" I asked. As they worked, I tracked who was speaking and relayed the conversation to the archive. They knew I was recording them; Bye's directive indicated I could choose to tell them or not, but not why the recording was necessary. No one seemed to think it out of the ordinary, nor did anyone flinch at my "promotion"—both Jeffers and Hurtado seemed relieved, in fact, and Gint just smiled and nodded.

"I mean I could tell she was hiding something. Nothing

in the genetic workup suggested a predisposition to addiction, and she claimed she was going sell whatever she got a hold of."

"Sell it? Interesting," said Gint.

"Interesting and creepy," Jeffers added. "Is there that much of a need for sedation here? Or currency? Sell it for what, there's nothing to buy."

"It was a distraction, Xhosa was sent to cause a stink so someone else could sneak in and get rid of Fiedler," said Hurtado. He looked around furtively, an odd reaction, as he knew he was being recorded. Did he believe in ghosts?

"But why Fiedler?" said Jeffers. "I mean, she was a weirdo, and wow, cynical, but why kill her?"

"You didn't believe her partner's explanation?" Gint asked, shuttling the dispenser nipple into the grid.

"That guy was as weasel as Xhosa, moreso," Jeffers laughed.

"Yeah, absolutely bought off, chooga bad actor, too," Hurtado added his own chuckle.

And so the afternoon proceeded, Jeffers and Hurtado flinging theories back and forth, without ever concluding who might be behind such a nefarious murder, while Gint prodded them with questions and I recorded the whole thing. I decided being Custodian was something like being a newshead.

The following morning, an FD specific newsfeed debuted, after the typically bleak external feed we all received. The feed began with Gardiner saying cheerful things, segued to Ms. Beaudoin, who declared the Facility "officially self-contained," that is, fully operational without recourse to the energy grid, and finished with a discussion of the various rumors about Fiedler's death, presented by two members of Team DataPsych, Siegleman and Bonato. The rumor segment featured snippets from archival footage, including Jeffers saying, "is there that much need for sedation here?," followed by Bonato's definition of pseudo-addiction, and how it might be relieved through the use of posiflow scripting. Though the whole feed seemed cobbled together, the last segment was almost incoherent, a pastiche, and I assumed it would create as many new rumors as it was intended to quash. Perhaps the Conclave would devote vidspace to a more comprehensive Q and A session before or after today's SOM, but there was nothing, as yet, in the morning schedule.

Paulie appeared at my door just as I was getting ready to leave for the SOM.

"Barking good time! Ready for the shit show?" He laughed, stepping aside to let me into the hallway.

"Yes, I'm very curious to see what you've arrived at."

"Yeah, well, just remember, I told you it would be dingy. Hey, so, the whole Fiedler thing was a sketch, right, she's not really dead, right?"

"I'm pretty sure she's dead, why would anyone say otherwise?" I nodded at other employees moving down the hall, ebbing toward the dining hall.

"It's a sketch, just trying to see how we'll all react. You got Custodial now, they should let you in. Or maybe not, ha—"

"I really don't get it, sorry," I said, and tried to disengage. I understood why people wanted to believe conspiracies, just as they wanted to believe in god or loa or rational thought: the world was not orderly, nor was it chaotic, it was beyond both categories, and conspiracies put boundaries on reality, made it coherent. I was too skeptical for boundaries, and so Paulie's squeaky rants just sounded silly to me.

The dining room crackled, the Fiedler rumor mill and expectation of the first SOM working together to remind everyone just how bored they'd been. The Runners brought us tureens of beets and and greens and platters of freshly grown chicken, and the nervous tension turned jolly, almost celebratory. There was an underlying sense that this was it, all the vague directives and weird restrictions truly were in service of the greater good, of a project we all could derive meaning from, and nothing could sully that meaning, that sense of purpose. Then the SOM began.

Gardiner appeared and welcomed everyone, did his little half-wave thing, and faded out. Then we were treated to an anatomographic journey through Dunwoody's body, from heel to brain, as the voice-over recited some very basic anatomical details and equated each one with a kind of tek, "the urinary system is the bodies' own water filtration and treatment system..." and the like, ending with the brain, and then a detailed print of an augmentation system. Given the open-ended nature of the presentation requirements, starting the SOM with very elementary material was not the worst choice, it could certainly help ground the audience. Unfortunately, the pedantic tone stayed consistent throughout, and quickly became remarkably condescending, especially given the musty, pedestrian nature of Team Tek's vision.

It was, as Paulie had warned me, incredibly dull, outmoded, predicated entirely on the idea that we would be able to upload human consciousness very soon, any day now, in fact, because look, we've made so many strides in tek, what with GoCrowd instant voting replacing inefficient pre-conglomerate apparatus, nanovirus scripts revolutionizing medical treatment, in-home extrusion modularity, and all the rest of the greatest hits from a few decades ago. It was dressed up with very non-specific claims about the new ments we'd been written, but was otherwise remarkably pedestrian, and draining. The resource question was quickly glossed over—apparently, all we needed to do was insist people stop breeding, lest we run out of energy to power all the quantacores necessary to house the current world population. I noticed people beginning to log out about halfway through, switching to backchannel chat or simply walking out of the dining hall. I noticed because I was just as bored and had put the SOM in bracketed screen mode, open on the surface of the table, right around the time the vid exited Dunwoody's larnyx. I felt sorry for them. For all of us.

Dunwoody greeted the general ennui of the remnants of the crowd with what I decided was characteristic obliviousness. He rose from his seat near the door to the serving area, applauding, and turned to face the rest of us, arms open as if to receive the flood of accolades. Some of the crowd who'd left had begun to drift back in, perhaps to see the Q and A, and Dunwoody followed their entrance with confusion, then started darting his head around like a bird, searching for something or watching something the rest of us weren't privy to. A few kinds souls clapped. Then he sat, like an imploded building.

Gardiner and Beaudoin's avatars faded into view, signaling the start of Q and A. The questions were pointed, verging on aggressive, and were just as dull and obvious as the SOM had been, recitations of the same questions that had dogged the whole mind-emulation vision from the start. It could work, of course, to help ameliorate so many of the social disorders that had plagued humanity, if only it weren't impossible. The whole session, which was stretching into its third hour, was redolent of first-year college scripts. And then, mercifully and with little warning, it was over.

"Told ya," Paulie said, scampering up behind me as I walked back to my quarters.

"Yes, you did," I said. "Please tell me the entertainment will be more...."

"Entertaining? Absolutely. Peachy D gave that task to the younger team members, poor guy. For sure, the entertainment will be memorable, and will blast away all the nasty effects of the SOM. Chooga!" He darted left, toward the elevator. Well, at least there was something to look forward to.

I tried taking a nap, failed, and messaged Gint instead, worried about our own SOM.

"It was embarrassing," I told her, and she nodded agreement.

"That has no bearing on our vision, dear. It's a teaching experience, they've shown us exactly what not to do."

"Alright, alright, you're right." She had a calming effect on me. She really should have been Custodian.

"First thing, we'll meet and begin a script, just put every idea in and then cut and shape. Have you heard any of Jeffers' or Hurtado's ideas yet?"

"Not in depth, we got distracted."

"That's fine, we're well ahead of ourselves with the duty script, why not devote the whole day to a plan for the SOM?" She was offering me the chance to assert my leadership, suggesting I assert and own this plan of attack. Well, ok.

"Good idea. I'll send them a document. Enjoy off-day."

"I will." Her faced flickered out. I usually spent off-day running training scripts, or old vids. I knew someone had formed an off-day netball league, and Paulie claimed Team Endo had all-day genital massage workshops. All of us were also on-call for any Médecins emergencies, of which there'd been none, but it didn't take much for an epidemic to flare up.

Just as I'd managed to unwind my anxiety, an invitation to my first Custodial Conclave popped up. It would follow Team Tek's entertainment, and a "collective review" of both their SOM and the entertainment was the first item on the agenda. Each team Custodian was expected to offer a summary of their team's workflow, and then there was an open slot for extra-agenda items. Now I was worried all over again, and nearly messaged Gint once more, then thought better of it. I'd done Custodial work before, in more challenging circumstances, why was I nervous? Part of the reason involved the nature of the work—when I'd helped run the Houston camp, after three of the Custodians died in a suicide pact, I had a clear agenda and a clear set of deliverables. Here, I still wasn't sure what we were supposed to be doing. All I knew was that Team Tek had flopped.

I worked on a plan for our SOM for an hour or so, then headed down to the great room for the entertainment. The buzz that preceded Team Tek's SOM disaster had returned, so Paulie and his crew must have been doing a good job stoking the coals. Motochairs, the kind used for various ported sport gatherings, were set facing a central dais. I sat beside Jeffers, who smiled in an unfocused way, then saw the invitation blinking. A wash of gentle colors and tones seeped over the room as I accepted the invitation, very ambient and obvious, but very pleasant and well done, nevertheless. I smiled back at Jeffers, who had already turned away.

I found myself relaxing into my chair as the color washes began to coalesce into shapes, then into a face, a light brown face of indeterminate gender, perfectly smooth, perfectly symmetrical. It spoke:

"Welcome to Team Tek's Wonderous Diversion, Act One, Scene One. What we will present to you this evening depends on what you have to offer us, and the rest of the audience. Let me explain: the music you hear, and the abstract visuals, even the face speaking now, is derived from cognitive architecture present in your mind. Everyone sees a different face, everyone hears different music...

and everyone will experience a different journey over the next few hours, spun from the fabric of your being. But what is being without other beings? Self without other selves? Just as the music you hear is shaped by your individual minds, the algorithm within which your individuality operates is collective, a composite of all the data you are sending us... you will each experience an individual iteration of a score composed, real time, by our datachoir. As you begin your journey, some of you will find darkness, some will find light, and the shape of the journey will adjust accordingly. You must work together, from within completely different worlds, to finish the journey with the best outcome... to win the game, remember, you are a team, and as a team, you will be what you will be..."

I heard the first notes of a tone poem and there I sat, at my granmè's knee, watching her snap peas. I could almost taste them as they snapped, could hear her humming a tune, and I turned to look over my shoulder and saw a hole, vast, dark, floating in the air, drawing the world into it. I turned back to granmè, afraid, and she smiled, and the world lightened, I could no longer feel the hole sucking at my back, then she laughed and was holding a chicken and with a single cut of her knife loosed the chicken's head from its body, lifted the thrashing carcass and let the blood drip on her face, then held it over mine. I could not move, all was blood, and then a fire roared up beside me, and I was dry, and a woman handed me a glass of rum and I drank. It burned my throat, all the way down to my bowels, and my bowels exploded and I was lifted, I was swinging from a swing dangling from a tree whose branches stretched across the sky. A hand pushed my back and I swung, higher and higher, off into the sky, toward the maze of branches, then I tasted metal, a metal bar in my mouth and I bit down, I was on all fours in a field of red grass, and legs fell around me and a crop bit at my thigh and I bolted, on all fours, down into a valley full of smoke.

I sat beside a roaring bonfire, at the knee of an old woman. She had yellow eyes and a bright red head scarf, and was stroking a huge black pig, who sat at her other knee. She smiled, toothless but emitting a strange red light from somewhere in her throat.

"Ou konn mwan?"

"No, I don't know you, old woman."

"Ou konn me, yes, mwen rele Marinette Bwa Chech, ou granmè konn me bon!" She laughed harder at that, then bent down and took a bite out of the pig's neck, blood running down her chin and blouse.

"Please, I don't understand," I said. The pig was trembling, but did not move or make a sound.

"You understand. I save ye, maybe, or I bind ye here, maybe, you got pick a right offering." She gestured toward a blanket strewn with animal figurines, pieces of bone, polished stones, a broken glass, a bottle of greenish liquid. My hand was pulled toward a small goat carved out of soapstone, and I put it on my palm and held it out to her. She smiled again and I wished she hadn't.

"Ah, ou konn mwan!" she shrieked, and then she was sitting in the fire, her chair and body at the center of the flames, blackening, turning to ash and flakes that rose and rose and began to gather above the fire in a clump, a burst of white light, and I was sitting under another tree looking at an owl that glowed brighter than the moon. It blinked, picked at its chest with its beak, and flew away. I watched it dwindle to a point, til it became one of the millions of stars spilled across the sky. I felt serene, even as the stars began to wink out, a few thousand at a time, and my mouth began to itch.

I sat on a metal table in an examination room, tile walls and floor, the itch in my mouth suddenly fierce. I reached in my mouth and poked at a molar that seemed the source of the itch and it broke, and something began pushing its way out of the hole, out of my mouth, something far too large for my mouth and I thought my head would burst and I spit feathers and an owl the size of a human, with human arms and human legs covered with down. The owl reached down and grabbed my penis and rubbed it vigorously, each rub causing a chorus of voices to echo: "no boy no girl no boy no girl," three times it grabbed and rubbed, then bent over and slashed my stomach open with its beak. It did not hurt, I stared down at my open belly, watched the owl poke among my guts and pull out my shriveled ovary, then pop it in its beak and swallow.

Light, waves of gentle light and the sensation of falling, but not as strenuous as falling, a soft gravity drawing every cell of my body downward, at different speeds, my body elongating, stretching into shapes and waves of gentle light, then the music began, and the face appeared again.

"Thank you for participating in Team Tek's Wonderous Diversion, Act One, Scene One. We trust you had an interesting journey. The current score for Crowd One is +27. Your current individual score is +11. Wondrous Diversion ancillary scenes will be available, starting tomorrow, for anyone who desires to raise their individual or crowd scores."

The wash of colors and ambient music played across my vision, while a small red light in the bottom right invited me to close the channel. I closed it, and the colors faded, slowly, and I saw other employees shaking their heads, one or two standing unsteadily. Beside me, Jeffers had tear tracks drying on her face, and she chewed her bottom lip. I closed my eyes and sat for a few minutes. It felt as though my mind were full of scraps of paper, blowing in the wind, in a tiny cyclone. The scraps settled, dissipated, and I opened my eyes. Jeffers was gone, as was much of the crowd. I knew if I didn't make it back to my room soon, I would fall asleep in the motochair

§

The alarm shocked me, I usually woke well before the alarm sounded. Then it all flooded back: the entertainment, staggering back to my room and passing out, fully clothed, the Conclave I was supposed to attend in 10 minutes. I splashed water on my face and ran a trimmer over my head, turned on the arrow to lead me to the meeting, and jogged out to the hallway. Paulie was coming the other way, and I waved as I passed, head down. No time today, Paulie.

"Great gig, huh?" he called as I went past. I grunted an affirmative and made it to the elevator. Mbete and two other people, a man and a woman, were already aboard, and they all nodded to me.

"Interesting entertainment, no?" said the woman, her voice rich, vaguely euro-accented, probably a designer speech filter.

"I do not see why they make it a game. This is not a game," Mbete replied.

"Oh, game structuring has proven far more efficient than other worker relation models," said the man. I tried to remember what he looked like, and had to stifle and urge to turn and stare at all three.

"Not a game, even entertainment, is not a game. It is serious," Mbete added.

"Games are very serious, of course," said the woman, and the doors to the elevator opened.

I peeked at them all as we made our way down the hall. The man, shallow-chinned, heavy eyebrows, bulbous nose, was Mikhail Siegleman, Team DataPsych Custodian, renowned workforce motivational theorist and former intellectual crush of mine. I still was somewhat awed by his presence, but like most people, my thrall with his theories spanned my teen years and early 20s, at which point the realities of the workplace intruded. The woman wore a Runner jumpsuit, and so could only be Euna Gessner, who I knew only from the bio provided at orientation: former Olympic Bossaball medalist, celebrated polyamorist, her enormous wealth derived from genetically-engineered domestic pet patents. She walked like she wanted to sprint.

The meeting room had a wall of old-style vid monitors, and a blank, black wall for ment projection. The chairs were soft, the table sparkling, and the meeting nearly as dull as Team Tek's SOM. I've experienced several styles of Custodianship, from people who were committed members of that class, and could distill most of those styles into three general categories: first, the hands-off, tell me what the situation is and what your plan of attack will be Custodian; second, the hands-on, let me tell you all exactly what you are going to do (and don't mess it up) Custodian; third, the offer me a range of ideas, and I will choose one and direct everyone to follow through, but predicting which one might I choose will be impossible as I base my power on inscrutability Custodian. I had hoped Gardiner was an odd enough duck that he might break the mold and offer a different style, but he followed the last style to the letter, allowing every Team Custodian an opinion, a report, and a chance, at the end, to offer something unscripted, then retreated with his advisers, presumably to decide which direction the project would take from here. The opinions, on Team Tek's SOM and entertainment were nearly uniform: bad SOM, great entertainment with excellent HR potential. Only Mbete repeated his critique that game architecture was not correct for the scope of the entertainment's potential. The reports were perfunctory—Team Endo even offered "nothing to report," normally a kiss of death (and certainly not true, if rumors were to be believed), but in this case, it met with a nod and a notation. And, no one had anything off-script to add. The only thing that kept me awake, reeling as I was, still, from the entertainment, was the presence of Barbara Gint at the table. I'd suspected there was more to her role than was on the org charts, and I felt more justified about being named Custodian of our team, but also more wary of meeting her placid grey eyes.

Mbete fell into step with me as we walked.

"No one understands, why it is bad to play a game with this," he said. I really didn't feel like discussing it, so I nodded and kept walking.

"I enjoy games," he continued. "You must be of a mind to play, if you play a game. When you mix the mind of the game with the mind of everyday life, everyday life becomes only another token to mark time until the game is over." We got on the elevator. I thought I understood what he was saying, so I offered a suggestion.

"The idea of keeping score is endemic to our culture, of course. GoCrowd, halos, they are all ways of keeping score. It may be that the game mind, as you say, has fused with the everyday life mind, but in a way where we value life first, but the score merely amplifies it, amplifies our selves."

He shook his head. "If that is so, the game will win and we will lose."

I wasn't sure what he meant, and as I caught a sideways glance of the scars rippling the side of his head, the absolute exhaustion in his eyes, I only knew I didn't really want to know.

Chapter 9

The following morning, before the news feed, I was privy to my first Custodial update. There was no indication of a Custodial update in my new employment contract, so it must have been a late-night decision to produce one. My dreams were shot through with imagery from Team Tek's entertainment, and rousing myself again proved difficult, so I didn't quite know what was happening until the update was nearly over. I didn't want to miss the news feed, so I waited to vid the archived version of the update. Thus I learned of the events in SinoGanra like the rest of the employees, without Custodial preempting. The viral agent ravaging Lahore had spread as far as Karachi, and so had reached the Indian Ocean. Beijing's response had been the deployment of a nuclear "curtain" from Tibet to the former Tajikistan, similar to the NAS nuking of Eastern Texas during the Red Gulf crisis, but on a much vaster scale. Without knowing if the virus was waterborne, it was a particularly pointless act, especially given the failure of the same tactic in the NAS, but as 35 million people had already died, their bodies unrecognizable, a certain amount of panic was understandable. That the "solution" killed another 15 million was somehow equitable to those in charge. I don't suppose anyone considered what all that fallout would do to the water supply from the last glaciers clinging to the Himalayas.

Maybe they'd already moved into a bunker underground somewhere and didn't care.

I sat and stared at the wall for several minutes before mustering the energy to vid the Custodial update again. It was Gardiner and Bye, strangely giddy, providing a response script for employees asking about Lahore, as well as a special back channel messaging key for "Custodial Emergencies." That was odd, they had encryption on top of encryption for anything they wanted to send, why would they need a specially designated channel? I decided to message Barbara Gint, since she was apparently some kind of Custodial envoy.

She responded instantly, saying she "wondered when I would ask," and offered to meet for breakfast in the lab, before our shifts started. On the way to the lab, I was passed by a runner wheeling a tray laden what I presumed was the breakfast part of the meeting, and Gint was already there when I arrived. The sense of sluggish disconnect I'd woken with was still strong.

"All ready to work on the SOM?" she asked, spearing a piece of poached egg on toast.

"Ah, yes, of course, but if I could first ask—"

"I'm joking, I know you have other questions for me. So, shoot."

"Pardon?"

"Questions, ask away." She wiped her mouth and took a sip of juice.

"Well, yes, first, you are a Custodian, obviously," I said. I tasted a forkful of egg: so delicious I almost forgot to listen to her answer.

"Not so obviously, really. I helped develop the new ments, as you know."

"Yes," oh my, I couldn't stop eating.

"And as a result, I was here to help set up the facility. Mr. Gardiner asked me to stay on as an adviser, in order to measure any adjustments we might make in the future, ment architecture reconfigurations, or, god forbid, anti-viral algorithms."

"Ah, ok, that makes sense. More or less what I had assumed."

"Also, Charity Bye is my partner. It would be very hard for her to maintain the separation, so, there you are."

"That makes sense. But why not tell us?" I meant "me," but she knew that.

She thought for a moment, staring past my shoulder. "Mr. Gardiner is very insistent on trying to control as many variables as possible while we are here, and in modeling all the social data we can. We knew you, and others, would gradually find out, and we wanted to track how and why the information flowed the way it did."

"I see. I assume I am not supposed to tell anyone else?"

"Correct, the official word is restricting that information to employees that require it."

"Ah." And if I did start blabbing? I guess they would just "track the information," and I would not be provided such information in the future Or maybe they would, to see how reliable I was. And, of course, someone else on the Conclave had already spread the word, I was sure. I was part of the Custodial SOM in more ways than one.

"What else?" She put her plate and cutlery into the tray the runner had left.

"Um—" my head felt like it was evaporating at the top, gently, but enough to distract me. "Oh, the special Custodial channel, why? It seems like encryption would be sufficient."

She smiled. "You would think so, wouldn't you? I think Salenas has convinced Gardiner to be very worried about what's happening in SGN. The special channel can, in an emergency, work independently of the net, using our own server farm. It's a test, also, to see if the quantacores we have operational can handle the traffic."

"Independent of the net? Why?"

"As I said, I think Salenas is behind it. He's worried the SNG situation might spill over and start knocking down cubesats."

"Cubesats? How? No virus could reach that elevation."

"None yet, no. There are reports trickling in, uncon-firmed, of course, but it sure looks like some kind of cubesat disturbance over the affected area. I think all the nukes probably have something to do with it, but we can't be sure. Yet."

Jeffers and Hurtado arrived, and our conversation turned to work and rumor monitoring. I noticed both of them giving Gint side-eyed glances, so they had surely heard something already about her special status. I sat, numbly running algorithms and recording conversa-tions, wondering which parts of what Gint had told me were true, which parts were false, and if all of it was be-ing fed to me as part of "tracing the flow of information."

By the pre-dinner news feed, I knew at least part of the truth: cubesats were going down over Asia, and the Lahore nanovirus was now waterborne.

§

Dinner was raucous, the dining room thronged with talk and whispers. A response script sent over the Custodial channel said we were to encourage all employees to work diligently at their SOMs, as the world needed this knowledge now more than ever, and that we had a backup intranet about to deploy. No one took the script very seriously, and word spread that the team Custodians knew no more than anyone else. One of the women in Team Military suggested, emphatically enough to be heard over the din, that we go up top, outside, as if seeing the sky would somehow allay their fears.

We got word of a shadow profile of the virus ravaging SGN, and met at the lab to start working up algorithms. Everyone knew the drill, and we were given a very general time-line: three weeks, give or take, well, two weeks. As the virus approached, we would get better profiles, but it would apparently knock out cubesats as it went, so at some point we would receive no profile data at all, which meant the virus was at our doorstep, and our water filtration system was in danger. It felt good to have something concrete to work on, even though the lack of complete profile data was frustrating. At 0300, Gint suggested Jeffers and I get some sleep, then rotate shifts with her and Hurtado. I'm sure I dreamed, because I woke on the floor, but I remembered nothing.

I got back to the lab at 0800, after getting a message that the Custodial emergency channel was now a Project-wide emergency channel. Gint and Hurtado both looked ready to drop, but a late feed of high-quality profile data had given us a lot to work with, so they also both seemed hopeful. Jeffers and I settled in, pecking now and then at the remains of a casserole a Runner brought soon after we arrived.

"This picture is shit, I need to adjust the contrast," Jeffers said. I signaled assent with a green light. Once I got deep into this part of my work, I stopped talking and communicated exclusively by ment. It was faster. Jeffers, on the other hand, still liked the sound of voices.

"Can I ask you a question?" she said, and I signaled green again. "No, like, in person."

I sighed, and flicked off the profiling interface. "Sure."

"Do you think this was really an accident?" she seemed sheepish, looking down at the table as she said it.

"Do I think what was really an accident?"

"The virus. The whole dingy scenario, the nukes, the cubesats going down. Someone said they heard about plans for 20 or 30 facilities just like this one, in different regions, that the whole thing was a set-up."

"That's more than a little ridiculous. Think about the resources necessary to pull something like that off."

"I know, I know, it's just—"she was starting to cry, I noticed— "it's all happening so fast."

"You've been in situations just like this before, so have I, you know response time is short, you know how quick-ly viral patterns can scroll their mutation scripts." I put my hand on her arm, like I was balancing a piece of wood there. Interpersonal compassion was not my strong suit.

"Yes, you're right, but, it's just, I don't know enough about the organizational structure here, I mean, if something did happen, I don't know nearly enough to trust, um, those—" she pointed upward with a finger, an oddly furtive gesture, since she knew I was recording her. Or maybe she'd forgotten. I checked: the recording channel was still open. Of course, if we lost net access, we would lose access to all that data, unless they were archiving it locally, which would be odd, and thus consistent with the whole project. She was right, the Custodians were a slippery crew, it was hard to feel comfortable when their agenda was unclear.

"One more thing?"

"What is it?" I said, flicking off the interface again. My obvious impatience made her cringe.

"Well, you've been in the, what, the upstairs," she said, hesitantly.

"I've been in the vidstage, and the Conclave was the floor below that. So, yes, but just there, why?"

"Just curious," she said, and went back to profiling. Just curious about what? A strange question that went nowhere, and which made it hard for me to focus the way I needed to, so I stopped to fetch us both some tea and snacks.

A Runner met me at the door of the dining room with a tray. I complimented her on their speed, and she grinned bashfully before slipping back into the dining room. People selected for Team Runner were highly introverted, very energetic individuals, great at focusing on repetitive tasks, generally non-productive in more social settings. Euna Gessner, the Runner Custodian, wasn't introverted at all, at least when I'd met her, but she did seem rather maniacally on task at the Conclave.

Back at the lab, I poured us both cups of tea and took a bite of a crescent roll. My teeth found something hard, and I pulled out a thin strip of plastic with "0300: Meeting Rm I-40" printed on it. It fell apart within seconds of reading it, and I looked across the table at Jeffers, to share my confusion. Her eyes were closed, deep in the profile. I decided the message was not intended for me, but for her, that it was utterly charming in its antiquated style, and that something conspiratorial was afoot. And, that it was exciting, a real life version of *Friend's World*. Then I remembered that people were dying outside, millions upon millions, and I was ashamed.

§

I was not so ashamed that I didn't walk, as casually as I could, down Hall I toward room 40 late that night, a few minutes before 0300. I lingered in the hall until 0305, then went in. The room was empty, and no messages were coming through my ments, so I went back to my room. I lay in my bed, playing with the little light Kirkus sold me, back in the real world, or at least a lot closer to it. As I'd assumed, the message was not for me, so it must have been for Jeffers. I spent the next shift trying to work up the courage to broach the subject with her, but could not. I left my pastry untouched, and pulled apart my sandwich wrap carefully before eating it. As we worked, more cubesats were reported offline, and the evening news feed we received was choppy and dismal. The virus had spread through China and pushed West into the ERC, and fear of the virus was prompting large scale riots in every major city on the planet.

Profiling the virus was going well, however. I was surprised no one had counter-engineered it yet. The basic script was simple enough, it was the mutation forks that proved prickly, and addressing those was a matter of isolating enough of a profile to render it defunct. With the data we had, I thought three more days of work would be enough to have a model, and one more day to replicate enough anti-virus. It was impossible that every nanocenter in the world had been swamped by the virus, speedy as it was. Something else must have happened, something more than nukes in the Himalayas and riots in the favelas everywhere.

My suspicions were exacerbated when it turned out my presumptive time line was a very conservative estimate: four days after we got our first, hazy profiles of the virus, Hurtado and Gint cracked it, and Jeffers and I had a model to begin replicating. Our news feed that morning, full of static and lost signals, had at last gone dead completely, and the emergency channel reported full cubesat failure, that is, the net was effectively gone. We were directed to get the antivirus ready for deployment in all air and water filtration systems, though not, oddly, for airborne dispersal outside. As Jeffers and I rushed through replication, the thunder began.

We knew it couldn't be thunder, of course. But the room shook, and we heard a great boom, then another, and another, cascading. It lasted four or five minutes, neither of us moved, or messaged each other, or, it seemed, breathed. Then it was over, or so the emergency channel signaled: "Remain calm. Sensors indicate multi-warhead nuclear detonation. Radar indicates zero remaining incoming warheads. Please return to your assigned tasks. More details as we learn them." We looked at each other for the first time since the thunder began. She reached out for my hand, and we both began to cry.

I'm not sure how long we both let ourselves sit there, weeping softly, but once we had exhausted our tears, there wasn't much left to say, so we continued outfitting the filtration systems with the antivirus. We fixed the script to the grid and let it run. We had gone back to not looking at each other, which suddenly made me nervous.

"I think we will know more, soon," I offered, weakly.

"I don't think I want to know more. I don't think—" she jumped up from her chair. "We need to go up top! Outside! We need to see what the damage is, we..." she slumped back down again.

"Let's take a break," I suggested. There was still luke warm tea and juice left from the morning, and some soggy little thing called a "danish" that the Runners in dining had cooked up. It felt stupid to eat, to drink, but I gathered the tray up robotically and set it down on the table. Jeffers didn't move. I cut the danish in half, poured tea for both of us, and watched Jeffers raise her head, shake it from side to side, and mutter "no, no," louder and louder, till she bolted upright, shouting "NO" as she ran from the room. I looked down at the danish, and the little rectangle of plastic sticking out of one side. I pulled it out: "0400: Meeting Rm K-72."

Chapter 10

Team Farm's SOM was postponed for a week, due to inclement apocalyptic conditions. Well, the second part wasn't included in the official notice, but the SOM was indeed postponed, and all employees were put on Custodial Alert, which meant we were to continue our shift duties and SOM planning until the Custodians could provide a full profile of what exactly had happened to the world at large. Paulie came to my room that evening and regaled me with conspiracy theories, several of which involved alien species who had been biding their time on the other side of the sun for a thousand years. I had dinner sent to my room, as did more than half the employees, according to Gint, who messaged me to say the filtration systems were fully fortified with anti-viral agent, and to chat about a lot of nothing. Everyone wanted to chat about nothing. I wanted everyone to leave me alone, for my little good angel to go quiet for a while, and let the big good angel chug along and listen to my heartbeat. The evening news feed was a replay of the previous emergency announcement, so I set my alarm for 0330, closed my messaging channel, and lay in bed, staring at the ceiling.

I, and everyone my age or younger, had been born into a world teetering on the brink of collapse. I had had mentors, at nearly every level of schooling, who fed me scripts about the universality of this fear across time, that humanity had dreamed of skies filled with fire as long for as we had an idea that the sky was a place. I understood this explanation, but it did not negate the fact that the threats we faced, as a species, were currently well beyond the dreams of any hair-shirted monk on a stony island. Considerable resources had been devoted to building orbital habitats, on missions to Mars and Io, and all were hampered by the same cynicism and incompetence that characterized every attempt at saving ourselves here on earth. These were my people, born into a dying world, raging to save it but without the energy to rage long enough, the conviction to do more than please themselves, to find distractions. And now the end was really here, it seemed, and so many of my people were dead, and I couldn't help but think they were the lucky ones.

Work had always been my distraction, my salvation, my only habit left to cling to, so I rose when the alarm went off and headed for Meeting Room K-72—it was work, surely, the work of finding out what exactly was going on, what sort of work the people who sent messages in pastry wanted me to do. The hallway was empty, the elevator, the halls of floor K, all devoid of people. I could imagine everyone in their quarters, unable to sleep, scanning dead channels, staring into space. The door to K-72 was already open as I approached, and I didn't hesitate this time, walking through and sitting at one of the conference chairs. Seconds after I sat, the lights went out, and I heard a voice:

"Please don't be alarmed. We must be careful. Please put the box in your head."

The lights came up again, and sure enough, there was a black plastic box on the table in front of me. I stood and lifted it, saw the hole in the bottom, then sat back down and put it over me head. I felt utterly ridiculous, but then again, humanity was murdering itself outside.

"Thank you," the voice said. I heard someone, no, a few people, pull chairs away from the table and sit in them. The box was blocking my vision, but I could hear perfectly.

"The box is unfortunate, but we must be careful," the voice repeated. "It blocks visual input 100%, and scrambles aural input enough to be secure. Naturally, it also blocks any ment transmission or recording."

"Can you hear me?" I asked.

"Yes," said a different voice. I nodded, and realized the gesture might not have the same effect with my head in a box.

"Manoushka Duval," said the first voice, "Custodian of Team Médecins."

Was I supposed to respond? "Yes."

"We are in a difficult situation, Mr. Duval," the first voice continued. "If we are to survive this situation, we need help, we need employees willing to commit themselves."

"Who are you?"

They ignored my question. "The situation outside this facility is dire, hence the situation within the facility is also dire. I know you understand that. I also know that you have seen how our Custodial Team operates, and that you must understand they are not the right individuals to lead us out of this situation. Gardiner, Bye, and the rest are operating without a plan, without an ideology, and they are not creative enough to guide us, they lack vision. We may be the last people alive. Do you think they are capable of helping us survive and thrive, here and on the surface?"

"To be perfectly honest, I haven't given it much thought." I heard chairs moving, motion, whispers.

"I find that hard to believe," said a different voice.

"I'm sorry you find it difficult. Like many employees, I have been in shock these last few hours."

"But you've seen how they operate, the obfuscation, the vague mission statements. Think about it now: are these the people that can lead us to a better world?"

My initial reaction was no, of course not, then I thought about the task ahead, and realized no one was truly up to the task. Then it occurred to me that I might be speaking to Bye, or Salenas, or even Gardiner himself.

"What do you offer instead? You wouldn't be asking these questions otherwise. What is your vision, then?"

More whispers. "We are not at liberty, at present, to reveal details to you. We must first have your commitment to removing the current Custodial Team. If you do not commit, how can we trust you with the details of our vision? How can we trust that you will not go straight to the top floor and tell them everything, jeopardize our entire project?"

They couldn't trust me, of course, and neither could I trust them. I was sitting in a room with a box on my head, they knew who I was, and I only knew there was some conspiracy afoot to remove the Custodians. I couldn't commit without more information, and they couldn't provide me the information I needed to commit. They knew this would be the end game when they put the message in the pastry.

"Why me?" Perhaps I could get someone to leak data.

"You are Custodian of Team Médecins. You have been to a Conclave, you have better data then the typical employee."

"I can't commit without more information, and you knew that before I put the damn box on my head."

Silence, followed by chairs scraping, a door in the back of the room opening.

"We will be in contact, Mr. Duval. Please consider what we've discussed here. We will signal you when events are about to transpire. Watch for the signal. And please, until that time, consider the fate of the species may well be at stake. You may remove the box."

I lifted the box from head, and again, the room was perfectly dark. The lights came up, and on the table in front of me was a smaller box. I opened it, and saw inside Fiedler's silver and turquoise necklace.

Was I meant to take it? Was it a message, that they had killed Fiedler, that there was, in fact, a conspiracy from the very start, as Paulie insisted? Or did they think I was friends with Fiedler, and wanted a memento? I lifted the necklace, surprised how heavy it was. It was worn in spots, and needed polishing. There were people watching me, I realized, watching as I manipulated the object they'd given me, watching to see what I would do. If it wasn't so large, I would have swallowed it, just to confuse them. Instead, I put it on the table, beside the case, and left the room. As I rode back up to my floor, I noted it was 0430, and that I was suddenly exhausted, ready to sleep, and comfortable with the idea that I might not wake up. What is it about the structure of the human mind that leads it to dream of oblivion, I thought, what possible evolutionary advantage can there be to lusting after the void? Our survival instinct was a tattered, befouled old flag laying in the mud.

I sat on my bed and noticed things on my table had been moved, that my wall unit was partially open: someone had searched my room while I was gone. Or had put something in it. I suddenly felt angry, manipulated, with nowhere to direct my anger. Just as quickly, my anger subsided, washed away with the world outside the facility, and I slid under the bed clothes and fell into a hard sleep.

§

The morning news feed was, well, sparkly. Someone had generated a head, a classic news feed anchor animatron, replete with enormous hair and a stiff smile that triggered far too often. Each script it read highlighted the work each team was doing, with twinkling music in the background, and plenty of neon glow. Then the head discussed Team Tek's SOM and entertainment with Dunwoody, or an avatar of Dunwoody, most likely, as he looked sprightly and well-tanned. They agreed that the SOM needed a great deal of work, and that the entertainment had been a roaring success. Dunwoody's delight at the success of the entertainment was enough to confirm that it wasn't really him. Team Farm's SOM, the head noted near the end of the discussion, was now scheduled for today. At the very end of the broadcast, there was an update on conditions outside, in the form of a weather map, but with additional overlays for "viral infestation" and "radioactive drift." It looked like a child had overclocked a vidpaint kit and left it running for a week.

A meeting tag spiked just as the feed faded out, indicating a Conclave in 20 minutes, breakfast to be served. Well, that was nice of them. I dressed, splashed water on my face, and went through the desolate halls to the elevator. The occasional distant voice, a scuttling of feet behind a door—the absence of people heightened my senses, brought the grey walls and flecks of white mold in sharp focus, snarls of tubing, the smell of old clothes and grease. The elevator screamed and shuddered as it rose, then stopped to allow Mbete to enter. His face was puffy, his eyes squinting, unfocused.

"Good morning, Colonel," I said.

"Not Colonel, just Mbete," he sighed.

"Of course, sorry."

We reached the Custodial floor. Mbete opened the doors, then stopped.

"Godsong," he said.

"What?"

"Godsong. My first name. My mother was a preacher, in Dadaab." He gestured for me to step into the hall.

"Manoushka."

"I am glad to meet you this morning, Manoushka."

"And I you, Godsong."

We went down the hall to the meeting room in silence.

§

The meeting room must have been soundproofed, because a roar of voices washed over us like steam from rejuvenator as soon as we signaled the door open. Everyone was talking at the same time, loudly, except, I saw, for the members of Team Custodian, all of whom were present, all of whom sat together, their backs to the wall. They had the glazed look of people frantically messaging each other.

"What are you going to do about it?" someone yelled, close to where I found an empty seat. They yelled it again, and I realized it was Mikhail Siegleman, and he was yelling at me.

"I'm sorry, what am I going to do about what?"

"The virus! Are you releasing the anti-virus to the wild or not?"

"I—well, we have released it here, into our filters, we are checking its efficacy—"

"The world is dying!" he screamed, and a sudden, blinding flash of light and screeching noise interrupted everything. When I could see again, I watched the rest of the Conclave regain their vision, shaking their heads and smacking their ears with their palms.

"Well. Now. People. Employees," said Gardiner, sounding out of breath, though he hadn't moved. "As we are all in attendance, ok, let's begin the Conclave, and please, respect one another's space, both physical and verbal. We will take turns voicing concerns, dealing with them, and then we can get on with the very exciting work we have ahead of us."

The silence that followed was more confusing than the noise that had preceded it. It seemed no one could actually believe we were going to hold a proper meeting. The silence became a weight, pressing down on everyone, until Euna Gessner finally broke.

"Mr. Gardiner, respectfully, what is going on here? I've talked two of my people out of suicide in the last 12 hours, the world outside is, what, gone? And we're having a goddamn meeting about—" her voice rose to near shouting, then her head snapped from side to side and she stared at the table. Her nose started bleeding slowly. Apparently the shock or augment blast or whatever it was could be delivered to individuals, in addition to the whole group.

"Please, please, I understand you are all under a lot of pressure. We have a new kind of deadline now, don't we?" Gardiner giggled, sneaking looks around the room. He had made a joke. Ha.

"I'm sorry, sir," Gessner began, then stopped.

"Mr. Gardiner," Dunwoody said, rubbing his hands together, "while I respect your need to maintain order, perhaps administering neuronal shock is not the best way to obtain, ah, authentic commitment."

"Good point, now we're working! Salenas?"

"The attention arrest script should remain in place until such time as employees have proven they can act in a professional manner, at which point it will be retired."

Some very subdued grumbling greeted his announcement.

"We understand the stress that you all are facing. We are facing it too, but the need to maintain a semblance of order and professionalism at this juncture is more crucial than ever," Bye jumped in.

"Professionalism?" It was Gary Manpeiler's turn to test the waters. "If the worst has happened, out there, then I don't think the word really applies anymore, do you?" His voice oozed out like oiled honey.

"Oh, gosh no," Gardiner said, "I think now it applies more than ever. For instance, you are right, we need to figure out if what we fear has really occurred, if it's really as bad as we think outside. In a non-professional situation, if we didn't understand organizational structure and dynamics, we might just go rushing willy-nilly up and out and find ourselves all dead of radiation or viral agents in seconds, and poof, no more human race. No, no, we need professionalism more than ever now, a sense that we all have a job to do to ensure our own survival, to help us flourish, to make as all be what we can be. I know, I know, I've said that before, but truly, let's think about the opportunity we have here."

"Opportunity?" Mbete choked the word out, and it fell like a bug that had flown from his gaping mouth.

"Yes, an opportunity. We came here to make plans, to develop a series of structures and directives that might help humanity flourish once again. But it was an exercise, and as many of you noted, the first obstacle was the most difficult: implementation. We could develop a model society, yes, but who would listen? I mean, wow, now they will listen, for sure! I mean, whoever is left, and I'm sure there are people left outside, let's not be rash. But really, let's see this for what it is: our chance to make our work mean more than any work we've ever done, maybe than any work anyone has ever done!" He slapped the table with the edge of his hand, making a meaty *thunk* that sounded like it hurt.

We tried to process his zeal. The alternative was, well, was what? We could go outside and, presumably, die. We could reject his message and try to live piecemeal, negotiating every meal, waste removal, power, pharma, everything we needed for daily life. Some team or other had hold of every part of this facility, and we needed them to all work together. The scope of the planning necessary was daunting, far more than it had been when the whole exercise was academic.

"Mr. Gardiner," LouAnn Manpeiler spoke through the general fog that had settled: "There has been a great deal of, um, talk—"

"Yes? Lots of talking, yes?"

"Well, sir, talk that perhaps you had something to do with the Lahore virus." She cringed, a dog anticipating a blow. The room held its breath. Gardiner laughed.

"Of course, of course, I understand, reactions of that nature are natural. But a moment's reason is enough to dispel such silliness. Just think, could I, even with all the resources I have at my disposal, release a virus that would spread just enough, in all the right directions, that it would cause various entities around the world to use nuclear weapons to try and contain it? Let alone, why would I do such a thing, but even if I was a madman of this type, consider the number of moving parts, of things that would have to go exactly right to bring about the situation we have outside. I find it flattering, really. Thank you, I admire your candor. Now, other general questions, before we begin the task of negotiating some kind of organizational architecture?"

There were more questions, some innocuous, some bizarre, some practical, and no more attention arresting scripts were deployed. We each left the room with an agenda for our teams, and a bare bones system of "credit" that would help determine the exchange of goods, services, and work, as determined by a script Team Tek would author. This pleased no one, especially Dunwoody, who wanted none of the responsibility, and only agreed to take it on once basic living income standards for all were agreed upon. That evening, at dinner, we were supposed to sit together, all the Custodians, as Gardiner and the rest led everyone through the plan, which, at this point, was only a set of directives for making a plan. We were back to square one, but all the other squares had been taken off the board.

"Manoushka, join me for a moment?" Mbete asked when we once again found ourselves alone in the elevator. I nodded and followed him to his quarters. Unlike on my floor, there was activity in these halls, men and women walking up and down, open doors with people inside playing cards, drinking.

"My floor is so quiet," I said, as we went into his rooms.

"This floor is all military. The end of the world, it is the end result of their training, what they were made for. Also, they do not believe it."

"What? What do you mean?"

"They are men and women trained to fight. One cannot fight if there is nothing to fight for, so they tell themselves stories, that the news feed was a lie, or a mistake, or that it will be only a week or two before they can leave. They must."

"Ah. The whole floor is the same team?"

"Yes. Yours is not?"

"No, we have Médecins, some Tek, some DataPsych, a hodge-podge."

"That will change." He plugged in a kettle and put teabags into cups for us. "Manoushka, I ask you this because I have seen what happens when people lose hope: are you prepared to fight?"

"Fight? Do you mean physically?"

"I mean whatever you mean." He poured the tea.

"I—I don't think I am. I don't think I want to be in a situation where I need to fight. I want to work." He sighed, blew on his tea, and sat back.

"I am glad. Because, there are many that want to fight, to be violent because violence, it is a seduction. Do you know why I am here, why I am no longer called 'Colonel'?"

"No, that wasn't in your file. Only that you served PonDafrique for a dozen years, that you joined NAS as a consultant, then left them as well. It was a well-scrubbed file."

"Yes, thanks to Mr. Gardiner. It was his idea, I am not a man who cares to hide things. I left PonDafrique because I wanted more money, more status. I cared for little else. I joined NAS, and two days later, I took a team of consultants to the Dakotas, an uprising of server teks and favela dwellers. We managed to catch them, all 12,000 of them, and took them to a camp in an old shale mine. Our orders were to kill them and shred the bodies for removal. I had done this a hundred times in PonDafrique. It is what we do, soldiers. There was nothing different here, the people were more white, and it was not so hot, but I looked out from my hovership at them all, 12,000 human souls, and something in me shifted, a tectonic plate moved and an earthquake happened in my mind, my soul. I could not give the order. I was finished as a soldier, I could not do what I was meant to do. The directive kept flashing in my eye, my men stood waiting—then it stopped, my Lieutenant gave the order, and I was released from my contract." He crossed his hands on his lap and looked at them.

"I am sorry. I heard nothing of the uprising," I said.

"No, it was not worth a spot on any news feed."

"I heard, from people in the favela near my house, about things like that. Unreported mass killings. I only ever half-believed them."

"Now you can believe them all."

"So, Gardiner—"

"Gardiner hired me, he says, because he needed soldiers with conscience. I told him soldiers needed to obey, not question. He said we would see, and promised there would be no weaponry other than stun sticks and our fists. I did not anticipate these," he said, tapping the spot on the back of his head where they deployed the augmentations.

"Yes, I can't believe no one else ever thought to weaponize ments."

"They did, but they were never strong enough. A small static charge, some visual disruption, and so easy to block."

"Block?"

"Some charged fabric, like a bandage, that was enough to keep signals from transmitting." He reached suddenly and grabbed my neck, his hand around the back, gently, but firmly enough that I sat perfectly still. He put something on the back of my head, leaned back. "Like so," he said.

I reached up and felt a mass of snarls on the back of my head, like a small, furry hand pulling on my skin. He reached up and touched his hair, then twisted it slightly. He was wearing a very realistic wig. I was fairly certain mine was not realistic at all, but it was not a full wig, so maybe no one would notice.

"For now, just to say this, without people hearing or seeing: a scut bandage, doubled, is enough to block ment transmission. Remember that." I nodded. "And you have access to many scut bandages. And you will not fight, but perhaps you will help those of us who will." He sat forward again, put his hand on my neck, and pulled the hairy bandage off my skull. It had been tighter than I realized. He put the thing in my hand, and I thought I could feel it wriggling.

"Now, let us go back and deliver the news, yes my friend? The employees must be wondering what is to become of them!" He laughed in a shrill cackle, like a hyena who just found a corpse. His eyes were overfull, tears rushing down as he turned away.

Chapter 11

The noise level at dinner was so low, I wondered if Salenas had deployed a preemptive attention arrest script to the entire dining hall. Everyone ate quietly, whispered requests for salt and pepper and water jug and tea canteen, avoided looking at one another—even Bye, Lem, and Beaudoin, the members of Team Custodian sent to appear in person, ate without speaking, though surely they were messaging each other and checking observation feeds the whole time. I only got two messages during the meal, one from Hurtado, asking to begin his shift three hours late tomorrow, and one from Paulie that just said, "aliens!," and included a grinning Grey Man head that spun thrice before turning to mist.

We'd all received the message to remain in dining hall after the meal, and even the runners came out of the kitchen and wherever else they lurked and sat together at a table in the corner. Every team sat together, in fact, something that hadn't happened since the first day. Soon after the last runner emerged from the kitchen and joined his team, the lights changed color, subtly, from white to a gentle rose. Bye stood and cleared her throat, and every set of eyes turned toward her.

"Good evening, employees." Murmured responses skittered across the room. "We have much to discuss, and I hope we can all maintain a professional demeanor. It is, of course, more crucial now than ever that we all work together to be what we can be. Agreed? Very good. Now. I have just forwarded you an agenda for this meeting, and as you can see, before we start break out sessions, we will have a word from our Head Custodian, Mr. Gardiner."

Gardiner's form, clad in a white jumpsuit with orange piping on the legs and sleeves, rippled into view in front of Bye, who sat down primly.

"Hello!" Murmurs, again, even less strenuous than they were for Bye. "Wait, wait, I can't hear you! Hello!" A few people shouted hello, angrily. "Wonderful, wonderful, gosh you are such a wonderful set of persons. Just the best group to undertake the task we have before us. Wow! Double wow! Ok, I can see how really terrible this all must appear to everyone. It was terrible for me, when I first understood the scope of has happened outside, and I don't even know the whole scope. I know that some very nasty radiation is blowing by the facility just now, not right on us, but let's look."

A map of the Western NAS appeared, with great swaths of red and lighter red oscillating across it. The camera zoomed out to show the whole continent, and how red it was, all of it, save for a few islands of yellow scattered near us, and up in the very north, smack in the midst of one of the largest dead shale fields, where no one could live, even without clouds of radiation.

"Right, I know, I know, pretty bleak. But extrapolate a few years—" the red began to seep away, slightly, then more and more, leaving several large yellow spots around the Midwest, and a few opened up further south, in Sinaloa. "See? That's only five years from now, and already the habitables are growing. And that's just our best guess, extrapolating from the weather data we can pick up, the last bits of net feed we managed to snag, and not even counting maybe some radiation-eating bugs, huh? Big bonus to the first person who splices one of those babies together!" He chuckled. His madness, which was apparent, was also remarkably focused and consistent. "Now, let me be serious for a moment."

His avatar sat cross-legged, about 5m in the air. This was his serious posture, apparently.

"We all lost people out there. And we all knew that it could happen, though no one really wanted to believe it. But we need to think of this as an opportunity, a chance to rebuild the world, bit by bit, the best world possible. And you know, it's happened before! At least two, maybe three, near-extinction events for our species, a volcano in Sumatra, the Baltic meteor a few million years before that—and what happened? Did we wilt away? No! We flourished, the best genes survived, and we prospered. And we can prosper again! Don't let yourself get all sad, don't let the darkness get you. You're better than that. You are the best at what you do, and you are special, besides. Think of how lucky it is that we set up this project when we did. If I were a religious type person, I might think it divine providence.

"So here is my message to you, and yes, I know you've heard it before: be what you will be. I know that is a good thing, cause you all are the winners. You've won. Give yourselves a pat on the back." He reached over his shoulder and patted himself on the back, and gestured for us to do the same. A few people actually did it.

His avatar, still floating above us in sitting position, faded out. No one spoke, and the sound of Bye's chair scraping the floor as she stood cut through the room like a rusty hook dragged along a drum.

"Very good, very well done, I think," she said, and put her hands together as if to clap, then thought better of it. "Well. As you can see from your agenda—"

"Fuck the agenda!" someone yelled. Other voices joined them, a general clamor shuddered forth. Bye pursed her lips, and the room flashed. It wasn't as bad as the first time, perhaps because I knew it was coming, but it still took a moment to get my bearings.

"So, we have an attention arrest script ready to restore order at any point, as you can see. I would much prefer you use your own sense of self-regard to maintain a professional attitude, but we can deploy the script if need be. Let's not need to, ok?" Gardiner's disembodied voice said as people shook their heads.

A furor arose to Bye's left. Lem stood and drew a stun gun, Beaudoin ducked behind him. The flash came again, then again, and when we had regained our senses, three men with bright red wigs and clown noses held Bye's arms. Lem was on the ground, blood seeping from his head. Beaudoin had vanished.

"People! Listen! We don't need to listen to these fools anymore! Who do you think engineered the crisis outside? Who do you think engineered the Lahore virus? Gardiner! You know it! You know it in your hearts! And you know he's right, we have work to do—but not for fools like him!" The wigged man picked up Lem's stun gun, pressed it to Bye's chest, and fired it. Her body spasmed and fell. "We must make our future! We must—" another shock, a brutal one. My teeth felt like they were about to fall out of my head, and my eyes burned. When we came to, the clowns were on the ground, their hands being bound by a man from Team Soldier. Lem was sitting up at the table, holding a towel to his head. The soldiers lifted the three men off the ground by their arms and sat them on the floor, against the far wall. They paused, then reached down and pulled off the wigs and noses. They were all member of Team Farm, including Hendrickson, their Custodian. The soldiers paused again, receiving messages, then they backed away from the bound men, who began to twitch and writhe. Gardiner's avatar appeared again, in front of the table, his leg projecting through Bye's prone body. "Oh come on now, people, let's try again. We can be so much better! You know," he started walking, holding his elbow— "some days, even when there's work to do, the best thing is to just stop the meeting early, and reconvene later. Let's do that, what do you say? Go home, get some rest, make love, play chess, watch a vid, whatever, and we'll all meet back tomorrow and try again. How does that sound?" No one moved. "Good, ok then, let's move it out, and have a great evening, ok?"

Team Soldier got everyone moving, helping Bye and Lem out first, then signaling us to leave in staggered groups, out the door and away from the dining hall. I sent a script to the lab and started extruding painkillers, anticipating serious trauma and migraine aid requests in the near future. I put my hand on the small of Jeffers' back, guiding her out when our table was signaled. Hurtado jumped up and almost ran to the door, twitching, vanishing into the crowd in the hallway. Jeffers kept stopping, looking at me, opening her mouth to say something, then shaking her head. We were the last Team to head for the hallway—other than the three soldiers and three former clowns.

Bye and Lem were already at the lab when I arrived, and had, in fact, already gotten the pharma and bandages they needed. "Painkillers already extruding, good thinking, Duval," Bye said, creakily. Lem stood near the door, waiting for the bioscan to finish. When they left, I checked the database, and was not surprised to find the scans Bye and Lem had just done missing from the archive. Self-wiping data screens, these folks have a long game planned here, I thought, and began answering requests for aid as quickly as my ments allowed.

§

After three hours of filling pharma requests, including all blends previously restricted by the Custodians, Hurtado appeared at the dispensary. He nearly bowled over Mick, the runner who'd been helping me distribute, then started checking over the list of requests without acknowledging my presence. I saw his hands were shaking. 10 minutes later, Jeffers arrived, gave us both a weak smile, and sat, staring at her messages. As I finished the final extrusion request, two more appeared: one for Hurtado, one for

Jeffers, both mild sedative/mood-relief blends with vi-taspikes.

"Ok," I said, and processed the requests. They both had access codes to the extruder, and I didn't feel like arguing.

"Just want to make it through tonight," Jeffers said, on the verge of tears. I put my hand on her shoulder.

"Still think they killed Fiedler, she knew the shit was going down like this," Hurtado said, fumbling with the sink handles, trying to draw a glass of water. He still wouldn't look at either of us.

"Who killed her? And what shit, exactly? The end of the world?"

"Yes, the end of the goddamn world, dingy bastards ran a game out there and it took down the whole planet. Or haven't you been paying attention, playing Captain Pharma for the Conclave?" His eyes swelled, glassy, full of fear and panic. I was surprised. His file had indicated experience with some fairly grim situations.

"So you think—someone killed, killed her because—why? What could she do, I mean, if she knew about what they were doing, and, then why did they hire her? Why hire someone who disagrees with you, so you have to kill her? That doesn't make sense." Jeffers was starting to rock slightly from side to side. Pharma, kicking in.

"I don't know, I don't know, I'm sorry But I'm gonna figure it out. I'm done, I'm gone," he said, and was, out the door and down the hall. I watched Jeffers rock for a few seconds, then moved my hand from her shoulder to her arm.

"Jeffers—Candle—go lay down. Everything is fine here. Go rest." She nodded, wiped her mouth with her arm, and left. A few more requests popped up, followed by a very insistent message from the Custodial team requesting attendance of all employees at a special meeting in the fourth floor fab warehouse, in two hours. 1400 seemed a strange time to have a meeting, but I'd just watched the HR director assaulted by people wearing clown wigs and noses, so perhaps it wasn't so strange after all. There was something encouraging about the speed of their response, actually, though it did cause another spike in pharma requests.

For the next 90 minutes, the requests trickled in. At 1330, I sat with Mick, fighting exhaustion, waiting for a few more to appear and make it worth his time to run them before the special meeting. He was a small man, slightly hunched, with too much brown hair hiding his scarred face, and he picked at the leg of his jumpsuit as we waited.

"Sorry, two more and you can deliver," I said.

"Yep. Keep moving."

"Good advice. So what do you think that was all about, anyway?"

He flinched, turned slightly away from me. "The meeting?"

"Yes, the meeting."

"It was a false flag operation scripted by the Custodians and using Team Farm to divert attention from their inability to properly secure the facility. I think." He spoke so quickly I had to take a few seconds to process it. "Or at least that's what people are saying."

"Really? It seems like that attention arresting script is a useful security apparatus. Not to mention the whole of Team Military."

"Easy to hack, the ments are easy, so easy. The military are—also easy." A second and third request popped up, and I ran them into the extruder.

"Easy?"

"Easy peasy. But not secure from the outside, too, outside attacks."

"Outside is, well, who do you think is left outside, that might be dangerous?"

"Don't know. If they are outside, they are dangerous." That was a good point. I filled the pouches, and he clipped them to his belt, smiled at me while looking a few inches above my shoulder, said "easy peasy" again, and darted out of the dispensary.

I flipped on the "waiting" script for requests and headed to the fourth floor. I'd never been to the fab warehouse, and it seemed another in a series of strange choices made by the Custodial Team. I nodded at employees I knew, but no one was talking very much, or at least talking to me. I suddenly felt conspicuous, my own Custodial status, such as it was, aligned me with a team that everyone was deeply suspicious of, and with some reason, though not because I believed them capable of a vast conspiracy. On the contrary, I was beginning to think they were simply, drearily, incompetent.

The fab warehouse was larger than the dining hall, though much of it was filled with shelves of supplies. Beyond the shelving were three tiers of metal bleachers, enough to hold everyone in the facility, all facing a large, transparent, plastic room containing a lab table and two small cabinets. It had no roof, and only by careful scrutiny could a door be seen, on the far wall. I sat on one of the top tiers and watched my fellow employees drift in. I spotted Jeffers, who seemed far gone, staggering slightly, and Gint, walking beside her, whispering in her ear. Hurtado must have beaten me there, as he sat in the front row of the bleachers opposite me, staring into space. A message popped into view, from Beaudoin:

"Is this seat taken?"

I turned and saw her standing slightly behind me, and gestured for her to sit.

"I thought you would be with the rest of your team," I messaged her back.

"I'm on the outside, now. I know less about this than you do, I'm sure."

"Ha. Don't think anyone could know less then I, at this point."

A small tinkling noise sounded, and the walls began to sparkle. The crowd shifted in their seats as the last stragglers, most of them runners, found perches and sat. A gong rang, softly, and then a smell like jasmine wafted through the room. A door in the wall behind the transparent room opened, and Lem appeared, followed by three men in shackles. They were the Team Farm clowns, Hendrickson and two others, all haggard looking, all bruised about the face. Three men with rifles completed the procession, the last one pulling the door shut.

Lem mounted the three steps to the transparent room, opened the door, and swung his hand, a smile playing at his lips. Hendrickson went through, as did the other two men. Lem followed, guided Hendrickson to the slab, bound him to it with straps, and chained the other two mens' shackles to some rings on the floor.

"Really, you know less than I?" I messaged Beaudoin.

"God I hope so." I noticed, beyond Beaudoin's profile, several bots scurrying along the shelving units, moving stock. They were among the very few bots I'd seen since entering the facility, and I found myself transfixed. A muted klaxon snapped me to attention, and I turned to see Gardiner's avatar fade into existence a few feet in front of the transparent room. It might behoove him to appear in the flesh sometime soon, I thought.

"Oh my friends, my dear friends. Wowza! I expected some chaos, some mumbledy mumbledy, but really, can't we all work together? We won't get anywhere without everyone helping everyone, that's why I want to accelerate our planning, get our SOMs demoed, so we can put together all the best ideas and deploy! I understand being frustrated. I understand being scared. But let's get one thing straight: we have an organizational structure in place already. If we decide to change that, become something better, wonderful, but for now, we operate within that structure, no exceptions. Anyone who fails to operate within that structure is really just being a jerk, and they are failing to be what they will be in an awfully big way." He turned, as if to walk through the transparent wall, and faded out just as he reached it.

Within the diaphanous walls, Lem touched the side of one of the small cabinets. It unfolded itself into a bot that looked something like a daddy long legs, but with four short side legs and two longer legs extending forward, toward the prone Hendrickson. Lem stood still for a few seconds, then, backed away toward the door. Two large drill bits extended from the legs of the bot and started spinning, slowly, then very fast, whining shrilly. The next noise caused the audience to clench itself like a stomach: the whining muffled and staggered as the drills met the heels of the Farm Custodian's feet. Hendrickson didn't move at first contact, then let out a scream that swallowed itself, and finally lost consciousness as a chorus of screams erupted from the audience. The two men chained to the floor in the box with Hendrickson wept together and pulled at their chains. Once the drills had gone several inches into his heels and up into his ankles, the bot legs retracted, leaving the drill bits sticking out like apple stems. Two chains with S hooks descended from the ceiling, and Lem attached them to small eyelets on the bits, then unbound the straps that held Hendrickson to the table. He looked out at the crowd, and the cringing, weeping men beside him, then thoughtfully revived Hendrickson with a small jar of stim. We watched as the chains pulled the farmer off the slab and lifted him into the air so that he hung upside down, shrieking, blood beginning to seep from his ears. I thought his eyes might burst, they were red as the blood on his face.

Members of the audience tried to leave, and fell, struck by the attention arrest script. Newly arrived members of Team Soldier had slipped in behind us, and they lifted anyone stricken and put them back into a seat, then gave them whiffs of stim. Everyone wanted to run, or kill Lem, or claw their own eyes out, but after the first few attempts at flight failed, no one left their seats. Most simply closed their eyes, or buried their heads in their laps. I turned to see Beaudoin staring at the scene, crying silently. I put my hand on hers, and she looked at it, then at me, and squeezed mine so hard I cringed. I was getting better at the expression of sympathy. Her face had the look of a ship broken on rocks, and I knew she hadn't known anything about this gibbeting, that she had been pushed out of the inner circle of Team Custodian, and that fear was consuming her. I sent her a message telling her to come to the dispensary after the "meeting" was finished. She nodded, and went back to staring at the swinging, now silent body of Hendrickson.

The other cabinet was a bot that removed the tongues of the two chained men, both of whom collapsed. As they did, Team Médecins received a message from Bye letting me know that both men would receive bioscans and cauterization from the second bot, and requests for pharma for both had been sent to the dispensary. I found myself thinking about the history of Médecins, of a time when human error caused so much suffering, before we developed the necessary tek to remove so much of that error from the equation. I thought about all the places in the world that lacked that tek, all the places where poverty ate at the soul, and then I realized all that suffering was gone, all those people were dead, or would soon be dead.

It was a grim comfort, and I felt something less than human for taking solace in the thought, but I did. I still do.

Chapter 12

The cheerful breakfast chime heralding the FD newsfeed woke me like a rat crawling in my mouth. I'd slept in the dispensary, anticipating a flood of requests after the spectacle we'd witnessed, but only three came, so I spent the night staring at the table, the chairs, the extruder, the bioscanners, the cleaning bots waiting at attention in their cubbies. I don't remember losing consciousness, but a splotch of drool stained the table. I tried to shut off the newsfeed, to no avail, tried boxing it, running it as backdrop, nothing worked, a voiceover recited the Alberta Pledge, the NAS, SGN, PD, and ERC sub-charters, as some ghost music and montages of pleasant landscapes ran. I tried walking, hit the table, and fell to the floor as wind blown fields of wheat glistened before me. After a few minutes of word-less soundtrack and imagery, Bye's voice, dripping like rancid milk, thanked us for our help and invited everyone to breakfast, and then to another meeting, at dinner time. As she signed off and I pushed myself up from the floor, a message directing me to a Conclave in 20 minutes flashed. Good god, what could be next, my little good angel said. My big good angel wanted nothing more than to sleep for a thousand years and wake to a world scrubbed free of human wisdom.

That was it, the bit that had been gnawing at me ever since the cubesats went out and we went into lockdown:

in some perverse way, I was glad, glad that humanity was on its last legs, glad the whole stupid, over-loud, garish party was drawing to a close. And glad, perhaps more perversely, that I was one of the folks who got to tidy up and dump all the half glasses and spent pharma patches down the incinerator. It was hateful, but undeniable. Part of me was happy we were over.

Beaudoin messaged me seconds after the Conclave invite, asking to meet beforehand, a floor below. I spent a few minutes arguing myself up out of my chair, then went down the hall to the elevator. I realized I didn't know where the stairs were, should something happen to the elevator, and jogged down the hall the other way. I passed a runner running the other direction, found a door marked "emergency" on my map, and pushed through to find a set of stairs like every other set of stairs I'd ever seen, only more so. Relief is an undervalued emotion, I thought, dragging myself back to the elevator, a wave returning to the sea.

There was no reason to meet with her, or with the Conclave, and I saw clearly that nothing I had ever done was with much reason. And, yet, there I was, and I thanked her and took a danish from the tray and thanked the runner (Cherish? Thanda? We'd talked, she wished for more sun). We were in the room just below the Conclave meeting room. Was she here to tell me I was next to be hung from my feet? Hence the danish?

"I—" Beaudoin looked as haggard as I felt, shadows digging into her face. It was an interesting face, even beautiful, intelligence lighting kind eyes, cheek and nose sculpted to compliment each other: she had the look, this morning, of a public statue. "You know—" she paused again. If she was finding it hard to speak or was dealing with multiple messages, I couldn't tell.

"I am glad to see you," I said.

"Oh, yes, yes, glad to see you too."

The rear door opened and Euna Gessner slipped through. I raised my eyebrows at Beaudoin, who, I think, grimaced.

"She means to say: 'Please don't be alarmed. We must be careful.' Yes?" She stood beside Beaudoin, arms crossed. I recognized the words, then could hear Beaudoin speaking them, could feel the box I had placed over my head as blindly as a duckling following its mother's ass.

"It was you." I looked down at the last bite of my danish, glistening on the neon plate.

Beaudoin took a breath and started again. "We have to stop this, this, I don't even know and neither do they, they've lost control of themselves—"

"Gardiner," Gessner spat.

"Yes, I gathered that from the last time we spoke," I answered.

"I'm sorry, please, I never thought they would go to the extremes they—" We all saw Hendrickson, dangling by his heels, blood so slowly moving down his body.

"We don't have time or space to wait around anymore, we have to move," Gessner said. "I mean, whoa, we might be the last people on the whole dingy planet, and these chirpas, well, you know, you know what we have to do, right?"

I felt suddenly nauseous. "I still have the same question I had before, when you had me blinded: what is your vision? I understand you think the Conclave lacks vision, I may even agree, I may not, but why would I think revolution, in and of itself, preferable to the existing organizational structure?"

"There is no structure, it's just power, that's all, obviously."

"No, he's right," Beaudoin said, finally raising her head, "what do we have to offer? Ok, listen: we don't even know if the world outside this facility is viable. We don't even know if the newsfeeds we received are true, the whole thing could be a hoax. I know the ment system, I know someone very skilled, and very diligent, could fake the sensor data we're getting, they could fake the newsfeeds, the whole thing could be a set up. Gardiner brought me in to show Salenas and the rest the finer points of ment scripting, advanced vid production, the usual routine, what I'm paid for, god. And they had me build an infrastructure..." her head went wobbly and her eyes slid out of focus. Gessner snapped too and shook her, making a small clicking noise with her teeth until Beaudoin refocused. "I made this scape, here, and I heard them talking, whispers, that it was an experiment, I know, I know the whole idea was an experiment but, an experiment outside the experiment, layers, of, meaning and I—" she started crying, so softly I had to bend over the table to hear her sobs.

Gessner put a hand on Beaudoin's shoulder, looked

back at me. "They fried her, for a day or two leading up to last night, then after the meeting, till an hour ago."

She had no encryption? The architect didn't know the secret passages? They must have erased them all, I guessed, I knew woefully little about ment architecture. "Can't she block it? I mean, she built it."

Gessner looked puzzled, then: "No, you dumb shit. Not with ments, physically. She's been in a cell for three days, they only let her out when she promised to sit near you. See now why we want you on the right side of this? God and Mr. Clean, they've already picked up everything we've said here, it's in the archive, yeah? Now, make your choice."

She helped Beaudoin to her feet, and they were gone, back through the door at the rear of the conference room. I had three minutes to get upstairs. I checked the map as I walked, not for directions to the Conclave conference room, while my arrow twitched faithfully on the floor ahead, but for the whole facility, a blueprint that might tell me where all these doors in the backs of rooms led to.

I was, for perhaps the only time in my life, the first one at the meeting. Had the situation been different, had I been at a six month gig scripting up scuba miners off the Chilean coast and the human race was still intact and I had not just watched a man hung from his feet, I think I still would have felt intensely paranoid, sure I was being watched as I fiddled with my jumpsuit stitching and cleaned my nails with other, dirtier nails. I smiled as Mbete and Siegleman soon joined me, the first plantings of a forest I could hide myself in. Then Hendrickson walked in from the eastern door, laughing, and I lost all sight of myself.

He came through the door, tossing his head back to hear what Lem said, laughing, they all were laughing, the whole room was laughing. No, half the Conclave was laughing, and half looked as I must, mouth open, mind churning but unable to light on word or phrase or concept. He sat, and Lem sat beside him, the man who'd drilled into his feet the day before, and Bye and Gint and Gardiner all sat, laughing, swapping snippets of conversation. I scanned the room for Beaudoin and could not find her, saw Gessner sitting at a far corner of the table, chewing a fingernail. Mbete, looking like a firefight was about to break out. Dunwoody, trying to laugh like he knew what the joke was but choking on it every time. Every other person at the table looked satisfied, even happy.

"Well, well," Gardner began, rising, and it was really him, incarnate, not a projection— "let's all give ourselves a big hand, Operation Grand Guignol was a great success, right? Wowee, great work, everyone!" There was applause, someone whooped. Gardiner's teeth were yellowish, I noticed. He stopped and looked at me, and kept staring, I looked behind my chair at the blank wall, felt stupid for looking behind my chair, turned angrily to face him and he was looking at Mbete.

"I understand, gosh, some of you really feel kind of wobbly about all this now. Am I right?" Mbete nodded. "Confused?" He turned to Dunwoody, who nodded. "Wondering what all in the crazy world is going on?" He looked at me, oh how I felt like nodding, held my head still, gritted my teeth. "Look: in any operation like this, where we're trying to establish order so we can move forward, some of us can be in the script, and some need to be outside. For verisimilitude, right?"

"Versimili..." Mbete failed.

"So it seems more real."

"I know what it means."

"Right, and holy mack, that was real, yes?" More applause, though muted, people waiting to see where the situation would spin.

"Sir!" Mbete stood. Gessner, on his left, and Siegleman, on his right, grabbed his arms and pulled him down into the chair. "Yes, yes," he continued speaking from his chair, "sir, my men, they knew about all this and I did not?"

"Well, yes, they did, we needed to change things around a bit, yes, but you're still Custodian—let's be frank, shall we?" Mbete nodded. "Your, ah, history as a soldier is somewhat tarnished, and I want to give you opportunities to polish it up a bit, get rid of that taint, but you seem really, well geez, reluctant to do what you need to do. The violence economy is dead, we get that, no more profit upstairs, so now it's even more real, we need you ready to be a soldier. If I came to you with the plan for Operation Grand Guignol two days ago, what would you have said? Would you have followed orders, or would you have flinched?" Dunwoody laughed suddenly, as though he just got it, the whole picture came into focus. The laugh was high-pitched and mad, and every head turned to him, then every head looked away as he sat, silent, twitching.

"I do not know what Operation Grand Guignol was. I

cannot answer that."

Hendrickson leaned over the table: "Sure you do, look, here I am. My boys are fine. It was a fucking vid, you get it, but more than vid, it was fucking beautiful."

Gardiner winced every time Hendrickson swore. I hadn't heard anyone say "fuck" with such relish outside a favela in a very long time, I realized. Not since I last saw Kirkus, in my hallway, a million years ago.

"I was not speaking to you, farmer," Mbete glowered.

"Listen boys, listen," Gardiner stood and crossed his arms. "Operation Grand Guignol was simply meant to show all the employees that we don't need to resort to the attention arrest script, we can affect all kinds of attitudinal shifts without being so, ah, crude." Salenas gave a snort, and Gardiner glared at him. "It's more humane this way, we don't want to damage anyone, we might be the only hope our species has at this point."

"How do you know?" Mbete blurted. His voice resonated with the suspicions of everyone at the table. Well, almost everyone.

"Oh really. Really? Ok, we'll go now, look at all the sensor data. No, no, not good enough, better yet, you get yourself geared up and go check, go ahead, go outside with a hand sensor. I'm not stopping anyone from doing anything except dying another pointless death," Gardiner said. I'd never seen him truly angry, and he wore it like a florid child.

"Yes, I will go."

"I will go with him," Gessner offered.

"Me too! Me too!" Dunwoody chirped. Eyes fell to me.

"I have no reason to go."

"One sensible employee among you, geez. Can we outfit them with rad suits?"

"Yes, won't work for the virus, however," Lem said.

"Release the anti-virus, it's self-replicating, will take three or four hours to clear 100km," I said. My voice sounded odd in my skull.

Gardiner squinted. "Of course, yes, it takes at least that long to get outfitted, and we can broadcast the whole thing, we need to have a meeting anyway and let everyone know they need to get to work, right? Show them how the org chart works, so to speak."

"And please, if I may, where is Ms. Beaudoin?" I heard a chittering, an insect noise, from the corners of the room. I could not read anyone's eyes, but they were all upon me.

"Who?" Gardiner asked, not missing a beat.

"Elaine Gardiner," I said.

"Elaine Gardiner?"

"No, no, I mean, Elaine Beaudoin, part of your Custodial Team, uh, su-pa-tek ment producer...," the words came like cubes of plastic pushing down my tongue, extruding from my mouth.

"Well, no, not here, I think Ms. Gint is our ment producer, are you feeling right-o, Duval?

There were a dozen or more people in the room, staring, and they all seemed arrayed at the end of a deep, narrowing hole, which I sat at the bottom of. Even the silence was like the silence of tunnels. I sat for three or four days, three or four minutes, Gessner like a bird spearing out of a tree: "You mean Gint, I think, she's right there, to the left of—" she pointed, and Gint was there, rosy cheeks atop sunken jaw, hunched, face oddly shadowed, as though she were wearing a heavy hood. She lifted a hand and shook it at me.

"Yes, of course, I, just lost track, such a long few days—"

"Indeed! Who wants ice cream!" Gardiner bleated.

§

Four hours later, the employees of Gardiner Group gathered in the dining room, in desolate little herds, for their evening meal and all-in meeting. I wondered what they did all day. I slept, this day, from the moment I got back to my quarters, dodged Paulie's request for real time, signaled the dispensary to release the anti-virus that had waiting in queue since we cracked the script, tore off my stiff jumpsuit, and collapsed on the bed, and stayed asleep until 10 minutes prior to the meeting. It was all-in, I had to wake up. Well—no, I had to.

If everything was augmented beyond the point of easy discernment, what was real, what was not, then they should just hold virtual meetings, I thought, avoiding the bald stares of other employees, if in fact there were bald, unmediated beings doing the staring. I assumed the news had flitted from room to room, and I was Custodial, accessory to the farcical torture performance of the evening prior. Everyone must know the clown revolt was also a set-up as well. I rested my chin on my fist and stared at the tabletop. I should have known, it seems so obvious, now, hackneyed.

No one sat with me, no one sat near me, not within three seats. The other Custodians avoided looking at me, even Mbete and Gessner, whom I waved at clumsily. I shouldn't have mentioned Gardiner, no, I mean Beaudoin, I shouldn't have mentioned—why did I call her Elaine Gardiner? Where did they put Fiedler's body? Were they manipulating my vocalization, no, I could see things, might taste and hear, but they couldn't make me do anything, that was well beyond. Well beyond what. Well.

The meeting started, Gardiner chipper as always, the rationale for Operation Grand Guignol revealed, people nodded, agreed it was worth setting limits, it all flowed exactly like a SOM. The next step, Operation Canary, was presented, Mbete and Gessner and Dunwoody all stood for applause, a full fly-through of the hazard suits next, then Q&A: did it need to be so graphic? Can we use the ments for recreation again? What about babies? Who is in charge of breakfast because I have egg allergy? But no one asked about Ms. Beaudoin, and for all I knew, I was the only one, aside from her team, that ever met her. I picked a fork out of one of the dispensers on the table and pretended to pick my teeth with it, always watching the presentation, then began scratching my wrist with a tine. As soon as it bled, I began making another line, until I had gouged a very shallow "EB" into my skin. I held a napkin against it. When I got back to the lab, I sprayed it with anti-coagulant, then scratched again, then spray, then scratch, until scar tissue formed.

Chapter 13

When I messaged the Custodians that the anti-virus algorithms suggested a 5-700km clear radius as of 0800, I was first commended for my speed, then drafted into the Externalization Monitoring Committee. Mbete, Gessner, and Dunwoody were the Externalization Team, along with Kull, a member of Team Endo who'd volunteered his services once he heard about the project. Team Endo's orgies, or whatever they were, had proceeded, I was told, despite all that had occurred in the last few days, and there was even talk of adjusting the contraception threshold at some point, once all the numbers balanced, so we could start making more people. Well, so some of us could. That's what Paulie said, in any case, he was the only employee left who spoke to me in anything other than official capacity. And even he said he'd never met Beaudoin, though he remembered scanning her record on the archive, since wiped clean. I wasn't sure I believed him. I wasn't sure I believed myself.

"They're gonna fry out there, no challenge. Kinky. And you get to watch, and maybe take the blame, get out, mon frère, just say no!" We sat in one of the conference rooms near our quarters. The more the sanity level of the project dropped, the more Paulie seemed rational.

"Fry? If the radiation was that thick, we'd all be dead already. And the virus is gone, so—"

"Maybe yes, maybe no, no es chooga."

"No, it's gone, I checked that myself."

"I don't mean it's not gone, I mean it never was, right?"

"This again?" I shook my head.

"Again, not again, different, a thousand ways you could put it together. Think they couldn't splice a script into your datafeed? Make it look like there's a virus, let you write an anti-virus, another script that look like you killed it? Easy peasy."

"Alright, but then, why?"

"Don't know, we're the rats, gotta find a way out the maze. I'm working on it." He winked at me.

"Working on what?"

"Here," he said, got up, went around behind me, and before I could think, flipped open my hard port and jacked something into it. It felt like a muscle spasm in my brain, and I felt a small thread of drool run off my lip. He sat back down, smiling. I would have asked him what the hell he just did, but I couldn't speak.

"No worries, just an encrypted channel. Really en-crypted, not this fake dingy shit the Custodials use." He winked. Gradually feeling returned to my face.

"Don't ever do that again," I slurred.

"If I'd asked, would you have let me?"

"No."

"There ya go."

A little pink cartoon pig head appeared to my left. "Chooga!" it said, in just the sort of voice one might ex-pect a disembodied pink cartoon pig head to have.

"What, you encrypted it in a kiddie vid?"

"Kinda like that, actually, under the radar and so forth, but so very hard to break, and I dig the little guy, serious cute, he is."

I sighed. I was too worn down to fight with him. "Just please only use it in an emergency, got it? No sudden bursts of conspiratorial insight while I'm trying to sleep."

"Ha, you really are an old man, you know?"

"Always have been."

§

I met the Externalization Team on the elevator, along with Lem, the sight of whom still made me shudder and look away. Kull had a large, wheeled case, presumably the rad suits and other gear. We reached the surface, and I checked rad and viral levels in the hall, then again in a small room the arrow led us to. Everything was fine.

"Ok, begin transmission, then gear check." The Externalization Team Mission would be broadcast to the rest of the employees, of course, so I checked the feed from their ments to the net, and once the team had donned them, I began scanning the rad suits. If the sensors were faulty and there was considerable radiation or contagions outside, the suits would do nothing, as everyone knew. It was all part of the theater, and I played my part meticulously, though I suspect I lacked feeling.

"All set," I said, and stood off to the side.

"Good," Lem said, and drew out two rifles from the case, handing one to Mbete, the other to Kull.

"What are those for?" Dunwoody asked through his mask.

"Use the ments," Lem said, through the feed.

"What are those for?" he said again, and we all heard him, everyone in the facility did.

"Protection. Once through this door, then across the bay, then out the main door, is an unknown situation. Unknown situations of this character require protection," Lem said, and nodded to Mbete, who signaled his assent through the feed.

"Oh, come on," Gessner said, pushing for the door.

Lem and I went back through to the hall, leaving the cart, watching the small window to the mid-right that broadcast the feed. It was, largely, from Mbete's p.o.v., switching every 30 seconds to cycle through the other team members' vision, then back to Mbete.

"Let's go watch from the next floor," Lem said, and I followed him to the elevator. "I have to trigger the door, so we won't miss anything," he said, smiling. I'd seen smiles like that before, and always something small and fragile lay broken on the floor soon afterward.

We descended in silence, watching the feed and the impatient Team waiting for access to outside. Lem led me to a small conference room, where the rest of the Custodial Team sat, except for Gardiner.

"Mr. Gardiner is suffering a stomach malady," Bye said, extracting the thought from my head, "and is watching the feed, yes."

I looked around the room before widening the feed scape. Everyone else, it seemed, was watching full screen. They were a haggard looking bunch, except for Bye, who always appeared perfectly formed, made of carbon fiber and synth gel. They stared, and I saw a room full of holes, shallow nooks dug in dirt that bugs might hide from a desert sun. And then I saw Lem, staring back at me, smiling once again. I flipped the feed on wide screen.

The view defaulted to Mbete, though there were toggles for each member, if a viewer chose to switch. The door was immense, I remembered coming through it a lifetime ago. As it opened, light shone through, sun light, rising as the door rose, and I started to cry. I could feel others crying, in the room and throughout the facility. The Team stood, staring, even as the door was fully open and our eyes all adjusted to the view, the concrete and the parked shuttles beyond, and the mountains and clouds and sky beyond that. Gessner and Dunwoody moved through the door, Kull followed, Mbete in the rear. It was a gentle spring day, trees rippled on the hills like a stream full of rushes. I almost sneezed.

Gessner and Dunwoody both took out scanners, and the readouts popped into the feed. It took a few seconds for them to sync, then the numbers began: normal, no detectable radiation, no contagions. I took a deep breath as they moved further out, Mbete scanning the facility slowly, conscious, perhaps, of the number of eyes seeing through his. Dunwoody chirped, "Looks good here," as he scanned a concrete pylon.

"Looks beautiful," Gessner answered, her voice hushed with reverence. One of the readouts ticked then, Gessner's, then ticked again, then went full red and streamed bad data like hornets. We heard her cry out, then watched, with Mbete, as she grabbed at the neck of her rad suit. Dunwoody screamed. They both thrashed, fell, twitching, Kull started running back toward Mbete then he, too, fell. Their suits were turning color in spots, growing mottled, and then we saw the door, slowly closing, as Mbete ran toward it. He dove through, rolled across the floor, and the feed ceased.

No one said much as they filed out of the meeting room. Minor key ambient music played from somewhere. As I reached the door, a message from Lem appeared: "I believe you should check your data." Right, they would pin this to me. Then again, it might be my fault. But it wasn't, I'd checked everything, unless of course someone set me up. I was 3 m away from the lab when the little pig head manifested and squeaked at me, "better strap yourself in! Wild ride ahead," followed by a sharp little giggle that made me squint. Inside the lab, Jeffers sat, eyes closed, at the conference table. I sat across from her and tried to message her, but she was off line. Then a drum roll, a pink wash of light, and a robotic voice: "What's really outside? Let's take a look."

What followed began just as the previous Externalization feed had, but instead of surges in scanner readout and the viral decomposition of three team members, the feed showed Mbete raising his rifle and gunning down first Gessner, then Dunwoody, then Kull, quickly, calmly, almost artistically.

I looked at Jeffers, still sitting with her eyes closed, still not responding to my messages. I tried to imagine her at home, a little girl, her parents drilling her as soon as she could be fitted with a port—they were both well-regarded EduTainers, she said, and had been relentless in stuffing her full of knowledge and ambition, until she had enough and took a job working viral response at a favela when she was only 17. She disowned them shortly thereafter, but they kept tracking her down and spamming her with invites to EduTrainer conferences, and finally she took out a personal firewall. I couldn't imagine how it must be to amputate one's parents, but I respected her strength, though I did find it callous. What was her birthday like? I stood, went around the table, touched her shoulder, and watched her slide off the chair onto the floor. I scanned her, detected pharma overdose, near death, extruded a template counter-agent, held it to her arm, and stopped. She wanted death, chose it, would the new Externalization feed have changed her mind? Had she even seen the first feed? For all I knew, neither was real. I took an oath, when I finished my Médecins thread, *non intercedere cum morte*, do not interfere with death, and death was hers to obtain. I sat back down in the chair her body was just in, still warm, and watched her body and the scanner, until it registered null.

A message from Lem pulsed red in my view. I wanted nothing to with him, with Facility Dàtóng, with Ivan Gardiner or Bye or anyone in a jumpsuit, anyone with two legs and two arms and a spine and a facility for language. But I needed to know what to with Jeffers' body. What had they done with Fiedler's body? Did Beaudoin even have a body? There were bodies outside, too, perhaps. Too many layers, too much everything on top of everything else, I knew exactly why Jeffers made her choice. It felt as though my little good angel and my big good angel were losing form, flowing together into muddy pool, a swirling of body and mind and whatever else constituted a person. There was a lot of silt in that pond, and it was too brackish to yield any reflection on the surface.

§

The message from Lem ordered me to a Custodial meeting. I ignored it, and went back to my quarters. I had never willfully refused a work directive before in my life, and it made me giddy. I got in my bed and slept and slept and slept some more. I woke because someone was banging on my door, stood to open it, and fell to my knees. Something was not right.

"Boo!" Paulie said, lunging past me once I managed to open the door. He sat in a chair, giggling to himself.

"Ah, look, Paulie, I don't feel so hot—"

"No, course not, you got no feet, no media in your metabolism, your *net*abolism, ha!" His eyes were red and swollen.

"I don't understand."

"The ments, man, the system is done, they shut it down," he said, then leaned across the table, "except for our little piggy, of course."

I looked around the room. It was my room. It was nothing else, no message box, no drop menu icons anywhere, no accents decorating the cleaning bots or their niches—I'd forgotten what ugly little things they were. And now they were inert, I noticed, two clung to a wall, one on the floor, in mid-scour.

"Yeah, the bots, too, just power and water and heat, that's all we got, like cavemen."

"It's so odd... so long since—" the little pig head appeared, or a crude, blocky version of it, at least, and it giggled along with Paulie. "How do you keep that on?"

"I got the key, compadre."

"Ok, whatever that means. So you shut everything down?"

"Me? Hella dumb thing to do, why would I? No, the Custodians did it. After the runners poisoned the Military, now everyone's—"

"Wait, what? Go back, what happened?"

"Runners saw the feed where Mbete shot their girl, next thing you know, all the Military is corpses. Except Mbete, ha, he's up with the Custodians somewhere."

"Oh no."

"Oh yeah. All the other teams are bunkering, each one got a floor, the main dining room looks like neutral territory, no one heard a word from the big boys, chooga! The doors are locked, nobody going outside, even if anyone wanted to, elevators all shut down. Time to find our own way to kill ourselves. Or..." he winked. Of all the gestures Paulie could have offered me at that moment, a wink was the most obscene. "Or..." he winked again. I had to stop him.

"Or what, just say it!"

"Ok, ok, sorry, trying to play the part, mephisto. Or, we let Paulie take us on a ride."

"What are you talking about, now" I sighed, instead of punching him.

"Multiverses, baby! Been working on this my whole life, just snap us out of this reality into another one, can't be much worse than this slagheap. Pretty simply to machine, really, I got most everything I need, just, well, not enough power."

"Power."

"Power. If you can chain together a relay on each of the top five floors—"

"No sir. Not a chance."

"Wait, wait, listen! No one even needs to know what you're doing, you just put one of these little guys on each relay—" he held up a tiny bot shaped a bit like a fly—"and it does the rest, it'll burrow in and connect all the relays so we can hit it! Take this whole dingy place out of one stream into another."

Well, it was work. I had no more work, really, I was a failing tool, and it was something. It was also the stupidest job I'd ever considered.

"Let me think about it," I said.

"Ok, ok, fair enough. But tomorrow, I need to know tomorrow."

"What is tomorrow?"

"Ha, good one! Oh, but, right, no ments, no clocks! Ha! Well, just, in a while, then."

"Right. A while. Let me think about it. And I want a contract."

§

Paulie laughed when I mentioned the contract, then stopped once he saw I was serious. I needed job specs, payment details. I needed to be wooed. I was also ready for any port, the storm was everywhere.

I lifted one of the cleaning bots and turned it over in my hand. It looked like it was made for scrubbing surfaces, or maybe just small scale dust removal, I knew nothing about cleaning bots, and why would I, they were unseen, quietly scuttling around when the room recognized I was out, or asleep. My mother cleaned our house, even after we got a full smart house when I was 10 or 11.

The shock of a message notice flashing into view made me drop the bot. It wasn't Paulie's pig, it was red and stuck with half a dozen "crucial" flags, and I opened it without thinking. Gardiner's face hovered in front of me. "Mr. Duval, hello. I know you must be so darn confused at this point, so I'd really really like it if you could come see me at your convenience. Reply to this message and I will tag you for access, so you don't have to climb the stairs." He giggled, and I watched his face fade away. The afterimage of his round face and tiny eyes lingered, and I gleaned the inspiration for Paulie's piggie icon. Oh well. Two offers were better than one. Or, Gardiner would giggle and say "gosh" while Lem killed me. Either option would do, though crawling into my bed and pulling the covers over my head also held promise.

I half expected I'd have to manually swipe the door, but it slid open automatically. An arrow even popped up above the floor, though it was blurry, twitching as I rounded corners. I took the elevator to the top floor and made my way along a grey corridor, as featureless and oppressive as every other corridor in the facility. The arrow led me to a small room, and pointed toward a door painted bright green. It was so vibrant, I had to turn my head, and kept it turned even as it slid open, even as I walked through into a wave of moist heat.

Gardiner sat cross-legged on a large platform covered with an elaborate Byzantine rug. The heat made me dizzy, and I fell easily into the wicker chair Gardiner gestured to with a sweep of his hand. The wicker squeaked forgivingly, inviting sleep and dream.

"Oh, Mr. Duval, my dear, dear sir. Such a fine, committed man, so much a part of the good work we've done here."

Madness I had seen before, men and women who had lost so much they gave themselves over to a cavern at the center of the soul, hollowed themselves out and fell in. And the ones who heard voices and wore their filth like a suit of armor, and those who ruled as though their fellow men were bits of kindling for the fire of their own need. The man smiling thin-lipped and pinkly sweating before me was something else entirely.

"What do you want?" My scalp started to itch.

"Ho ho! Still full of vim, I see, but I fear I hear a cross note in your voice. I understand, of course, this is surely the most strenuous employment application you've ever undertaken, but you understand, we have to be, um, choosy, yes?"

My tongue was full of stone, I had to think to lift it. "Sorry? Application?"

"Of course, of course, you think me so inhuman as to subject people to the charade on sale here? An application, yes, this is the completion of your application for employment with Gardiner Group. And you've done very well, I might add. If you accept, simply signal assent, and we can get you unhooked from the application script and start working on—start working on—start working on—"

His head turned slightly to the left each time, his right eye twitched and sparkled. I felt myself begin to float up out of the chair, and pushed my body, weightless, toward him. A silver disc materialized in my hand, and as soon as I was close enough, I shoved it through his words, into his mouth. His head began to flicker and fade, and I launched myself backward, pushing against his chest with my feet.

The gravity did not return until I was on the elevator, and even then it was weak. The world continued to twitch in time with the Gardiner glitch, "start working on—start working on—." I pulled myself along the corridor to my room, pulled myself down onto bed, and held on, listening to my little good and big good angels cooing to one another, snuggling on a feather bed the size of the sky. I had done good work, they told me. A tranquility born of satisfied exhaustion held me above sleep a while, then it, too, gave way, and I sank into an ancient, empty sea.

Chapter 14

Time was broken and fluttering, full of black spots. Paulie and Kimba, one of the runners, sat across from me at a table crowded into a storage closet. The shelving that surrounded us was bare. I liked the way the row of holes on the shelf frame looked, their predictability, not a square or off-center space among them.

"Mulch," Kimba said.

"Oh, duh, of course!" Paulie slapped his hands together.

"And so they were mad, we ruined the mulch, so they wanted us to give up something."

"What, now, what, they mulch the bodies?" I asked. "Is that, I mean, flesh can be mulch?"

We weren't here to talk about what the Farm Team did with corpses of the Soldiers, but a little gossip was necessary to make everyone feel more at ease.

"Well, they do. Or something like mulch, but they figure we're too dumb to understand."

"They are way arrogant," Paulie offered.

"Farmers always are," Kimba said.

"Ok, so," I pushed the dialogue forward, "you can help me get access to all the levels I need?"

Kimba nodded, staring at his hands. Like most runners, he didn't do well with direct questions or eye contact. His beard jutted out to a point, and his skin was dark and mottled with pocks along his forehead. He was also hugely muscled, which made his reticence all the more disconcerting.

"Great, so, I just need a graft or—"

"Chip. There are chips, under skin, I can fetch an all-access one for you."

"Ok. And in return, I give you dispensary access."

He smiled, sideways, a bit like he was having a seizure. The gesture rattled me, I couldn't remember how I'd gotten there, in that room, with those people, plotting to help Paulie with his absurd plan. Disconnected patches of reality, my new life script. People, lives, bent smiles, reality, all unfixed concepts, bleeding into one another. My unease passed as quickly as it came, a face in a crowd.

"This is gonna be so motostank, man, we are gonna take this place AWAY!" he yelled, and Kimba twitched.

"You just made that up, the 'motostank,'" I said.

"Yeah, like it? New days coming, new parle necessary, captain."

I shook my head. The plan was already grafted into my mind, somehow, I couldn't vid it or map it, I just knew where to go, which one of the tiny bots to flick at which relays, what Teams had holed up where, and as soon as Kimba chipped me, how to get in every door and stairwell. I was a bot myself, I guess.

Kimba got a chip, too, with access codes for the dispensary. I warned him the extrusion scripts might be shut off, but he brushed my caveat aside, with a wink to Paulie. I wasn't fond of Paulie's management style, it was far too familiar, and this job offered nothing in the way of creativity, or even agency. But it was a job, in any case, and since reality was, it seemed, collapsing in a heap around me, it was all I had. I was being mounted, I realized, like a loa was about to ride me up through the facility, at the behest of a lunatic who though he could shift us all into a different universe. It had been decades since I though about any of the things my grandparents had done in the name of God and culture, about the lessons they tried to teach me and which I ignored, embarrassed of their weird ignorance, and since I'd arrive at the facility, my mind kept returning to them, to the loa and the twins and of course, my two angels.

Then I was in my room, sitting on my bed. I didn't remember how I got here, or why I came, but my kit was packed on the table before me, the bed was stripped to the mattress, and someone had put the inactive bots back in their niches. A tiny bell chimed, and I knew it was time to begin my work.

The first relay to tag was on level nine, where Team Endo held their love-ins. The elevator opened and took me down. I wondered if everyone on the floors I passed could hear the elevator grinding and humming, if they held their ears to the dead walls and wondered who rode, what Custodial fiat was about to be visited upon them. I exited to a hallway that reeked of sweat, vinegar, and lilacs. Lit candles were strewn haphazardly along the floor, a quick sniff of which was enough to identify them as the source of the lilac smell. I headed for the main conference room, guided not by an arrow but by something like an itch, an overwhelming desire to head down the hall, turn left, and stop at a pair of grey metal doors, on which someone had painted the word "heaven" in neon pink paint. I could hear moaning coming from the room beyond, and the door opened itself when I touched it.

"Well hello," a voice to my left said, and a warm, moist hand took mine. I shuddered and yanked it back as my eyes adjusted to the low light. The entire floor of the room, with the exception of the small square of concrete I stood on, was covered with pillows and mattress of all kinds, and the pillows and mattresses were covered with people, mostly nude, writhing together like something spied under a log in the woods. Candles burned in stands and on shelves mounted in the wall, and couches and a few large, plush chairs stood here and there, also covered with people. A young, naked woman bobbed up and down in a kind of hammock, suspended from the ceiling, each time lowering herself a bit more toward a weeping bald man's flaccid penis. I felt sick, and the warm hand touched mine again, more lightly this time. I gagged, pulled my hand back again. The hand was attached to LouAnn Manpeiler, who knelt beside me, her black hair escaping in greasy strands from a bun at the top of her head. Her naked body was a glistening assortment of crooked angles set with wrinkles and folds and the odd mole. Her breasts were small, her chest concave—I was struck with how much she looked like a plucked pigeon, smiling as though I was a crust of bread on the sidewalk.

"And who sent you to our little nest, dear?" She tugged at my hand and began walking, picking her way between the moaning and writhing mounds of skin. I followed.

Her buttocks moved like a sack of dried beans on a runner's shoulder.

"Ah, no one, I mean, I just heard about it, and—" Paulie's script was too bare-boned for lying, apparently, it was my job to improvise and I was failing miserably.

"Of course, just got your wings on and flew down... Tell me a more interesting story, Mr. Duval." She reached the far wall and sat in a chair covered with a red sheet. A large man snored beneath a blanket in the chair beside her, and she reached beneath the blanket and gave him a pinch, all the while staring at me. Gary Manpeiler gave little yelp and shook his head.

"Gary, hon, Mr. Duval has come to visit," she said, absentmindedly fiddling with her vulva.

"Really?" he said, rubbing his eyes. "Well, he must be an angel, then."

"Hee, that's just what I said, that he flew down!" She slapped his shoulder.

"Right. This is the script: I'm here to help get the power turned back on, full power, that is, the local net and bots and all the rest. I was trying to be secretive, but I'm not good at that, so there it is. The relay for this floor is—" I let my finger float up, felt my body turn to the left, pointed at a comer of the room opposite where the Manpeilers sat— "there. All I have to do is open the hatch and do my work, and I'll leave you to your... work." The sound of moaning, of flesh squelching against flesh, rattled my teeth.

"Oh, is that all?" I couldn't tell who'd spoken, and now they both laughed, too loud, wiggling in their chairs.

Their lips looked blue in the candlelight.

"Y-yes, that is all."

"Well now, we all have needs, don't we?" Gary said, rubbing his arm where LouAnn had smacked him. "So many of our team mates, they have needs, who will provide for them?"

"I don't understand."

"Simple, dear," LouAnn chirped, "we have needs, you have needs, we must work out some kind of exchange."

"Let's make a deeeeaaalll...." Gary cooed.

"What kind of deal?"

LouAnn grinned wider, got up from her chair, and slid her naked buttocks along my thighs as she moved sideways to sit on Gary's lap. "A good snuggle would be a nice start," she said.

"And then we'll want to see that brave, brown maypole up and ready. Love is all, Mr. Duval, and I fear my own arbor vitae has been rather tired since the world ended. Yours might be the example we need, here, young and vital, if I could clench myself around it, myself and the missus alike, we might find our own cosmic equipment returned to their state of ready access. What we need, Mr. Ducal, is your love, at once and without condition."

My stomach churned, bile laced my throat. "No, that is not an option," I answered, trembling.

"Prude," LouAnn sneered.

"Calm, my love, calm...." Gary said, petting her shoulder. "Mr. Duval, tell me, what gives you meaning in this fallen world, why do you live on in a concrete bunker, watching your fellow beings toy with one another?"

"I'm working."

"Working. Indeed. Freelancing, I suppose, no longer in the employ of Gardiner Group?"

"I, yes, I am doing a job for another employer, and am operating under the assumption that Gardiner Group is defunct, hence I have no contractual obligation to them."

"So that is your meaning, that is what makes your breath shine in the night? What makes your sleep untroubled, what makes—"

"At present, it is enough, yes."

"Love is all, my dear, don't you understand?" LouAnn began, "the soft, moist flesh of another person, driving your mind up through all the pain and all the boredom until it *explooooodes* and everything is color, all the colors and all the flavors at once bursting forth. It's what the universe wants for us. It's the key to something greater, the only way we can unlock the door and see beyond..."

"I have no interest in seeing beyond, whatever that means. If you want to exchange, I can give access to the dispensary, and scripts for pharma that will—"

"Shit on pharma! It might make him hard as that wall, but it's false, a false god, the key is broken, the vision tainted by demons!" LouAnn lurched up from Gary's lap and grabbed my groin in one hand, my shoulder in the other. "You will fuck me, you dirty little sexless thing. You will fuck me and make me come and then you will fuck Gary and he will absorb whatever strange essence you fucking neuters have, the nanos in his blood will leech you dry..." hands grabbed me from behind and pulled, I fell on a mattress and LouAnn's vulva was on my face, grinding up and down hard enough that her pelvic bone mashed my nose shut. I got a hand lose and shoved her aside, she weighed less than a sheet, and then other hands flipped me over and tugged at my jumpsuit, then tore it, I felt my thigh and buttock suddenly exposed to air, then someone pried my jumpsuit and ass apart and another hand grabbed at my scrotum and one in my mouth and I screamed and writhed and bit down and tasted blood. There were more screams all around, I bit harder and pulled flesh from bone and spit it out and I was released. I staggered toward the relay wall, pulled back the curtain, and flicked the bot that had migrated up to my finger the closer I got to the relay. I saw it land, orient itself, and scuttle away, then someone struck the back of my knees and I fell into a gathering of flesh, mounds of it piled like laundry, some covered with thick hair, some shaven and slick, and I felt myself sinking into it, until flesh covered my head and pulled me down.

The universe was dark, and warm, and I breathed but I did not breathe, my body moved as it did when inhaling, exhaling, but what they took in was not air, I could push it with my hand, like a gel. Lights flickered on, and when my eyes adjusted, I saw I was in a kind of bubble, in a large warehouse room. Paulie's pig appeared, granted me another inane giggle, and pipped, "this might sting!" A crushing weight descended on my chest and with it, a panic, I saw the lights suddenly brighten, the gel was flushing away and I choked and coughed until my throat was numb. I heard my father, snapping at me for being weak, felt his hand on my shoulder, then laughter, the man never laughed.

The light shifted and I saw Kimba, laughing, shaking me, hard, reaching back a hand to slap my face.

"No, no—I—"more fluid discharged from my nose, and he held his hand. I was sitting on a metal grate, fluid seeping off my body, starting to shiver. Kimba stood at the edge of the grate, hands on his hips, grinning, pocked cheeks pouching around his lips.

"Have a good trip?" he chuckled.

"I, what was that?"

"Extraction bubble, suck you right up through the floor."

"A what? That's not possible," I looked down at the grate, tapped it with my fingernail.

"Oh, you an expert now? A transportation genius, perhaps? Conversant in all manner of secret tunnels, trapdoors, passettos, and bab al-sirrs?"

"No, no, I'm—I'm sorry."

"Think nothing of it, friend. Welcome!" He stood aside and waved his hand slowly, revealing to my eyes the wonders of an empty warehouse. I looked, then looked back at him, trying to raise my eyebrows in a question, but unsure if I'd actually made them move.

"Come on, let's go eat." He hooked my arm and yanked me off the grate, then let go and strode toward a door in the far wall, leaving me to stumble after.

"We owe much to your generous trade, you know," he called over his shoulder.

"Ah."

"Even though, certainly, we would have succeeded

without the dispensary, well, the pharma just made it so much easier, and so much more fun!"

He pushed through the door. The room beyond was smaller, and might have been a canteen once upon a time, or the office for the warehouse we'd just left. Now, it seemed to be the setting for a strange equestrian event: a crude track was marked on the floor, with very low hurdles made of old cartons and trash placed every few feet, and a runner astride a woman from the DataPsych team goaded her onward as she clomped on hands and knees around the track. Two other DataPsych members were similarly mounted, apparently waiting their turn. The woman circling the track reared back and made a whinnying noise, and I saw it was Bonato, one of the talking heads from the internal news feed. Her whinny brought great whoops and hollers from a gaggle of runners watching from a small stand of bleachers, which in turn drove her faster around the track.

"She's all in," Kimba said, "took to the races like a fish—no, wrong, like a horse to a horse track, I guess!" He was beaming, rubbing his hands together and shifting his weight from side to side.

"I don't understand. What is this?"

"Why, it's the power of pharma, my friend! And our animal natures." He paused to touch hands in some kind of ritual with another runner, a taller woman with short, dirty hair and a wide, dirty face.

"I still don't understand. I don't really care, to be honest, I'm working, and—"

"Yes, yes, working, I know, working for a new boss,

same as the old boss, ha, good one, but listen, Duval, you are stuck with the grubs for a few hours, so relax. Enjoy the entertainment, my chooga Médecins."

"Stuck?"

"Stuck, as in, waiting for the next phase, the bot you dropped off down below needs time to do it's work, before you can get on with yours. Paulie didn't tell you that?"

I shook my head, and he laughed again. "Come on, null set, I'll buy you a drink."

He led me past the track, where a new steed was shaking his head and drooling gently, through another door to a short hallway. "We got the good stuff, you know, trade the farmfolks upstairs for it, when's the last time you had a proper beverage, anyway?"

"I'm not much of a drinker."

"No? Well, end of the world, maybe it's time to start." We entered a large conference room with a bar, tables, and a large cage in one corner. A few runners sat at the tables drinking, another polished glasses behind the bar, and two DataPsych members sat slumped in the cage, heads lolling, eyes closed.

Kimba directed me to a table, went to the bar, and returned with two glasses and a jug of clear liquid. He filled the glasses, threw the contents of his down my throat, and gestured to mine.

"If you don't mind, it's been a long day already, and—"

"Drink it, really. Not kidding."

I sniffed it, but it had no scent, so I closed my eyes and did as Kimba had, throwing the liquid at my throat. It burned like I'd swallowed a torch, my whole head shook, and the air rippled with a faint tinkling sound. "Delicious," I choked, and saw Kimba frozen mid-smile. Everyone in the room was frozen, the drink the bartender was pouring hovered in mid-air. The tinkling increased, louder and louder, then stopped altogether as the world resumed its forward progress.

"For later," Kimba said, handing me a small glass bottle.

I thought of a thousand things to say, none of which made sense.

"So, what do you think of the revolution?" Kimba said.

"The what?"

"This, my friend," he gestured at the cage and the nodding DataPsychs in their filthy jumpsuits, "is the revolution, the proletariat taking control of the means of production, get it? Well, not so romantic as that, maybe. We got control of what they want, the ones who seek to rule, cause really what they want is to be ruled, to be animals, to know that power, the only thing they believe is real and is right. We give them what they want, and don't have to take their shit anymore. Works for everybody."

"How? I mean, I'm guessing, you give them pharma?"

"Not just any pharma, supasupatek pharma, our own brew, makes it so the only thing gets them happy is humiliation—or more pharma!" He slapped his leg.

"Where did you get the script?"

"What, you not listening?" He tapped his finger on the side of his head. "It's our own brew, what, you think like these shit apes, that we Runners, we too dumb to do the big work, the big thinking? You went out and got some fancy halo, come on, anybody can get those threads, friend, I got more threads from the greynet than you could believe. Runners for doing the dirty work, can't make friends in meatspace, give them another scan, put them together in a big green nursery, teach them to mind their manners and do what they're told. Might as well put in a request script: wanted, one revolution, delivery due at the end of time." He took another slug of the liquor. I wondered what he did while the room froze, watched as his body jumped an inch forward as he rejoined time.

"A nursery? Not really."

"No, not really, but they might as well have done, we all took the aptitude screen, didn't put tower folks like you in the same track as me, did they? Because your brain so much bigger, you got more processing power? You know it, you speak the right language, those aptitude scripts are made for you and people like you, keep you comfy enough. Who you think writes them?"

"And if they let you write them, everything would be fine, equality all around," I shrugged.

"No, course not. I'd be too busy trying to keep these people here," he swept his hand around the makeshift bar, "from killing you all." He smiled and took another swig of liquor, and when I blinked, he was standing behind his chair, raising his glass to me. I answered his toast, and we left the bar, weaving between the frozen patrons of the tavern, pausing every now and then to take a sip when the tinkling grew too loud.

We made our way to a set of quarters exactly like the one I'd had a few floors above. It might have been directly below my quarters, in fact. I sat on the bed, he on a chair, and we let the tinkling grow unbearably loud. When it stopped, I was exhausted, my head throbbed, and my tongue felt like someone had made a plaster cast of it, then yanked the cast off before it was dry.

"You get used to it, null set. Take yourself a little nap, I come back and get you when it's time to deliver the next bot."

I nodded. As he turned to leave, I mumbled at him. "If I'm such a worthless, privileged *enbesil*, then why help me?"

He shook his head. "End of the world, chooga, one way or another this is it. Even if the man lying about what happened outside. We all know it. No point being mad and righteous, now, we got ponies to ride. What is it, enbesil?

"Ah, stupid person, a fool," I said, not sure how I knew.

"Yeah, well, we all enbesils, then, friend, we all still here."

I lay my aching body down and stared at the ceiling. My grandpère once called my father enbesil, I remembered his face, fallen, that great stony face, like a cliff crumbling into the sea. The entirety of my life had followed that motion, a collapse into oblivion, foam, waves that never reach the far shore. But it followed from a remove, I had watched it happen from a hill, or on a vid, or it wasn't my memory at all, just my mind taking hold of scrap and knotting a quilt from it, each new knot pulled tight as another came loose, faded away, then the threads, too, fading.

Chapter 15

Kimba woke me and led me to the relay without saying a word. His eyes were laced with red veins, and he had a large bruise on his face. The fact that I could see the bruise on his blue-black skin meant it must have been fairly deep as well. I flicked the bot onto the relay and heard Kimba grunt. I turned and saw his red eyes were tearing.

"Are you alright?" I asked him.

"Ya, ya, what about it, next floor up for you, for you, for you—" he pointed at the roof, then pointed again, and again, stuck just like Gardiner had been, looping, the world looping around me. I reached in my pocket and there was a disc, some kind of flat black nanocarbon this time, instead of silver. I thrust it into his mouth, and the ceiling above him opened, and I floated up and through into the floor above.

The pig icon popped up in the corner of my eye, and I imagined it gutted, pulling its entrails out as its legs kicked on. "Good work, kid! Go get'em, kid! Only three more floors till boomsday!" I had not felt such hatred for anyone or anything, virtual or real, in a long time. Ever, perhaps. My body relaxed when it blinked off, my jaw ached from gritting my teeth, and the smell of rot blew over me on a warm breeze. I had emerged facing a dead end, so I turned and walked toward the smell and the heat, and saw a faint greenish light in the distance. The hall was empty and sparsely lit, and my steps seemed to grow louder the further I went, then they began to squeak, and the squeak softened into a woman's voice repeating "step, step" each time I did. I stopped, held my foot above the ground, and put it on the floor. Now my steps made no sound at all, and the green light shone from around the door at the end of the hall. I lifted my hand and the door slid open. The shrill wheezing sound that drifted to me as I stepped into the green glow was discomforting, but not so discomforting as the fact that my hands appeared to have shrunk to half their normal size, which caused me to shake them violently as I walked forward, following the tug of the Farm Floor relay. A railing stopped me from falling 30 feet to the concrete below.

"Hey, Duval!" I recognized Hendrickson's voice, calling from somewhere below. As my eyes adjusted to the light, I saw row upon row of green-lit nanofarms, 20 or so shelves high, and beyond them, the grey metal doors of the meat labs. "Down here, look, the stairs, your left. Your other left."

I found my way down, glancing every few steps at my normal-sized hands.

"Made it, eh?" Hendrickson looked, as he usually did, haggard but healthy. The image of him dangling by his feet hung at the corner of my mind, flickering.

"Yes. So you know why I'm here."

"Sure, although I don't know why any of us are here, I won't bullshit. I don't even know if you're real, how about that!"

"I, yes, I also have been having trouble discerning

what is real and what is—what is not."

"Right, every day I think, 'what is it now, the Tek boys fucking with me, or us, or whatever', yes, I thought that had all been shut down, our supament hamster world, but it looks like even what I think is up for grabs." He turned and walked a few steps, then stopped and waved for me to follow.

The whine of the nanofarms grew loud enough to make me feel nauseous. Hendrickson let his hand drift along the side of one as he walked, humming loudly to himself. He led me between the two meat labs, to another door and, thankfully, a room with normal lighting and no whining to infect my stomach.

"Sit," he said, directing me to an overstuffed chair. I fell into it and immediately felt a sense of mild elation. "Comfy, yeah?"

"Very," I agreed.

"It exudes a kind of topical pharma, very mild, a tiny bot farm in the seat." I could find nothing wrong with the idea. I loved it, in fact, and I was very glad that Hendrickson was not, in fact, dead.

"An exceptional idea, I'm sure many people would take comfort in furniture like this."

"It's not really for comfort, Gardiner had it shipped down, Lem used it for information extraction."

"Ah, well, that, too, makes great sense, certainly people who are in a comfortable and pleasant state of mind—"

"No, I did that, reprogrammed the little bastards, put the big cushions on—filled with spun fat, by the way, grown in the meat lab, emulsified, dried, makes great pillows. Lem had the bot farm set to cause pain, he really thought that would work. Fucking Napoleon knew pain-based info extraction was a no-go, for shit's sake, that Lem, that EuRusCo training, dark age stuff. But, like I said, he made a fine pillow."

"What, I'm sorry, is—" He waved a hand to silence me and smiled, then pressed the top of a small desk that had popped out of a wall. He had strong hands, I trusted everything about him.

"Let's talk about why you're here, and what I get in exchange for letting you do the job, and what else. What else? Nothing, just the job."

"Very good, I would—"

"As I said before, I'm not certain that you exist. I'm also fairly sure that without enough power, a lot of power, no one could pull off a full sensory environment like this one," he spoke almost too fast to understand, and rapped the desktop, "but that doesn't mean you are really here, or that I'm not strapped down getting fed all this end-of-world nonsense. I've been interrogated before, so I know the signs, like the way you smell."

"Oh, I never thought, ah, do I smell?"

"No, not at all. Not even a little," he said, rolling his chair over to sniff near my ear. It was all I could do to resist hugging him. "You have no scent, but then, I don't guess I do, either," he said, offering his hand for me to smell. I suspected he wanted me to say he smelled, so I did.

"Oh, no, you smell wonderful."

"Bullshit." He tapped the desktop. I wondered where

the rest of his team had gone, and why my heart was suddenly pulsing hard in my chest, and why I bothered, why any of us bothered dragging our way through this broken world. "There, sleep mode. I can tap this table and make you feel good again, just tell me what I need to know."

"Right. Well. You haven't asked me anything." How much I hated him, I felt it flood back, felt good for hating him and knowing it was true.

"Are you real, or an AI?"

"I cannot answer satisfactorily, as you know. You must have a Turing script—"

"And you know, if we are in a sim, the Turing script is corrupt and useless. I just want to hear you say it."

"Why?"

"I don't know. Whoever is running these scripts, and I think it's Tek guys, Gardiner and them are too null to figure that out, and Tek wouldn't do it just cause the Custodians asked nice, nicey nice. It could be a third party, someone hacked us remotely, but all the supatek ment shit they shot us with was supposed to be total firestorm, but I guess we have to admit the possibility."

"Every time you open your mouth I see you hanging by your feet."

"Huh?" He looked genuinely surprised. "Oh, that, well, that was Gardiner, of course, the whole thing was pre-scripted before we even got here. It was part of my contract, along with the growth mods, I never would have agreed to either but wowza, the resources they offered me...."

"I still cannot trust you. And I can say, yes, I am real,

and you can say yes, and we can go on not trusting the other, and then what?"

"I just wanted to come and develop better strains, get some really hardy nano going here. You know? Just figure out how to produce enough food, then share, no profiteering, no favelas, enough for everyone to eat. I suppose Gardiner knew I planned to set it free, but I didn't think he cared. This can't just be about money again, can it?"

"I don't understand."

"Are you working for Gardiner?" He stared. His eyelids were heavy, gray as rain cloud, but his eyes burned from under their shade.

"Of course. So are you."

"You know what I fucking mean!" He tapped the desktop again, and the world burst into purple flame. My blood felt like broken glass beneath my skin. When the pain subsided, Hendrickson looked ready to cry.

"I work for Gardiner Group. Gardiner Group has not been in contact with me for several days. By the terms of my contract, I am allowed to subcontract when my employer is incommunicado, unless that work somehow contradicts the original contract. If this contradiction were present, I would not be able to complete—"

"Mumbledly mumbledy, save it. Who are you subcontracting for?"

"Paul Levant."

"I fucking knew it."

"Yes, you said you did when I arrived."

"I did?"

"Yes."

He sat back and stared at the ceiling. "Yes, I did. I remember. I got the message. Bot on the relay, hook the power back up. Then I could flip the baffles on again, not have to hear that screeching noisy noise anymore, get some proper lights in here. I'm losing my mind, sorry."

"I understand. Now, can I affix the bot?"

"What? Oh, yes, let's do my part first, I get something too, a free gift! Extra bonus! Levant said I get to give you a tour." The pig popped up, winking at me. "He thinks it's all a data dump!" It chirped.

"Fine, a tour."

I hated farm tours, everyone, other than farmers, hated them. They were always the same: peeking into tubes full of bots too small to see, performing repetitive info scripts, playing at building plant matter, and the meat labs were even more boring, and they stunk. Everyone hated them, and yet everyone went, because farmers were, by and large, perfectly willing to let a whole camp starve otherwise. Most everyone I knew simply ate the extruded protein, and the real stuff was a delicacy. I had eaten fresh nanogrown twenty or thirty times in my life before coming here, and I had to admit, they had a right to be arrogant. It wasn't quite like real farm grown, the stuff I remembered from my childhood, but it was so much better than extrusion.

He led me out among the shelves. The whining started again.

"I think you will find some of our projects very interesting," he said.

"Ah." They were not very interesting, though the script

in/out efficiency was impressive enough. But not so impressive it warranted twenty minutes of explication. We wandered.

"And finally, the base corporea all comes in here," he said, stopping at an eight meter tall cylinder, tucked near the end of the rows. "All waste material from the pre-fabrication process, from the sewage flow, everything. Normal farm, these three tiers wold all be devoted to extrusion, but we cull it off the side." He pointed to a braid of smaller tubes that cascaded down the side of the cylinder and vanished into the floor.

"Ah."

"And here, opposite the extrusion vessel, the compost bin." Tucked between the cylinder and the wall was a large, square, lidded container. "I won't open it, since our compost is, well, is what we have to work with. Ha. Right?" He elbowed me in the ribs.

"Right. Like, waste."

"Like, yes, waste. When the Runners went on their little rampage upstairs, we filled this baby to the top, though they spoiled a lot with their stupid poison. Had to dump fecal waste in a freezer! But now, well, it's a cyclical system. We produce the food, waste back in, can't go on forever, of course, even with all the good quality mulch stuffed in there, we'll run out of viable foodstuff for the current population in roughly seven years."

"Mulch? I thought—"

"Raw material, vegetable matter, fecal matter in a closed systems, bodies of the deceased, in our case, lately. Are you a prude, now?"

"No, I understand where our food comes from. I just wondered why you called it mulch."

"What else would I call it?"

"On previous tours, it was called 'fodder' or 'chump'."

"Ah, well, ideally the matter in the compost bin is only meant to supplant the grown material, help feed it as the bots drive the script. Can't grow a turnip in three days otherwise. But, our core cutting scripts need to be fed regular revitalization threads, which they haven't gotten, so they decay into uselessness, and here we are, eating our seed stock, so to speak."

"So, we need organics from outside, if we are to survive."

"Oh shit, boy, now I see why Kimba calls you 'null set'. Who still thinks we're going to survive? You? That why you pulling this shit for Tek?"

"It's a job. And yes, I think it is the only chance left, as this point."

"And what is their big answer, up in the tower?"

"Ah."

"Ok, better question: does their answer mean the end of all this? Of me?"

I looked around the room. The whine, the green light, I could see why he was losing hold of things.

"No. They mean to shift the whole facility across multiverses."

His mouth hung open for a few seconds, then he laughed, and laughed, harder and harder, pushing against the ceiling of some madness.

"That is the funniest little bit I've heard in..." he

laughed again, catching his breath.

"Where is the rest of your team, Mr. Hendrickson?" I thought I knew, but asked anyway.

"In the freezer, of course. Well, most. The breeders are back in the breeding bay, trying to make babies. Ok, not babies, I just call them that, not really babies when they don't have heads, right?" He started laughing again, and I worried he would never stop, so I grabbed him by the shoulders and shook. He stood erect again, a good half a meter taller than I.

"Forgive me, Mr. Crusader. Let's get you to that relay, so you can blow us all the fuck up, shall I? Oh, but wait, I almost forgot." He staggered off down the row of shelves. "Come, come! Your extra bonus!" I found him in the corner furthest from the room where he'd tried, so lazily, to interrogate me. Farmers. Too full of self-importance to even do a proper information extraction.

"First, your work:" he pointed at the relay, set low on the wall, and I flicked the bot that had crawled out onto my hand toward it. "And now, here, my sir, is your bounty." He tapped one of the shelf windows, and it slid back, letting out a cloud of greenish vapor. I peered inside. Along the lattice within, a clump of vine and leaf, a more vivid version of the grape, perhaps, but instead of grapes, clumps of what looked like fingers, wriggling gently.

"Closer! Look! I made them for all the Gardiner employees—" I bent forward so my head was inside the unit. It was so hot I held my breath. What I took to be fingers were actually tiny human figures, tiny brown figures, tiny versions of my own body, writhing and wobbling their tiny limbs. I felt sick again, and banged my head on the shelf trying to pull it out. Hands grabbed my legs and lifted, pushing me into the tube, Hendrickson yelling "everything is compostable!," or maybe "everything is combustible!," or I heard nothing, shoved face-first onto a bed of a thousand tiny, wet bodies, all my own, surrounding me, holding onto my face. It was warm, and not so terrible, each of my cells separating from the other, sluicing off of bone, bone into marrow and crumb, as I was distributed across all the lattices. The last thing I felt was a tug, and then I was looking through piggy eyes, looking out of the avatar Paulie stuck in me, looking at the inside of my own cortex, chirping at myself, "get it together! Work to do! Work to do!" And then I was sitting upright, and Hendrickson was across from me, in the comfy chair, and his own eyes were open and lifeless, drool dried on his chin. He was even worse at information extraction than I'd thought, or else he'd turned the chair all the way up and committed suicide via settee. I looked past him at the door, and felt the tug of the next relay. Two more. Two more and I could retire to a sunny beach in an alternate reality, where I could plant my posterior in the sand, instead of on a chair.

Chapter 16

Though I knew most of the soldiery were dead, poisoned and butchered by the runners, I did not expect everything to be so clean. Mass murder is typically a very untidy affair, but here, the halls were white and spotless, they seemed freshly painted, and someone must have had limited cleaning bot access, not a feather of dust or grime anywhere. Also, there were no people, and nothing in any of the quarters, all the doors sat open, all the rooms devoid of any signs they had been inhabited. Everything had been scrubbed.

The tug toward the relay led me to the first closed door on the floor. I checked my hands, confirmed their normal size, and waved one at the door. Down a short hallway was another door, and behind that, was Mbete. What was left of Mbete, rather. He was propped on a large table butted against a wall, tubes from the ceiling attached to his armless, legless torso. A spotless white sheet was bunched around his pelvis, draping over the edge of the table down to the floor. His face was worked earth, bled and crusted over a thousand times, eyes the color of decaying fish. I touched the top of his head, hairless and sticky, where sweat had dried and been re-hydrated into a glaze. The reek that should have fogged the room was absent, someone must have powered the bots in this room as well, even the sheet was as spotless as the rest of the floor. A metal chair faced Mbete's perch, and I sat and waited for something to happen The relay tug had led me here, but no further.

My hands rested on my knees, my spine held my head aloft. I knew these things because my idea of my body was alive, still, despite the mangling and dissociation it had experienced since I took Paulie's contract. Somewhere in the minutia of the employment document was a clause defining any simulated dismantling of the body as part of the work, I was sure, just as I was sure that the body I felt myself peering out of was my own. The seamless shift from bodied to sim, from persistent reality to the feed that caused me to experience being pulled through the floor, or decomposed in a nanofarm, was excellent, from a connoisseur's point of view. Again, I was struck by the sophistication of the tek here, how all encompassing it was, and without any apparent direct link. Obviously, the danger was in remote manipulation of individuals, everything real could be directed by strong actors, but all sorts of baffles and hatches would spring up as soon as it was made widely available, before, even, it had happened before, the tek ecosystem was too wild for dictatorial dreams. Or it had been, before everyone died. If everyone died. I still had some small hope that Mbete had something to tell me about outside, about his mission there, about who he worked for and why, and what I was doing here. I just wasn't sure he could speak, or think, for that matter.

I stood and went and touched his head again.

"Mbete," I said, softly. "Godsong..."

His head lolled from side to side, then a brackish grin opened up at the bottom of his face.

"Oh, my brother, Mr. Manoushka, you have come..."

"I—I didn't know what had been done to you, I'm sorry."

"No, no..." the head fell back, then snapped forward. A cleaning bot appeared and began to scour the table where Mbete had let a long strand of drool fly. "I deserve everything, I am a soldier, I understand they..."

"Still. This is not a way to live."

"I am not alive, of course."

"You seem alive to me."

"I am being prevented from dying. A funny sort of living, at the least."

"Well." I couldn't tell where the relay was. I almost wished the pig head would pop up. "What can I do?"

"No, no, even if you could help, even if you could stop my breathing and kill me, I have no doubt you would occupy my place next." His words rattled, each into the next.

"Why? This was, it was the runners, yes? Their revenge for—" For what? I suddenly didn't know where the floor was, and I swayed in my chair, holding tight. My arm throbbed, and I saw the letters "EB" shining bright red. Beaudoin! Had he killed her? Who was she?

"Yes, for killing the External... for the feed they saw, that we all saw, where I shot the other members of the team. And I deserve it, every pain I suffer mine, only mine, I will not share!" He began rocking, and everything fell back into place. How did I lose those memories? Something was burrowing in my head, chewing it up. I needed to finish, fast.

"Yes, but why? Why did you kill them, I thought, after the Dakotas, when you stopped yourself from committing genocide—"

"That was a lie," he said, trying to smile again. "So much of what I am is a lie, but that was a simple script, just like your script about being a Médecins, about your immigrant family, your big and little angels, that nonsense about Marinette and the owl and—"

I shot up from my chair and grabbed his head with both hands. "No! I am not a lie, I am not a script! Perhaps they have turned you inside out and made you forget who you are, but I know. I know who I am." I let his head drop, and said it again, to my chest: "I know who I am."

"Of course you do, forgive me. Let me tell you what I know. This is a game, and the game is winning. I was a soldier, not a very good one, certainly not an officer. My script was given to me by Gardiner, just as the script for the Externalization team was a script. We did not go outside, both feeds you saw, both were scripts. I shot them all in the head, in the hangar, the doors were never opened, we all would be dead if they were. You did not eradicate the nanovirus, your results, another bloody script. Gardiner is the game, Gardiner wins. You see, my friend? It was all a lie, all a game."

The laser scalpel on the table in front of him was not there a few seconds ago, I was fairly certain. Still, it worked, and I felt it warm in my hand, fought the urge to nick a few centimeters out of his jugular and watch the blood surge in little spouts. He was smiling again, trying to laugh I think, but all that came out of his ruined mouth was a choppy wheezing. I felt a tingle in the bottom of my foot, dropped the scalpel, and pulled back the sheet to find the relay under Mbete's table. I flicked the bot toward it, stood up, took the scalpel once again, turned it on, and thrust it into Mbete's left eye. His head hissed and deflated, spraying a fine yellow mist from the hole I'd made, up into my nose and eyes and mouth, and I fell to the ground, coughing. When I could see and breathe once more, I saw that I was on the next floor above, where the Custodial team had held sway, where the rostrum lived and a woman who never existed fed me ice cream that also never was.

I had reached the end, ready to chain the last of the relays, ready to complete my contract.

[Subject 336136 keriport application of decryption lattice stack overflow. Stop recording.]

"Mr. Duval. Good morning."

The ceiling, the lights, a delicate rose color, stippled panels no obvious joinery no flicker, soothing, undersea.

"You will experience some disorientation for the next few hours. Please rest and focus on regaining diachronic coherence."

Voice within voice, someone to the left, other noises, a warm feeling up through the center. Everything is getting smaller.

My stomach. Hurts. A sharp pain, also dull, something pushing through it. I can turn my head, feels like bags of water are hanging from it, sloshing in my ears. A lab of some sort, old-style pharma pump, offline monitoring is used, as used, can use, I can't see it, where and when I know them, brutal alloy frame with variable skins readout direct VR port like a broken clam shell on the side, I know these machines. Loas work them, no, I have used them, I am no loa. Let the self fall where it may, all six consciousnesses falling together, a shuffling of cards.

"Mr. Duval." I open my eyes. I did not dream, but I remember, I remember who I was as if it were a dream. And I remember the face of the man who spoke. He is my jailer. His pale, bent head, his wave of fading orange hair, his name is Deebs, I hate all of him. He keeps smiling.

"Mr. Deebs," my voice comes from somewhere below.

"You recognize me, good, remember my name, good," he said, ticking off items on a list. "How does your body feel?"

"Fine."

"Would you mind lifting your left hand for me?" Left. "And the right?" Now, should I clap? He is ticking, ticking, itemizing, logging, adding to the mountain of data.

He stood to leave, still smiling. "Can I get you anything?"

"I want nothing." He nodded like he knew I would say that, how I would say it, when...

§

I don't remember being brought back to my cell, they must have stuffed me with pharma and wheeled me here. There was food on the table, and I ate it, grateful for its tastelessness. Everything that happened at the Facility had washed back to me, flotsam after a tsunami drifting ashore, and I lay on the cot putting the pieces back together. I remembered Lem and Bye holding me at gunpoint, Gardiner appearing and trying, again, to convince me that everything I'd seen was part of a job interview, and how, after I flicked the bot onto the relay, the whole Facility shuddered. How the cleaning bots Paulie had re-purposed tore into Lem and Bye's flesh. How Paulie laughed, when I found him, and told me he had been controlling Gardiner's avatar ever since Operation Grand Guignol, Gardiner had never even set foot in the Facility and was, thus, likely, dead, maybe even mulch. I remembered Paulie feeding me a script, I remember rejecting his next contract offer, his shrug, his lockdown of all the doors in preparation for the "shift" as he called it. I crawled up through an air duct, using the light I bought from Kirkus, and emerged into fresh air, ready to die, and not feeling surprised when I did not. And then I remembered, again, the explosion.

Other memories floated through, as is memories' wont, and with the help I suppose, of all the pharma they'd pumped in me. I saw Clara, one my of first term node partners, showing off her new ments, back when the rest of us still used lenses or headstocks. I felt my Manman's eyelashes on my cheek, after I had been crying. The flood of memory soon became overbearing, like being crushed under an avalanche of garbage at some favela, and I slept. One of the masked guards woke me later, poking me with the end of a prod, then leading me out the door at the end of the hall, the one I thought I would never walk through.

We followed a hallway to an elevator, then another hallway, and saw no other people, not even other guards. The walls, the floor, the way the lights were placed, the inset doors and switches, everything reminded me of the Facility, but not precisely; there, the sign for "E-3" used a different font and color scheme, here, where we stopped, the door swipe was set much higher. It slid open and I was prodded into a small conference room, an octagonal table surrounded with chairs, topped with a pitcher of yellow fluid and a dozen cups. I was pushed down into a chair, then felt the door slide shut behind me.

A few seconds later, a door in the opposite wall opened, and Mr. Deebs entered, in his grey suit and shining shoes, followed by Ms. Bye and Mr. Lem. Bye's hair was longer, and a much lighter hue, and Lem's face was fuller, almost paunchy, and he wore something in his ear, but it was them, without a doubt. They were all smiling their alligator smiles, perhaps there was a school for interrogators that taught them how to use the smile as a knife. I knew my mouth was hanging open, eyes too, but I couldn't see around their heads to their reason for being.

"Mr. Duval," Deebs said, sitting across from me as the others followed suit, "let me introduce you to Ms. Latour, one of our rehabilitationists, and Mr. Bent, who does DataPsych work for us."

"Hello," they both said, inclining their heads to exchange v-slips. There was no net here, they were not used to it, they were not stationed in this jail, then? I shook my head. No v-slips, you strange apparitions. We live primitively, here. I felt a surge of violence, a sudden compulsion to grab them both by the neck and throttle them until their faces went blue, until their eyes burst. I felt my body rising from my chair, heard noises rattling from my mouth, spittle. A hand grabbed my shoulder and pushed me down and I felt a pinch, heard the hiss of pharma, and I stared at the whorls in the tabletop, watching how they spun slowly, like dancers in a ballroom, like clouds rising off the plain.

Chapter 17

Deebs was there when I woke, of course. He sat, legs crossed, hands crossed over his legs, a small brown stylus of some sort crooked under a thumb. Smiling and nodding. I felt a churning in my stomach, a sourness that I felt might come rushing out, and I propped myself on an elbow so I could be sure it would douse him.

"Mr. Duval," he said, waggling the stylus.

"Mr. Deebs."

"You had quite a, well, violent reaction to Ms. Latour and Mr. Bent. Doesn't fit your profile at all, not at all. Could you tell me what happened?"

"You know what happened," my throat was raw. What kind of pharma had they given me? Not indexed to my bioschema, certainly.

"I'm afraid I don't, other than you reacted to Ms. Latour and Mr. Bent at a level of intensity that triggered a security protocol. If you could explain what about them was so, hmm, difficult, for you, it would help."

I sat up and swallowed. "How did you do it? Extract them from the facility, so the people I knew, the ones I saw die, were only avatars? Or maybe you skinned them from Bye and Lem's records, found doubles, or maybe you're exploiting the same ment adjustment they did at the facility, blasting it in wireless—"

"Please, please," he said, uncrossing his fingers and

petting the air in front of his knees, "calm down. We have gone over the data we captured, and I recognize the persons you have named, but please, take a breath, and I will bring up footage." He pointed with the little wand, and I saw the back of a holoscreen while he fiddled with it. It spun, enlarged, and I saw the contents of my skull, played back with a bit of fisheye at the edges, some brownouts when heads turned too quickly, but otherwise, fairly smoothly. It was the Custodial conference room, a meeting, and the image froze when my gaze fell on Bye and Lem, sitting beside one another.

"Now, to the left is Charity Bye, to the right, Josip Lem. Both known employees of Gardiner Group, both now presumed deceased." Another screen popped up beside the still shot. "Here, we have Mrs. Latour and Mr. Bent. Are they the same people?"

Of course they were not, they weren't even close enough to make a mistake. Latour and Bent were the people I knew from the Facility, Bye and Lem, I didn't recognize at all.

"No, of course they are not."

"What you have experienced is a fusiformal inhibition, very common to subjects undergoing the keriporting procedure. A kind of limited prosopagnosia, in which the subject overlays the faces of new people with the memory of what they've experienced—in other words, you saw Ms. Latour and Mr. Bent as Ms. Bye and Mr. Lem becuase your mind is still rebuilding itself, after prolonged memory reconstruction and extraction. And, well, because we did not entirely succeed in removing the Confidentiality block."

"The Con—" and it came back. My brain would collapse, was collapsing. "Ah."

"But, all is not lost, we did succeed in decrypting a great deal of it, in fact, we decrypted the most essential folds, leaving only your handshake to complete the process. But we can speak of that later. For now, I would like you to rest, and tomorrow morning, we will meet with Latour and Bent once again, to help debrief you, to review the data we gathered, and then you will be in a position to complete the handshake."

His words sounded like gobbling, phonemes falling down the stairs, down a waterfall. I nodded and lay back on the cot. He made talky noises, stood up and made other kinds of noises, then was gone. My big good angel was sobbing, my little good angel was drunk, and the world was awash with the whispers of the dead, spirits leading me this way or that, according to their whim. The whispers told me I should rest, while my mind settled into a puddle. All because I wanted to work, because I was seduced by Gardiner's employment scripts, his ment upgrades, his queer manner and his vision and his ruthlessness. I only wanted to do something significant, even as my species careened off a cliff. I was such an easy mark. Any cheap hustler could have spotted me a kilometer away, and one did.

§

For the next several days, I sat and watched footage. Rather, Deebs and Latour and Bent and I sat and watched footage, stopping and replaying while they made notations, asking me question after question, often circling back to ask the same question again, as though I was lying or deranged or both. They were very interested in the glitches, and where the silver discs came from, and why I shoved them in people's mouths. I didn't know where they came from or why I did it, though I remembered doing so clearly. I watched Hendrickson hung from his feet half a dozen times, and cried a little the first time I saw Beaudoin again, but my jailors didn't care that such a person did, in fact, exist, if only on the screen. They were looking for whatever pattern would lead to the "handshake," which Deebs explained was a pattern or scene I could think about, and which would then unencrypt my head and let me feed them the data they wanted. He would not, however, tell me what that data was. "It isn't important, and may inhibit your ability to provide the handshake." Deebs is a sneaky little man, and part of me hopes I simply die before he can get what he wants.

I wake, and he is there, sitting beside my bed. They are feeding me pharma again, surely, maybe tracking my brain activity, so he knows when I am about to wake, or to be woken, remotely. I wake, and we watch footage, then I eat, then we watch footage, then I am taken to a stim tank, then I eat, then footage, then sleep, then I wake and Deebs is sitting there, smiling.

"Good morning, Mr. Duval."

"I see nothing good in it."

"Well, perhaps we will find something in it to cheer you up. I received notice earlier that we may have found the pattern necessary for the handshake."

"Ah."

"Which means, of course, that we will be able to un-encrypt, and you will no longer be in danger." He kept tapping the side of his leg, which meant he was agitated or excited.

"In other words, I will be unnecessary, and you will kill me, I suspect."

"Of course not, why would—please. Are you ready to go?"

"Why not?" I said. I flushed my mouth and took the protein bar left beside my bed while I slept. I wasn't sure why I still ate. Habits, compulsions, what else are we?

Latour and Bent were waiting in the conference room. I'd grown to hate them as well, though neither said very much, presumably because they were messaging each other, and when they did speak, it was to agree with Deebs, or ask me a technical questions, like where I was standing, what I was wearing, at a given point in the footage. That they were Deebs' willing subordinates was enough for me to detest them and their toady ways.

"Now, this really is exciting, despite your reluctance, Mr. Duval. We believe we have found the pattern, and all you have to do, is watch it, then visualize it, and you should be given handshake protocol."

"Fine."

"Yes," he continued, "and we don't know quite how the protocol will, ah, appear—manifest, I think is the technical term," Latour nodded, "but we are very sure that you will know it when you see it."

"Fine."

"Yes, well, Mr. Bent?" We watched some kind of montage, footage of hallways, hallways I traveled down in the Facility, but sped up. Hallway after hallway, devoid of people. Walking to dinner. Walking to the lab. Walking to a meeting. Walking to deliver Paulie's bots. And, finally, crawling out the duct to a world that was not yet dead. I felt a shuddering in my spine, and felt Deebs and his minions flutter with excitement.

"Yes, look, look at the activity here," someone said. They were huddled around a holoscreen, poking at it like rabbis arguing over the Talmud.

"Excellent, Mr. Duval. Let's watch it again, We need you to watch it enough times that you can vizualize the sequence."

And watch it I did, 10, 20, so many times I lost count, all the while Deebs and Latour and Bent twittered and pointed and grinned. After the replay stopped, I would close my eyes and see the footage, neon outlines inside my lids. I watched the hallways rumble past and suddenly saw how lonely I was, like an elevator plummeting, how my facile connoissurship of employment, my halfhearted attempts at *Friend's World*, my compartmentalized rejection of my parent's affection, of their legacy, were all just ways I had sought to reject a world I felt rejected by. I had no desire for sex, and so stood outside what was normal and good, and rather than find my way to other people platonically, I had made my loneliness into a caricature of autonomy. I was alone and lost, and cold. Hallway after hallway, door after door, a scrolling maze leading down into the ground.

"Are you ready, Mr. Duval? The pictograph looks very good, all you need to do is visualize, then offer the hand-shake." Deebs was brimming, aglow.

"I can visualize," my tongue was so dry, my words felt like lumps of chalk, "but I don't understand what you mean by 'offer the handshake.'"

"You will see, once you have reached the end, but first, we must connect you one more time."

They took me down the hall to a lab and strapped me in. I swore I could hear a "click" as they connected with my port. The walls were pink, again, the ceiling, this is where I had awoken, perhaps. It didn't matter.

"Very good, let's begin. Please, if you would, Mr. Duval, begin the visualization."

Hallway leading to hallway leading to a duct, and I emerged into fresh air and saw it, a swirl of lines carved in the air, abstract until the mind began to register its sys-temicity, and then I could not look away. I could not look away, but I also understood I did not have to offer any response, it was my choice, after all this, all I had to do was assent, like I'd assented to Gardiner's contract. I just had to think "yes," and I would live, perhaps, or at least die better. Deebs would have what he wanted, and the world would go on turning, everyone alone, as alone as I. So I refused.

"Mr. Duval? Excuse me, Mr. Duval? I think we've hit a snag with the handshake, I—"

"No." I wish it felt good to say, but it did not.

"Excuse me? Again, please?"

"No, I refuse, I have had enough of this game. The

game is rigged, always the game will win and we will lose." I closed my eyes.

"I can't—no!—you must—" He shook my shoulder, then began, I assumed, furiously messaging his staff, or some masked guard, or perhaps his mother. A surge of water rose up from my toes, warm water rising through my body, and I could not breathe but had no need to breathe and instead of panic, I felt myself dissolving, no pain, no struggle, just bits and pieces detaching, floating away, so slowly and with such perfect logic it made both my angels stop and stare, entranced.

Chapter 18

H e's got brain function back."

"Well, shit. Let's see what the little grub has to say."

Clive Buss hated most parts of his job, but he hated shepherding grubs with homebrew ments something fierce. Coming up from the favelas to steal jobs from hardworking Nassers, they were scum and would always be scum, feeders, suckerfish. It was easier when they died, just call POP and show them the crude, melted port stuck on the back of a burred head, common as cancer.

"He was gone forever and a day, damn." He hated Tiki almost as much as the grubs, but at least he was certified, took care of his family. But soft, Tiki was soft.

"Yeah, ok. Give him some wakey wakey." Tiki bent and flipped a switch on the unit, wagging his finger in air. The brown, skinny, dirty man, way too old for a job scrubbing power coils, twitched and gasped.

"How ya doing, supatek? Can you see my finger? Follow my finger." Clive moved his finger, watching the man's eyes. He was tracking, thank god. Cleaning up after a fry was not what he had in mind for the end his shift, the BlueBoys made him nervous, every question they asked had another question hidden inside it. When POP says drop, you drop.

"Ok, good, now listen, are you listening?" A nod, tentative but enough. "You are in the recovery room at Speck

Industries. You came here to apply for a job, do you re-member that" Another nod. "Good, good, now here's the thing. You have a homebrew ment, right? And you can't use those for doing employment scripts, I mean, you know that, right? You burnt little shit?"

"Clive!" He spun at the sound of Mr. Guro's voice, a dog caught with his head in the garbage.

"Mr. Guro, sorry I—"

"Enough. Give me the sums." Mr. Guro was imposing, if one was not used to truly imposing people, as Clive was not. His narrow, crooked frame lent a gravity to his high-cheekboned face and eyes that seemed both angry and lost, as though they had forgotten the source of their an-ger and so would take it out on whatever drifted past in the interim.

"Right, uh, this gr—this applicant has non-certified augmentation, good enough to pass our initial scans, but too crude to accept the script correctly, so the script was anoma, anooma—"

"Anomalous."

"Yes, that. Sir." Clive looked at the dirty tile floor and wished he was playing hoop with his daughters.

"How long?"

"Sir? Oh, uh, basic interview script, 35 minute run-time, and he's been under for—" Clive bent and checked a readout on his holoscreen. "457 minutes, sir."

Mr. Guro raised an eyebrow, waved a hand in Clive's direction, and left the room. Clive knew the hand wave meant he should transfer over the grub's feed to the ar-chive, clean him up, point him toward Guro's office, and get the hell out of the building. The grub was drooling a bit, Clive noticed, and he felt something approaching satisfaction for the first time that day.

He polished the grub the best he could, trying to ignore the smell and the weird little noises it made. It would be another 30 or 40 minutes before the grub could talk, he knew, if, of course, it ever talked again. He set the feed transfer running and wheeled the grub down to Guro's office, leaving him in front of Guro's unattended desk. Why he still used a desk Clive would never know, but he hoped one day to find Guro slumped over on it, dead from some virus or other, something green spilling out of his nose. I can dream, he thought, and headed for the lobby to pick up his day's pay.

Guro watched him leave in a rear view screen, one of five or six he might have open at a given time. His mother always told him it would freeze his brain, trying to follow so many feeds at once, but she was a stupid woman, an old wives' tale script made flesh. And once she finally got ported herself, after years of swearing it was unnatural, she spent most of her day plugged in, just as he anticipated. He considered anticipation his most valuable skill, bordering on premonition, and the tingling sensation he felt when something unusual was afoot was, he knew, a kind of mysticism. It was this sensation that gave his cold, rational persona its secret power as he stalked the halls of Speck Industries, Cleaning and Reparation Node 921, searching out clues, peering into the future.

The body on the other side of his desk did not radiate potential clues. Light brown skin, short brown hair, unfocused hazel eyes, a wide, slack mouth slightly parted, sunken cheeks: a perfectly average favela dweller in every way, including the apparent absence of any prospects other than sickness and death, hence the homebrew ment, hence his application at Speck. Guro felt a twinge of sympathy as he scanned the man's activity chart. He couldn't imagine being trapped in an interview script for seven and a half hours, but then again, everyone knew the risks of non-standard augments, or were supposed to. He only hoped the poor bastard would regain enough brain function to walk out of the facility under his own power. If not, the paper work would be ridiculous.

Guro ran a surface scan, saw that the subject's heart rate was slowing, brain function settling down, and that he had stopped drooling. As he waited, he fed the subject's name and retinal scans into DSS and BlueBoy datastreams, though he knew Clive had already done so. Manoushka Duval, 37 years old, Haitian refugee, arrived in Half Moon a little less than nine years ago, no living relatives, the usual gaping data hole prior to arrival. Well, Manoushka, let's see if you are still a person.

"Have some water," Guro said, pushing a bottle across the desk. Duval's eyes settled on it, and then a bony hand, poking over the edge of the desk mousily, took it up. He drank, lost some down his chin, drank again. Guro pointed at a slot in the desk and a thin rag appeared. Duval wiped his mouth.

"Mr. Duval, it is my duty, as a licensed Gardiner GRX-13 Script Server, to inform you of the legal penalties incurred from use of non-licensed augmentation hardware in the processing of a 23D Employment Preamble Script. Per NAS Code 11 dot 6 dot 5 dot 9b, I am required to halt every two minutes to confirm your comprehension. Mr. Duval, do you understand what I have told you?"

"I, it—" Duval stammered, dropped his chin to his chest.

"Subject confirms comprehension." Guro flipped the archivist off with a grand sweep of his hand. He hoped Duval recognized the gesture, that he wasn't going to go further, that he was in fact interested in something non-standard, like buying Duval's footage. 457 minutes, the grub could eat for a year or two. Get drunk, even.

"Sir, I—where is this?"

Guro sighed. Basic comprehension was steady, but he didn't want to spend the next hour trying to orient the subject. "You are in my office. I am Mr Guro. The office is part of Speck Industries, Cleaning and Reparation Node 921, Lower Oak Block, Half Moon, New York, NortAmeri-Stat. You came here this morning for a job interview. Do you remember arriving this morning?"

"I, vaguely, coming here—"

"You were applying for a position in Remote Power Scour, and you provided us fraudulent credentials, and accessed our Interview Script with an unlicensed augment. Your port," Guro tapped the back of his own head, "is not licensed, and the hardware, while more sophisticated than many of the unlicensed ports we see here, is clearly non-standard. We know is is non-standard because of the non-standard way you interfaced with the script."

"I came for a job," Duval muttered, bits of memory coalescing.

"Yes, and the illegal port you used to access the job interview script caused a serious anomaly. The script runs 35 minutes, but you were unreachable for 457 minutes."

"Unreachable? I'm sorry, sir, I don't understand. I—I remember, now, something, just wanting to work, some kind of work."

"Unreachable, yes, disengaging any anomalous script is fatal to the subject more than 70% of the time, and is a class 3b Felony. In such cases, we let the script run its course." He felt a twinge of guilt as he recited the company line, most of which he had composed. For the first time, he was bothered by the presence of the backslider subroutine in the interview script, meant to trigger massive surges in random brain activity in subjects with non-standard ports. It was how he made most of his income, launching favela dwellers with bad port hacks into a hallucinatory jungle of their own composition, then selling the resulting footage to a rabid audience in the towers.

"So, please, sir, I know the hole is illegal, I should not have done it." The subject, Guro noted with disgust, was crying. Word had spread through the favela that Guro paid well, he had seen a few subjects three and even four times through their interviews. No more than that, as the one who'd come through four times, a squat, ornery girl, had died during attempt five, so he'd had to establish a limit of three passes. Duval was clearly clueless, and Guro remembered how tiring the whole process had been at first.

"Yes, yes, I know, everyone is sorry. But what you have done is illegal, and carries a very serious jail term. There is a way, however, for both of us to work toward a situation of mutual benefit..." As Guro explained the exchange, noting the subject's raised eyebrows at a very low-ball initial offer, he also reviewed the footage summary, the pattern of extreme, spiralling surges and vivid orange stripes throughout that indicated high-quality product. The summary was no insurance that the footage would be worth editing into something marketable, but was close enough, especially when the pattern was this intense. And the subject, well, he was clueless. Guro almost felt bad, but he was more angry at himself for not anticipating the kind of windfall Duval represented. Where was the tingle?

"So, our offer is acceptable?"

"Oh yes, yes sir, I, I know you could send me to jail, you are being very kind."

"Right, right, very well, you will have to do a retinal signature, also a thumbprint, please, of course you cannot use any kind of messaging hardware for at least three weeks, and I recommend you have whatever hardware you use be thoroughly checked. Perhaps by whomever you pay to have said augmentation removed."

"Of course, sir, of course." He wouldn't have it removed, Guro knew. He'd go back to the favela, pay chit crackling with funds, and he'd flash it around until some agent keyed him in, then he'd be back for another "interview," here or somewhere else in Lower Oak Block. Or someone would kill him and steal his chit, that was another possibility. In any case, the retinal scan and thumbprint were enough to protect Speck Industries from any legal threat, and to grant them full rights to Duval's footage. It was done.

"We're done, the funds are on your chit. Do you need me to activate the chair to guide you out, or can you walk on your own?"

"I, yes, I can walk sir, thank you..." he bowed as he retreated, walking backward through the door before turning to scuttle down the hallway and out the building. Guro uploaded a snapshot of the footage summary. hree seconds later, he had his first offer, and 37 seconds after that, he entertained thoughts of finally moving his mother to a different facility, out of the apartment they had shared since the day he was born.

Duval walked stiffly down the street, glancing up at the cams, stopping every few feet to re-establish his balance. He rounded a corner, then another, found himself at a train station. He waved his chit at the gate and boarded, not sure where it was headed, the names and numbers on the signage swirling, unreadable. His head was still a mess of stimuli and memory, and every few minutes he had to clench every muscle, overwhelmed by the sensation that he was being sucked down into an abyss. But he knew to board this train, and to get off at the station with the bright yellow pillars, and to follow them out to the street. He knew to go right, and to duck into a small alley that wound down below street level, and by the time he had reached the ancient metal door, he had remembered a lot more, like how to peel the fake print from his thumb and find the scanner beside the door, hidden behind the false window.

He went through the door, placed his hands on the opposite wall, and tilted his head back, his eyes wide open. A reddish mist brushed over his face and dissolved his retinal tints, causing red tears to trail down his cheek. A light scanned his face, and another door opened, and a body flew out and grabbed Duval, held him in its arms, head buried where his neck met his shoulder.

"My Anna," he said, remembering.

"Oh, João, oh my sweet," the woman said, sobbing gently into his shirt collar. His name, he knew it, though he was Manoushka, too, and would be for a while longer, he knew. Anna was not to know about it, how great the struggle was to reclaim his identity after burrowing, he remembered that promise well enough, keep the details from her, keep her safe. But she knew, despite his intentions. She'd seen, last time, when he lost a week staring at the tips of his fingers, she saw every time, but he no longer let details come in a torrent, and she no longer asked. He could smell the sweat in her hair, and his skin felt like cheap bed clothes. He saw over her shoulder the faces of men and women he knew, names that slid just out of grasp. It was something like home, he knew, but he wasn't sure what "home" meant, or what he wanted it to mean. He knew Anna's touch was drawing disparate elements of him together, fusing them, a tuning fork placed against a box humming with life.

Chapter 19

For the first day and half after returning from Speck Industries, João slept. It was his fourth time burrowing, so he knew what his mind and body needed, what ghosts they would see, what spasms would seize him. For six months, he'd lived as Manoushka Duval, studied the details of his scripted life, tried to dwell on his memories, tried to imagine how food tasted in his mouth, what his mother's voice sounded like. six months of preparation, seven and a half hours of work, then six more weeks until he no longer had Manoushka's memories or saw the faces of avatars from the burrowing pasted onto the heads of his friends and family. He hoped it would be six weeks, in any case. His last reemergence took four weeks, according to a note he left himself, one of half a dozen he found in a speakeasy spool in a locker in his quarters. Other notes told him to drink a bottle of water every half hour, that he needed to wait for a contact before acting, and that he should not trust Barnaby, whoever that was.

Anna tended to his sleeping, and when he woke, she helped him dress.

"You are so warm," she said, trailing her hand across his forehead. Her fingers were long and thin, her palms small and round, her skin the color of wheat. Every time she smiled, he saw Elaine Beaudoin, both their faces, superimposed on the other, so nearly the same. And then not at all, and then again, ghosts of earlier burrowing, Celine, and Neek, a fluttering of faces beneath and over Anna's face, the flickering of the lights above making it seem her blonde hair was undulating like reeds in a stream.

"It's all that sleep."

"That makes no sense," she laughed, "and besides, you've always been warm."

She put her hand to the side of his face and leaned up to kiss him. He flinched. She withdrew her hand, her face reddening. She stared at the floor.

"Sorry."

"No, no, it just takes time, you know—" He put his finger beneath her chin and lifted her head. "Just give it a little time." He bent down and kissed her, his stomach clenching. Her mouth was soft and giving, and the disgust he felt made the world shudder. He sat stiffly on the bed. All the ambient noise vanished from his left ear, and he clapped his hand to the side of his head and moaned.

"Oh Manny, what is it? What can I do?" She was at his side on the bed, her hand on his knee.

"What?"

"What can I do? I can get a Med in here, let me call—"

"No, I mean, what did you call me?"

She stared. "Are you alright, love?" She had been through this with him before, the last time he burrowed, but her voice was unsteady.

"You called me—never mind, I'm sorry, really, I'm fine. Let me get ready, I'll go do the OI check, then I'll come back here and we'll eat and read to each other, how does that sound?"

Her smile came out of hiding. "That sounds perfect, J."

She watched as he got a robe and towel, touched her lightly on the head, and went through the door, on his way down the hall to the shower. As the door closed behind him, she turned on her scribe and began her report.

§

João watched Carmine scratch his ear with a stylus. When they met, 11 years ago, prepping for his first burrow, João had assumed the stylus was an stylistic affectation, something meant to call attention to Carmine's Psych credentials, as were his bushy eyebrows and pinched, slightly distracted manner. Now, he thought Carmine just used the stylus so he could scratch his ear with it. Carmine poked at the holoscreen, then went back to scratching his ear, and João laughed. Carmine's eyebrows went up.

"Something funny?"

"The stylus, yes. Why not just get a small stick for the scratching, and use the pupil interface for the holoscreen?"

Carmine looked at the stylus. "I prefer the tactile, it helps me maintain my connection to physicality. I do a great deal of work via augmentation, and having certain, ah, totems, is important to keeping the basis of augmented reality in view. That is, the non-augmented world."

"A totem, interesting. So why don't you prescribe them? To folks like me, I mean. As part of training, or something."

The eyebrows furrowed. "Let's get started, shall we?"

"Sure, yes," João said. Why was Siegleman so prickly, always? He was supposed to be a motivational expert.

"Very good. Name and rank?"

"João Sandoval, Lieutenant, Infiltration and Dispersal Unit, Upstate 206."

"Good," he squiggled with the stylus. "And, where are you?"

"I am in your office, Upstate 206 Cadre Center, Half Moon, Sector 3, NorAmeriStat."

"Good. Why are you in my office?"

"I am undergoing an Ontological Incoherence check. You are trying to figure out if my last mission has done lasting damage to my sense of identity, or otherwise damaged my brain."

"Very good. Now. What was your mission directive?"

João paused. Something, something, he knew there was something he was supposed to ask, some protocol, and then, there it was, a flower blooming up from the mud.

"For that data, I respectfully request your security scan."

Carmine smiled. "*Very* good. Transmitting scan."

João's augments lit up for the first time since he'd been back in the facility. The shock was electric, and it was all he could do to hold his head up, though he did wince.

"It's alright, it hurts quite a bit to have them thrown on like that. Proceed when you feel comfortable."

João closed his eyes and waited for the brightness to soften. He checked Carmine's scan, entered his own to confirm, and opened his eyes.

"My mission was to infiltrate Speck Industries. Speck

Industries is a cleaning contractor, and black marketer of vid they swipe from applicants with pirate ports, typically favela residents. They feed them self-generative script agents instead of employment application scripts, then threaten to turn the applicant into the authorities for pirated ports if they don't sell the footage to them. Then, they sell the footage.

"Clients of these vids include various decision makers at elevated levels of NAS governance and military. Obviously, these clients do not view the vids on secure channels, so my job was drop several trojan payloads into the feed that would then replicate across an impromptu network. Once activated, the payloads should propagate and disrupt the entire NAS security net."

Carmine smiled. "A perfectly scripted response, João."

"Well, I was told memorizing it would help the recovery period. By you, I was told this."

"Yes, you were. And now, less formally please, how did the mission go?"

João paused again. His memory of the mission was an opaque cloud, a monolith that followed him, a few steps behind, silent, watching. He knew he had to spill it all, purge the false memories to start working through the next phase of recovery, but he also knew it would make him cry, at the least, and likely lose control of his bowels. He lifted his head and began.

When he had finished, Carmine nodded, said something João couldn't make out, and flicked the holoscreen off. João wheezed, looked at the hair he had pulled out, sitting on the table. He tasted blood, licked a raw spot in his lip. He didn't smell shit, and gave silent thanks.

"Breathe. Deep, deep breathing," Carmine said, in time with the gently pulsing lights flowering in João's display. He found himself floating, the whole room felt as though it were sinking, everything dragging down, down. The lights stopped, and he felt pleasantly empty.

"Yes, now, your account is fairly consistant with the summaries I've viewed. Pretty wild stuff, very supatek, as the fashionistas say. Story-within-a-story, some archeological exotica, plenty of retro futuretek stuff, nanovirus threatening the species, that always gets eyeballs, should be very, very successful. A big hit. Of course, there will be lag and glitching, as you work through it. The memory is an imperfect tool, as you know."

"Yes," João agreed, cringing at the cliche.

"But, I'm not seeing anything troubling at this point, no profound chasms in the data, so let's continue with the program, daily in-person appointments, agility training, nothing too strenuous at first. Do you recall Point One Point Seven?"

He knew it was a prompt, meant to trigger some pre-burrowing data point, but his skull was scrubbed clean. He stared. Siegleman clearly wanted to trip him up, make him say something actionable, so he could tell Gardiner and get him fired, or worse.

"That's ok, it's only the first day. So, I'll tell you, and tomorrow, you should remember. Point One Point Seven is an index for the number of agents who have successfully burrowed three or more times and survived without some trace of OI: Zero. We are confident, that is, you were confident before embarking, and I am confident now, that we have a thorough, secure program in place, and that your case will raise this number to one. Do you understand what I've told you?"

He nodded. Flecks of memory were drifting back, he knew he'd heard these words, he knew he believed them, even had been involved in developing the program. But he could not, he realized, recall his name at the moment. He nodded and smiled, and got up to leave.

"João?" Ah.

"Yes?"

"Get some rest."

He nodded again, flicking open a notepad in his display where he wrote the name "João" down as he left the room. Someone here was working with him, someone would tell him his real name. It was just a matter of finding the other agent, or agents, the one who would contact him and make it all clear.

Chapter 20

Three days after their first meeting, João noticed a dark flicker within the tranquility pattern Carmine used during their sessions, a moth-like fluttering at the periphery of his vision. He said nothing to Carmine, or to Anna, or whoever those people were, whatever agents of whatever agency—nothing was right here, but the differences were subtle. He wasn't still hardporting, he could tell that, the smells and tastes were all too distinct, too round for a sim, yet all the details were wonky, unstable, somehow. All the doors took too long to open, for example, and some gave a hiccup in the middle, stopping, then sliding, then stopping, then sliding, and no one seemed to think it odd, or at least odd enough to mention, and then the messaging script that sent the morning news wobbled slightly between verbal and textual, an obvious, though hard to detect, sign of a surveillance funnel buried inside it. Maybe it was just a general inventory of the population, maybe it was meant for João alone, there was no way to tell, and no way to build even a brief veil script to stop it, given how constantly he was monitored: Anna was there when he was not with Carmine, and he hadn't seen anyone else, he couldn't even eat in the canteen yet. The news feed was his only connection to the word outside his room, other than an archive of old vids and edu packs, which of course also had surveillance funnels festooned at every point and angle.

For the rest of the week, he listened to the feed, and watched the vids, and pretended he was recovering, and looked for more glitches to catalog. The feed was familiar to the point of eccentricity: nanoviral self-contagion, rugby union and Seepak Takraw highlights, and of course HutCo broadsides and dataspin. It was HutCo that he worked for, he knew, HutCo that set him burrowing, HutCo that held the keys to revolution, to getting all the eyeballs and dissolving the fat heads of NortAmeriStat once and for all. Or at least that's what the feed said, and João felt a stirring when he heard the scripts flowing by, he couldn't tell if he had believed long ago, or if he was being stimmed. It felt like faith, but now it was on the other side of a pane of frosted glass, and he knew it would never be the same, the security and commitment that gave rise to a swell of passion were all but gone.

He turned the news down as it segued to a breakfast drama. Anna sat at the end of the bed, watching him. "Did you sleep well?" she asked, seeing his lids twitch open.

"Yes, fine," he lied. She stood, stretched, and sat on the bed beside him, tracing lines in his hair with her fingertips.

"It's your first rest day, you made it through the week," she said. "We have clearance to take a walk up top, if you feel like it."

"Yeah, that would be great, I'm getting nine kinds of claustrophobic in here." Anna's eyes flickered, and he knew she was recording their conversation.

"I'm sure," she smiled, and bent to kiss him. They hadn't made love yet, had only just made it to the stage of comfort where they could lay in each other's arms, but the kisses were a regular, and welcome, aspect of his emergence. He still felt a vague disgust when her mouth touched his, but increasingly that sensation was washed away by a flood of familiarity and pleasure. Only when the sense of well-heing subsided did he wonder how much was coming through his ments, how much was pharma hidden in his food, how much was pre-burrow conditioning.

"Well, let's have some breakfast and get ready, then," she said, and lifted the extruder door.

"Anna," he ventured a short time later, wiping his mouth, "where are everyone's halos?"

Her mouth dropped, and for the first time, he saw a chink in her therapeutic persona. She was crestfallen, and then just as suddenly, her face was a sun-drenched harbor once again.

"Ok, let's think this through, this is good." Her voice was deliberate, controlled, but also hesitant, as though reading, or remembering, a script she'd decided was obsolete. "Yesterday, do you remember, we went over the Revolution White Paper? The Six Principles?"

"Yes, I remember, of course."

"Ok, good, let's remember them together, then."

He sighed. "Sure. Principle One, Growth is accomplished through Belief. Principle Two, Belief is Deliberate." Anna nodded encouragingly. "Principle Three is, ah, Belief is Manifest in the Marketplace. Principle Four, the People Must Arbitrate for Growth. Five, um, Five is Success and Freedom are Deliverables. Principle Six: Growth is the Only True Success."

"Good, very good. Of course you know them, you helped write Five and Six."

"Yes, I remember." He didn't remember.

"Now, to accomplish Growth, what must we do, as part of HutCo?"

"Deliver... ah, access and freedom to the people."

"Yes, especially those who are denied it, the disenfranchised."

"Right, I know, I get that part, I just—"

"Wait, let me finish," she said, her lips tightening. "Think of all those people in NAS work camps, all the people in favelas, waiting for food drops without hope of anything better, all those eyeballs just waiting for something to believe, something to help them grow and succeed and attain self-actualization. Now, what do those people all have in common?"

João blinked. "Ah, I don't know, poverty?"

"Yes, but, think: they all have halos. Again, this is a symbol you helped us isolate and understand as being central to the re-branding campaign. The demographic without halos is too minuscule to worry about, so—and I can see you now, the presentation you made for the Board, it was just so winning—so, we attack the halos as a symbol of a repressive and corrupt corporate entity, as indicators of wealth and prestige, and we wipe them off everyone's heads and free the people from the yoke of credentialed servitude. Please say you remember, those are your words, please remember...."

He saw that she was stricken once again, near to

tears. *A bravura performance*, he thought. *But I know my role, too.* "I... I feel it, my intellect doesn't quite obtain, but I feel it, I feel the words and feel myself saying them, I know how I felt in the conference room, giving the presentation, but I can't remember who was there, what day it was...." He turned his head to the pillow and pretended to stifle a sob.

"Oh, oh, but that's good, that's a step, we know this, everything won't come rushing back. Sensation first, cognition after," she cooed, stroking his neck.

"Right. Oh, that feels hella good." She stopped petting for moment, then continued. Why? "What? What did I do?"

"Nothing, just, you never, talked like that before."

"Like what?'

"You know, slangy, vidspeak. 'Hella'. But yes, actually, you did, last time you emerged, you would ramble in Calibabble while you slept, I forgot about that."

"Calibabble? Really. That's—that's just sad," he snorted ruefully.

"It was funny, tell the truth, and it was only a few days. Nights, rather. Do you remember anything about that burrowing? The one before this, I mean." Her hand rested on his collarbone.

"Not much. More like flickers, faces under faces, smells that make the color of the walls change." Why was she asking? He thought he was supposed to keep those details from her, not talk about it, and she wouldn't ask, that was the deal.

Anna stayed quiet, annotating their conversation.

"Well, that's good, keeping them in their boxes in important. You will let me know if you start to remember, if
they start to leak."

"Am I talking in my sleep now? Why are you worrying
about this?"

She stood and held her hands together. "Yes. You are
having sleep episodes, which is perfectly on script, don't
worry. We just need to monitor the memories as they
return, so we can help you box them up. You are right
on schedule, my dear." She smiled, then popped a new
meeting point into his calendar. six days from now, with
Barnaby Quick.

"Barnaby?"

"Yes, do you remember Barnaby?"

"No, I thought saying his name aloud might stir something. I know him?"

Anna shook her head. "Oh yes, you know him. You
blocked him for a long while during your last emergence,
too, hurt his feelings a bit." She snorted. "Tomorrow, Carmine will start massaging some of these memories, get
them flowing again."

"Yes, he told me. Not sure I want to remember."

"I know how that feels," she said, turning away. "Ready
for your walk?"

Each day, they walked a bit further, and each day, Carmine fed João pharma and ment scripts that helped him
embed the places he walked within his identity matrix.
And every day, João resisted, waiting for some clue, some
contact to emerge. The canteen, the gym, the North garden full of dwarf azaleas and moon flowers, the transport

bay—everywhere João walked and sat and talked with people, he felt the familiarity seeping in, wearing away at his resolve. He began carrying a small pin in his pocket to poke into his thigh when he felt himself drifting into automatic behavior, like when he first met Barnaby. A stone wall of a man with military posture and hair that looked like it would draw blood, he was Godsong Mbete, or, more correctly, Mbete was skinned from Barnaby, his appearance incarnated from João's existing memory of Barnaby. Anyone viewing the vid of his burrowing would skin Mbete differently, whatever their understanding of "imposing North African male" incarnated, as Barnaby was nothing if not imposing. He was also unnervingly loyal to HutCo, reflexively cunning, and smarter asleep than most people were awake.

"Good work," he'd said, his voice deep and resonant as a vid star, and João melted, even letting his eyes moisten as he shook Barnaby's hand. A few well-placed jabs with the pin helped the tears flow, although later, in bed beside a sleeping Anna, João wondered later if he had overplayed his hand, as he watched transcripts of the pitched ideological battles he'd had with Barnaby over every detail of the Revolution White Papers, Action Reflex Vidspaces, the Training Scripts, every element of HutCo's marketing identity sculpted from audience snap polls of meetings where Barnaby and João sparred.

Carmine fed João these archival vids gradually, following the therapeutic script strictly, attuned to changes in the subject's identity matrix, mixing the professional with the ceremonial, the private with the unexpected.

João felt the shifts in emphasis, and struggled to retain the kernel of resistance he could feel Carmine's script grinding against. He knew the person in the vids was him, that the ideas espoused were his own, that the kisses he shared with Anna were heart felt, just as he knew the person he watched was even then burrowing, playing the role of a kissing, arguing, committed soldier. Then he would pause the feed, look at the bare grey walls of his quarters, at the gleaming skin of Anna, at the worn edges of the table they shared, and he would question: is this kernel simply the remnants of the resistance script I internalized before burrowing? Am I losing coherence by pretending to gain coherence? He had searched everywhere he could think for hidden scripts, backdoors, physical coding, and all he had to go on was the speakeasy spool that told him to "wait for a contact before acting." He wondered if the spool was simply part of the therapeutic script, meant to help break up the resistance kernel, the way nanobots blasted arterial blockage into parsable chunks. But the dark flutter remained at the edges of the tranquility pattern, and the person in the archives called João knew something the person watching those archives also knew, and he felt it, ticking against the insides of his head like a tiny hammer.

Chapter 21

By the fourth week of therapy, the fluttering glitch in the tranquility pattern had grown too large for João to pretend he could not see it. It could be a coherence test, he thought, so he told Carmine about it, and that it was giving him a headache.

"A glitch? Odd, let me see." Carmine switched the pattern on in his own feed, his eyes half-closing. "I don't see the effect you describe," he said, after a few seconds. "What part of the feed?"

"Southeast, extending up almost to the Eastern quadrant."

"Hmm," Carmine tapped at the air, tweaking the pattern. "No, not seeing it. Let me recalibrate, just hold your head as still as you can for a few seconds." He twiddled in the air again, then refocused his eyes on João. "Ready?"

"Yes." The pattern began, cleanly this time, delicate, soft twinklings of color, a susurration of almost-heard chimes, and then the darkness burst forth, from the Southeast, spreading across his entire vidspace, and there, in the center of the cloud, pink words flashed: "Do not trust Carmine." They flashed again, a third time, and then the cloud vanished, and the tranquility resumed.

"And, the feed better now?" Carmine asked. João opened his eyes and nodded at Carmine's smile, wreathed in the overlay of the pattern.

"Yes, much better, thank you."

"Interesting, we had a similar glitching the first time you burrowed, but not since. Do you remember?

"No, I've remembered a lot of that emergence, but not this particular effect."

"Well, I can put the report in tonight's archive for you, see if that helps."

"Of course, thanks."

"Remembering every detail is not as crucial to onto-logical coherence as is the sense that every detail is po-tentially accurate, things can be verified form the archive, as long as the scaffolding is strong. And your scaffolding is assembling rapidly, I am strongly encouraged by what I've seen these last weeks."

"Good," João nodded.

"I'm not ready to authorize a return to active duty, but I think it important for you to have access to the op-eration as it unfolds, since you have devoted so much of yourself to its success."

"I—yes, I would like that, I still can't put it together, but I am ready to. The archive must be very deep."

"It is, but I think it better that your introduction be interpersonal, augmented with archives. Barnaby has agreed to meet with you later and serve as guide."

João twitched. Don't trust Barnaby. Don't trust Car-mine. Don't trust anyone. Don't trust yourself. "So I will find out the details of why I was charged with disrupting the NAS security net?"

"I would guess yes. Do you have any thoughts about it? About your mission? Any recall?"

"Only the mission script itself, I couldn't find anything in the archives, really, nothing comprehensive. Of course," he added.

Carmine chuckled. "Of course. Your instinctual grasp of protocol is so thorough, I thought you might have started putting it together. That's ok, better that you don't, and focus on the broader aspects of coherence."

"Like why I can't stand lassis."

"Right," Carmine chuckled again, "like that. Food preferences, sleep patterns, all those reactive bits of identity starting to aggregate, I'm so glad. You've done so much for HutCo, I'm glad to see such progress."

"Thank you. It feels to good to, ah, become myself again."

He ventured a smile, even as the tiny hammer ticked more loudly in his head.

§

Anna led João to the conference room to meet with Barnaby after lunch. They went through three sets of security doors and a retinal scan before reaching a third door, made of wood and carved with intricate, apparently random geometrical patterns. João found himself staring the designs, entranced, while Anna sent an entry request. The door swung open, rather than sliding, and João took a step back. He felt Anna's hand in the small of his back, reassuring him, and stepped past the door to a room dominated by a table made of the same wood as the door, and carved with similar designs.

Barnaby, seated in the far corner of the room, nodded.

Two other people, who João recognized as Candle Jeffers and Cheta Hurtado, stood and nodded as well, smiling. He realized they were messaging Anna, all their eyes flicking in sync, nodding slightly despite themselves. The table swam before his eyes, and he sat hard in an empty chair, trying to look anywhere else, to focus on the other faces, the ceiling, the slight discoloration on the wall behind Barnaby.

"Welcome back to the conference room, João," Barnaby said, rising from his seat. The others joined him, including Anna, and to João's dismay, they began clapping softly.

"Ah, thank you, please, sit, sit," he mumbled, brushing toward them with his fingers.

"Yes, yes, full of humility, as always. Or should I say, a dismissive attitude toward praise?" Barnaby said as he sat back down.

"I don't know about that, just want to get back to work," João replied. He was quaking, and clung to the kernel, feeling it about to wash away in a tidal outpouring of memory.

"Yes, certainly. Yes. Ah, please, let me remind you: Tofer Bell and Malachi Cortez," he said, sweeping his toward Jeffers and Hurtado. João knew them, he could feel the camaraderie, the love, even, he'd shared with them. Flashes of working closely, of Cortez the jokester breaking the tension, of Bell giving João level headed advice time and again, of the three of them on a trip somewhere, a desert facility, the meaningful glances of people who share a belief and work together to make it real, who share failures without complaint and success without interest...

"Yes, so good to see you both." Cortez let a tear slip out, and grasped his hands together in front of his chest, one atop the other. João remembered the gesture as some greeting they shared, so he returned it, as did Bell, and, after a pause, Barnaby. João turned to smile at Anna and saw that she had slipped out without his noticing. How, through that ridiculous door?

"Carmine tells me you are emerging very well, beyond all expectations, is what he said, actually," Barnaby ventured.

"Yes, I suppose I am, I'm glad to hear his confidence."

"He's said he might have to rethink the whole emerging process," Bell offered. "Says you're rewriting the script."

"Well, that's good to hear, though I can't really take credit."

"Right, yes, humility, we got it," Barnaby interrupted. "Let's get on with this, time is very tight, as you might know."

"I—no, I really don't."

"Well, what do you know?"

"I know what I was sent to do, why I burrowed. I know HutCo is devoted to breaking the NAS monopoly, and that disrupting the security net is key, as is getting rid of halos. And I know that somehow our success is predicated on market share in the favelas... but that's it."

"Sure, that's something. That's most of it, generally. Bell, maybe you can give João an executive summary?" It came to João in a flash: Barnaby called Bell by her family name because he was higher up the food chain. João had noticed, in the archives, Barnaby called João by his first name, so they must hold the same rank, which made Cortez and Bell João's underlings. Was one of them his contact?

"Sure," Bell said, and saw a messaging link request appear. He accepted, and Bell shifted noisily in her seat. "Holy, wow, this is weird. You taught me most of—sorry, let me get to it."

A map of the NAS appeared, with their borders glowing red, and a dense network of green and yellow lines woven throughout the interior. "This is the current NorAmeriStat augmentation net, in green, and the yellow is all hardport infrastructure. As you can see, they have a strict monopoly over all content service, in all geographical regions." João nodded. "Now, if you turn the axis and look at vertical integration, you will see huge gaps in service." The map rotated and began a slow horizontal pan, so that the green and yellow lines were less dense thicket than a bank of clouds, floating above a dark plain. "Now, some of that empty space is indeed empty space: dead zones, energy deserts, that sort of thing. But a lot of it is just untapped market, favelas, intake camps, places the NAS has denied service, for no better reason than they couldn't profitize it—"

"They always claimed it was for security, that the favelas were full of terror elements, but that's birdshit," Cortez jumped in.

"Ha, as my esteemed colleague says, that was how they marketed keeping those populations in the dark, but as I said, they couldn't figure out how to profitize it, and of course, they were trying keep the unwashed from intruding in their customer's feeds. Refugees in *Friend's World*? Not only would they disrupt the ecosystem, the worry is that they would start agitating for corporate citizenship. Which is, as I'm sure you recall, exactly what we want." She bowed slightly and waved her fingers left. The map overlay faded away, and a chart forecasting market-share appeared in the Northwest quadrant.

"What you see is a very, very conservative projection of what our marketshare would look like if we could access those markets. Access to underdeveloped markets would, in turn, lead to new content creation, which in turn would lead to access of that content from six percenters in the existing market: those fashionistas who look for new content, laser edge supatek stuff, and where they go, the rest of the eyeballs follow.

"All of this movement is based on being able to knock the NAS security net down and grant access to anyone who wants it, which means installing our own protocols so that even when when they bring the net back up, we have our own access ramps installed. It's all perfectly legal, the NAS Corporate charter specifically allows these kinds of hacks, because they never thought anyone could manage it, or they hired away anyone who got close."

"Such as, anyone from HutCo?" João interrupted.

All three sets of eyes dropped. "Of course, I would try to forget him, too," Barnaby said, and flicked his fingers across the tabletop. A dossier popped into João's feed, and he saw Paulie Levant's face, and the name... Paul Levant.

He scanned the file briefly, brilliant script writer, nanobiologist, and traitor the NAS hired away from HutCo after he nearly broke their security net remotely, without even having to burrow. His bio was the same as his bio in the Facility Dàtóng, his face, his name—and yet, João had never met him, he defected more than a year before João was brought aboard at HutCo.

"He's the only one we lost. The only big one. We take care of our people," Barnaby promised.

"I remember," João answered. "Please continue."

"Yes, ah, y-yes," Bell stammered. "To disrupt the NAS security net, we needed someone to deliver a payload, and then to seize the access ramp, another payload. Delivering both payloads would be difficult enough, but the resulting disruption would be too easy for the NAS to bracket, we needed multiple delivery points, and so we needed several agents who could burrow deep enough to deliver them. You, Mr. Sandoval, developed the training regimen and identified the agents who could pull it off, including yourself. You were the last of six agents to return, and all six have had successful emergence processes thus far, I am happy to report. The payloads are scheduled to drop—" she paused, receiving a message— "in the next 48 hours. Once they do, we hope you will join us here to watch the progress, as HutCo's vision for a new, more equitable market produces a thousand blossoms!" She had fallen into boilerplate, he thought, or maybe for the true believer, boilerplate was gospel.

"Why yes, of course," João nodded, "and that's it? We just have to watch it unfold, no more work to be done?"

"The payloads bang the doors open, and we got our own hella good content ready to roll, all kinds of demos and trailers, a bunch of coupon series, mandauras to replace the halos: we are ready, sir, as soon the shit breaks, we go in," Cortez said, bobbing his head excitedly.

"Mandauras?"

"To replace the halos, our proprietary system, much more equitable."

Barnaby was staring at him, half-smile a tease or provocation, João couldn't tell which.

"Do you think it will succeed?" João asked him, at least in part to stop that smile.

"I trust the predictors, which suggest a 37 percent success rate. About 30 percent more than we ever managed before. I know we've had our problems, João, our disagreements, but we worked through them, and now we are on the verge of something revolutionary. I do think it will succeed, and I think you will be known as a great hero. And I, well, I will be know as a tactician who could not fight."

João sighed. He remembered Barnaby's penchant for melodrama, how his narcissism loved to dress itself up as victim and parade around the conference room. "You are just as much a hero as I," he said, and everyone in room smiled, because no one believed what had said, except for João, who did not think himself a hero at all.

§

Anna appeared soon after, touching João lightly on the shoulder and guiding him to the canteen. She was particularly gentle, as though she thought the trauma of the meeting might disrupt him. Instead, it had made the hammer bang louder in his head, had made the kernel tighter, stronger, more sublime. He had loved some of those people, as he had loved Anna, but he knew it was another role, and that he had to truly feel love to play the role correctly: love is as easily monitored as any other strong emotion, and any agent worth their salt knows how to make the readouts look right.

"So, you had a lot of memory wash, then?" She asked, popping a greenie in her mouth.

"Yes, but nothing overwhelming, more like backfill, like remembering all the work I did with Bell and Hurtado, I mean Cortez, not the work itself, but the sense of working with them, some sights and smells, the usual. And what a baby Barnaby can be, I remembered that."

Anna laughed softly. "Yes, he is a famous child, that's sure."

"Really, don't worry, it was very integrative," he reassured her.

"Good, I'm glad to hear. Washroom," she said, got up, and headed for the washroom. Or to give a report, João thought. He dipped a greenie in pepper sauce and munched, flipping through the backlog of messages that had gathered while he was in the conference room. Most were marketing materials, some news blots, a reminder from Carmine to check the updated archive, nothing worth reading beyond the tag. He felt a sharp prick in the back of his neck and jerked his head around, but the crowd of people eating, sitting down, getting up, chatting, and swapping messages was too dense for him to pick out a source for the sting. He reached around to rub it and the pain was gone before he could touch it. That was it, he thought, that was my contact. He waited, closed the message window, opened all the ports he had access to, and sat, waiting. He was sharply aware of the stink of the food in the tray, of the noise of the canteen, of the grease on the tabletop that would never come clean, no matter how well engineered the bot.

"Do you want more?" Anna said, hand on his neck exactly where he'd felt the prick. No, could she be his contact? She was too close, it was preposterous.

"More? Oh, no, I'm full, thanks." He answered, guiding her hand down onto his chest and holding it there. "Let's head back, I have a lot of archive to look over."

"Ok, love," she said, and as he watched her swerve gracefully between tables and diners, he wondered if he could play the role of lover so completely that it stopped being a role. If he could, it would be with Anna, he thought, and then he remembered that she had probably just gone to submit a report on his behavior, and that she certainly recorded their love making sessions, and that she knew he knew all this, and nothing was not a role in this world, everything was the conscious projection of a stance, or training one's unconscious to behave the way one intended it to. There was no privacy, because there was no private life to retreat into, there was only image and projection and role, so yes, pretending at love was as close as he or anyone else would ever get to the real thing.

Chapter 22

The contact arrived later that night, while Anna was asleep, or pretending to be asleep. It started as a small pink dot intruding on an archival history of the most recent NAS-ERC police action, and João thought it was another glitch until he shut off the archive to restart it and the dot remained, the size of a toenail, hovering near the Eastern periphery of his vision. He couldn't reorient to look directly at it, and he couldn't figure out how to access it, so he just sat, propped up on pillows, waiting for it to do something. Then it giggled.

"Chooga!" The dot doubled in size, and morphed into a cartoon pig. João felt vomit rise in his throat, and swallowed. Anna moaned beside him.

"What—no." João messaged the pig.

"No? Whaddya mean no, Captain? You kept the kernel alive, couldn't get the backdoor open without your help. You is the supatek to end all supatek, my friend."

"Paulie?"

"Paul, yes, it's Paul. What is this Paulie? Some post-burrow affect?"

"I suppose. It's what you asked to be called in, in, in one of the holes."

"Really? Sounds like me. But it sounds stupid, too, don't call me Paulie." The pig winked.

"Ok, Paul, pig, help. I'm not sure my memory is right.

I'm not sure anything I know is right. Am I working for NAS?"

The pig giggled again, a singularly unpleasant noise. "NAS? Hardly. But now is not the time. Tomorrow, they do a security wipe from 2013 to 2027, I will deposit a better jack in your feed then, and we can discuss what comes next. I hope you will remember more by then."

"But—no, I can't. I mean. I don't even know what to say." He felt the kernel shaking, his mind loosening, slackening away.

"No worrying, just keep to the kernel, and I'll give you a reverse monitoring, so you can see what reports everyone is filing on you, when they file them." A tiny flash of light shot across the Northwest quadrant, then came to rest near the Western periphery, as a small square of quicksilver. "You can look at some archived reports, too, just need to be in proximity of the person who filed it, so the net can't sweep you. See you soon, Captain!" The pig winked out. João worked his breathing, focused his mind to bring down his levels so he didn't get flagged by the security net. Thankfully, it was night, and dreams made for erratic readings. He looked at the silver rectangle thoughtfully, then flipped it open. Anna's last report sat on a silver tray. He peered over the tray at her face, slack in sleep, eyelids occasionally darting. He did love her, and knew she had a job to do, and yet—the report was all quick bullets, indexed to the body monitoring graph of the evening. "Says he is full, not accurate," was tagged to the reading of food satisfaction index, "it was very integrative" was tagged true, as were all the other comments he'd made at dinner, other than the one about being full. So he was doing well, masking his kernel, telling lies and resisting the sort of biochemical changes that lies produce. He wasn't sure how he was doing it, but whoever had trained him had been thorough, and he felt the contentment of a job well done. Now, if he only knew who or what he was working for, if he knew the terms of the contract he was under, or if there was a contract, or if he was finally sliding into incoherence, they were all equally plausible after a visit from a cartoon pig's head.

He spent the next day toying with the mirror, grabbing reports from Anna and Carmine and two people sitting behind him in the canteen, archiving them for later, when he could view them without distraction. His session with Carmine was a recapitulation of the meeting with Barnaby, Bell, and Cortez, and discussion of the protocol for the payload meeting. João's presence would be entirely ceremonial, which Carmine assured him was "just as important as content upload or deliverable broadcast." After lunch, he went for a walk with Anna up top, through the glass garden to an overlook where they could see Half Moon favela 31 tumbling down into the valley like a spill of toy blocks.

"It's hard to imagine, we're so close," Anna said, "in a few hours, all those people will have access, thanks to you."

"Thanks to many people, not just me."

"Yes, but my sweet, you above all. I know you are humble, I know, I love that about you, so I know you will never say it, so I will: when the people in those dingy houses wake and find themselves able to join the rest of the world, they will see your face."

"What?"

"Your face, that's the icon."

"I'm not sure I like that idea." João shifted his weight from foot to foot.

"No, you didn't like it before, either, but it was a concession to Barnaby."

"My concession? And what did I get in return?"

Now it was Anna's turn to fidget. "I really shouldn't— this needs to wait until Carmine—"

"What? It can't be that serious, what did I get?"

Anna sighed. "Barnaby didn't want tek microloans. He thought it was enough to give people access, let them find their own tek, most of them have some homebrew ments, even some crude hardports, but you wanted a loan program, so anyone without ments or hardports, or who just wanted an upgrade, HutCo will provide them funding. Barnaby wanted none of it, especially because the loan terms were so, um, favorable. You convinced the audience, all the polling went your way, but Barnaby still held the keys, so you had to give something up."

"My face."

"Your face. It's a nice face." She lay her hand on his cheek.

"Thank you for telling me. I'm not surprised Barnaby failed to mention this deal at our meeting."

"Well, it could be Carmine didn't think you were ready yet."

"Yes, it could be." João leaned over and kissed Anna's

forehead, closing his eyes as he did so he could flip on the mirror without her noticing. As her morning and lunch time reports flowed in, he kissed her again, this time on the mouth.

§

All of Anna's reports were perfunctory, as were Carmine's, as were the two anonymous observers in the canteen. Everyone seemed to think João was making excellent progress, that he would be ready for the payload drop, that his identity was exceptionally strong, even as it rebuilt itself. João found himself disappointed, he'd hoped for more drama, perhaps some skullduggery, poison pen reports from a faction loyal to Barnaby, instead of dull, slightly over-reverential data ticks. He had almost dozed off in the middle of Anna's evening report when the pig head blinked into view, and the giggle flared.

"Ho! João! Doing some light viewing, I see!"

"Paulie, eh,—Paul, can we do without the giggle? Really, quite a headache."

"No good? Sure, how about this?" A low, throaty chortle sounded, less sharp than the giggle, but even more unsettling.

"Can we just do without the laugh, period?"

"Sorry, Captain, that's the key you fed in before we started this project. It's indexed to your neural net, I can change the pitch, the tempo, but the laugh stays, it's the handshake that gets me in."

"Yes, let's talk about that, too. Why do you need to get in? What the hell is going on?"

"Cool down, don't want spikes on your monitor, that could seriously jeopardize the narrative."

"Ok, ok, I think I know what that means. Now: tell me."

"Tell you, tell you, ok, sure. Lets unwind the thread, Captain. First, let's talk about what you are doing right now." The pig winked.

"I am messaging with a cartoon pig."

"Right, right," Paul sighed. "What I mean is, you, your body, what is it doing right now—don't answer, save the snarky, just let me talk, because right now, your body is in a ProjecTank about 3000 kilometers from where you believe your body is. You are outside of Denver, the Denver terrabubble, in a ProjecTank, making a vid series for Gardiner industries."

João felt a laugh burbling up, and swallowed it.

"Got it? I mean, can you assimilate that, my comrade? You are an actor in a vid drama. A well known actor, not quite supatek, but well known enough for character roles, for a pretty substantial branch, actually, and thanks in no small part to me, if I do say."

"What? I. But. Wait a minute, let me think."

"Think later, listen now. Your name is Jacob Gratta, and in this particular branch, you obtained the rather challenging role of a soldier and espionage expert in the employ of a corporate entity known as HutCo. Well, that's not challenging, what's challenging is that your soldier is a 'burrower,' one who goes undercover in vidspace to gather data, release trojans, build backdoors, and generally mess with your enemies security net, and because you are a burrower, you get to play multiple roles! Excellent, huh?"

"Shut up."

"Nope, listen: this whole story within a story thing is a device I, in my capacity as your talent guru, pitched to Gardiner VidPro, and of course they ate it up, and man, the audience is eating it up, too, because they all think you are going to fry yourself, they all want to watch the wreck, basically."

"I am not physically present, in this room." João looked past the pig at the wall. It did seem a bit... wobbly.

"Oh geez. Right. You are an actor, and I'm your talent guru, so it's my job to guide the narrative, to push you down certain story arcs, but now I've broken the secret wall, too bad. Not supposed to let the talent know, self-awareness ruins the performance, blah blah blah."

"This is a vid?" He ran his hand over Anna's shoulder, making her murmur and sigh.

"Yes, Captain, that's what I've said now how many times, I don't understand why you aren't getting it. We planned the reveal extra carefully, this is when you should be ready to remember."

João felt no tug of recognition, no clamoring in his mind for coherence and solidity. He felt, instead, hollow.

"Ok, well, let's keep going, maybe something will click. You, Jacob, are playing this role, and a lot of people are following your arc because they think you will fry, that your mind won't be able to handle the shifts in identity, and your brain will go all grey goo. And of course they want to see that, the shitters, slumped in their HomeTanks, waiting for you to fry on worldwide vid. It's a sickness, and that's why we built the backdoor for you, so I could break the secret wall and feed you the rest of the plan."

"The plan? Sure, of course, there has to be a plan."

"Hey, Captain, it was your plan, I'm just the script-writer here." The pig shook its head ruefully. "You really aren't remembering, are you? Anyway, the plan, the chooga plan: you are gonna drop the biggest, most supatek payload ever into Gardiner's system, just like you are pretending to, up in fantasy land, and that payload will for real bring the whole shitty net down, yeah! Can you get to that? I mean, finally, get people out of their Tanks, get them out into the streets with the rest of us, the ones who keep things running so they can pretend we don't exist, that the whole shitting world doesn't exist, the one falling down around us. It's for their own good, like you say."

"You can't be serious," João mumbled.

"Serious as a right hook, I am. And you are too, like I said, it was your plan."

"But—no, this can't be real. This is a symptom of emergence, my mind turning on itself, going OI. I invented you."

"Yeah, maybe, but then why the kernel? You know its true, it'll come back. Give it a few hours, you'll remember, the filthy air swarming with nano, the rain that cuts into your skin, the protein blocks that taste like wet ash... do you remember when you first found me? Banged through the net and knocked me out of my tank, I was just a kid, messing around on some anarchist feed, you remember?"

"No."

The pig sighed again. It sounded like air squeaking out of a balloon.

"Then I guess you're just going to have to trust me, until you do remember."

"Trust a cartoon pig?"

"Hey, don't shit on the pig, friend. You said I could pick whatever icon I wanted."

Now it was João's turn to sigh. "Explain to me again why destroying the net would be a good thing?"

"It's like this: there are a bunch of people with money, and then a bunch of people who are almost starving. The ones who are starving, they take care of things like solar farms, mine bots, sanitation, they do work, in the world. The ones with money, they spend most of their time on the net, sure they get up and walk around every few days, but basically, they stay plugged in, watching vid, buying and selling access rights, swapping their eyeballs for dosh— hell, it's a cliché, even, the story everyone told about the new supatek, it will split the world in twain, how many vids have there been with that old trope? You're in one now, kinda, but you are selling the revolution, so no one will have to do anything *really*, about anything *really*, they live through you and vids like this one. Hell, most of them laugh at it, at the idea of economic equality, it's quaint, an affectation of a past age. My parents, I told them, after you showed me what the world was really like, I told them it was wrong, the net was just about power, any poor shitter steps out of line or goes crazy from the stink of the sewer they're fixing, little light comes down from the sky pokes a hole right in their skull. You showed me that, remember? Guy stood up, said no, I won't go into that river of shit, satellite popped, body crumpled. And I told my parents, and they laughed, they said yup, that's what you get, it's an act of terror, they said, people could get sick if the sewers backed up..."

João wasn't sure, but he thought the pig might be sobbing. The head was twitching, pixelating.

"Alright, alright, I understand. I don't remember, so I can't trust you, but for the sake of argument, how am I supposed to drop this payload?"

"Right, action!" The head flashed pink, the eyes bulging. "It's simple, really: you have to fake OI, get sent to the restricted zone. Your character evinces Ontological Incoherence, big tragic finish, eyeballs cry, your character goes to the rest home for broken soldiers. Structurally, since they will think you are really fried, it means your connection gets put into quarantine, until they can purge you. Only have a few seconds, between quarantine and purge, but that should be plenty."

"Won't that fry me for real? And what about everyone else in vidspace, won't they get fried, too? How many people is this going to kill?"

"A few, maybe, older folks, folks who are pure vidspace and don't even go out, addicts, some of them might get blasted, but not many, it's basically harmless, just flipping a switch."

"What about all the bots, how will people access maintenance bots if, I don't know, the grid overheats, or someone doing surgery, all those remotely accessed—"

"Geez, I wish you would just remember. The payload will leave all the infrastructure intact. We're not stupid, you know. We're just ejecting the bastards from their comfortable little tanks, making them look at the world they've created."

"And then what?"

"And then we make a better world, I guess."

"No plan?"

"No plan for that."

João shook his head. It was almost morning.

"You'll remember," Paul said, grinning, "and when you do, just try to keep from setting off alarms, ok?"

"I don't even—how does someone fake OI?"

"You're an actor, Captain. It's in your blood."

"And all this time, I though I was a soldier."

Paul laughed. "Oh you are, a soldier in the ratings war. Ha, that's even what the call the series, *Ratings War,* it's been on forever. Except now, you get to shut the war down."

Chapter 23

The night before this next payload drop was predictably sleepless for Jacob. He first fixated on the idea that there was no end to the drops, that he was stuck in a loop of payload dropping and emergence, forever, then tried to settle himself, pumping the tranquility scripts all the way up. Carmine spent most of the day's session asking him about the series of emotional spikes the previous night, which Jacob was able to excuse as increased anxiety dream activity, triggered by his anticipation of the upcoming drop. "We'll probably see the same effect tonight," Jacob predicted, and Carmine agreed, both in person, and in his report, which Jacob snagged later, walking by Carmine's office. That evening, he and Anna attended to a comic vid, trying to relax. Sadly, the vid was not particularly funny, and it only made Anna and Jacob more anxious, and for the first time since he'd emerged, they squabbled.

"I don't know why, you decided, look it up," Anna said.

João blinked. He could feel his heart rate was slightly elevated, a tautness in his head and neck. He was angry, but he could not remember why, or what they were talking about, and why Elaine was in his bed. She was Celine, she was Neek, his manman would be so happy, in bed with a woman.

"João?"

"Did that to me?" He said. She called his name again,

and he heard all his names, all the roles he'd played, at once, a cluster of names on top of each other, fighting like a pack of dogs for dominance. She put her hands to side of his face: "Look at me. João. Look here."

His eyes slid back into focus, and he saw her, and smiled. "Sorry, I'm sorry, Anna. Just, I slipped off the rail there for a minute, sorry." Her face was very red, and she was crying.

"Follow my finger," she said, and led him around the periphery, then messaged him a color index. He opened it and ran the script, sent her the results.

"I'm ok, really. Too much emotion all at once, nervous about tomorrow, that awful vid—"

"It really was terrible," she laughed, and he joined her, quietly.

She recommended sleep pharma for both of them, and he agreed, trusting the pink pig would wake him and give him further instructions. He'd not remembered anything more about the person Paul described, or the world he detailed, or the plan he supposed to be part of. He struggled against the pharma, cascades of drowsiness and memory intermingling, until the memories became both more clear and more fractured, and he could not tell if he was dreaming: talking into a speakeasy, Runners riding DataPsych folks like ponies, Euna Gessner's head exploding, putting both hands through a window to get at the stuffed monkey inside, his mother, hair wreathed in morning light, hunched over the corpse of his baby sister, Mr. Deebs, carrying a can—he let them wash over, refused them all, held to the kernel like a barnacle clinging to a pier. And then, all at once, we was awake, but the pig was nowhere to be found.

The mirror was still operational, and he read through Anna's reports, and Carmine's, and wondered how much their own talent gurus were guiding them, instilling them with a sense of reverence that skewed their reports, how much they struggled to make the end of his arc tragic, or heroic, or were they trying for a larger part for their clients: Carmine misreads Jacob's coherence badly, he falls apart, Carmine goes on a narrative of redemption. Or maybe Jacob would be the hero and the face of the revolution, but Anna would get to assert herself more as a shaper of policy and marketing, using his fame to push her own agenda. There were so many angles, and he wasn't even sure that Paul was real, or that the mirror was real, or if both were symptoms of a serious break-down, of incoherence. If I'm supposed to be faking in-coherence, I'm doing a hell of a job, he thought. And a voice answered: "You cannot know if you are acting or not, if you are manifesting a simulation of incoherence, or truly becoming incoherent. It will occur, and you must hide the kernel deep, if the kernel exists. If it is not suffi-ciently deep, they will know, and your plot will be discov-ered. If it does not exist, then everything you know is a symptom of your decohering. It may be you have a thou-sand names, it may be you have lived a thousand lives, and each supplants the last, crushes the lives that came before under greater and greater pressure, strata of past identities fossilized, subsumed in magma, borne down to the core—except there is no core, only churning, only the action of solid to fluid to gas and back again, only fire, only the darkness between."

He looked down at Anna, aware he had had been mouthing the words in his head, hoping he was not actually vocalizing. She did not stir. The pig was nowhere to be seen. Jacob focused on the tick tick of the kernel, the tiny hammering that stayed steady as a metronome as the memories came again, tidal, the memories and names and all of it, each wave louder, each wave more diffuse.

Anna shook him shoulder gently. "João? Love? Wake and eat, my dear." A cup of something hot, a plate of yellow protein supplement, a purplish vegetable mush of some kind.

"Yes," Jacob mumbled, trying to shake the fur from his eyes. He had not slept, but lay like a shipwrecked man, tossed at last to a stony beach. "Thank you."

She smiled and bent to kiss his forehead. He recoiled slightly, but enough that she felt it. He liked Elaine well enough, but she knew what he was, why would she try to force this intimacy on him? She frowned, and he saw her enter net space, messaging someone, checking some chart or another. Neek was such a stickler for documentation, he found it alternately endearing and annoying. Now it was annoying.

"Come on, Neek, enough, I'm awake."

Anna snapped back to stare at him, then held her hands in front of her, palms out, tips of her thumbs together: "João. João. João. Nine Six Element Seven. João."

He shook his head again. Something in his display flickered, and he took the cup from Anna, drank, and felt a burst of pharma, some kind of stimulant. "I'm ok," he said again, "Anna."

She pursed her lips and furrowed her brow, but he ate and chatted and somehow convinced her he was alright. As they walked to the meeting, he built a flag for "João" that would pop into a corner of his display whenever she, or anyone else, used that name.

Carmine met them in the lobby of the general meeting room. Jacob saw that the meeting room doors were larger versions of the elaborately carved door to the room where he'd met with Barnaby. He found it difficult to pull his gaze away from the pattern, whorls of line and angle that seemed both symmetrical and asymmetrical, a key, a code, a handshake.

"Feeling well?" Carmine asked.

"Yes, fine, just a little nervous," he replied.

Carmine performed a few perfunctory scans, and did a final report, which Jacob did not bother to snag. It would all be over soon enough.

"Look a little tired, have trouble sleeping again?"

"Yes, some, Anna gave me some pharma, that helped, but I woke and had trouble getting to sleep again. Nothing to worry about, just nerves, really," he said, pushing against the need to call him Siegleman, to call him Santoor, to punch his pasty shitting face in.

"Good, good, maybe something to help make it through the meeting, then?"

"No, I mean, if you have something in case, I can take it if I feel shaky."

"Yes, just the thing, just like you scripted it. Here, you

can pop it in your thigh, less obvious that way." He handed Jacob a palm-sized pink pig's head. Jacob stared.

"Here they come, put that in your pocket," Carmine said, as Mbete and the rest of the luminaries paraded around a corner, flunkies in tow. Jacob gasped, he's seen so many of them die, and he'd killed at least one, maybe two, but not them, avatars, skins, he repeated to himself, they aren't real, we are all just skins.

"Ah, the man of the hour—of the next century!" Barnaby bellowed, slapping Jacob's shoulder. Jacob managed a weak smile, and a wave to the newsbots hovering above.

Barnaby swiped the air and the doors to the conference room swung open. Jacob found himself entranced again, then felt a hand at his back, Anna's, pushing him along. The conference room swept to the left, away from the doors in an enormous, gently curving arc. At the end of the arc, the room swelled to surround a huge, wooden table, several dozen chairs, and, on the wall, an old style vid projector, the kind used during product launches and other ceremonial occasions. It was religious symbol, and most people found it cumbersome and hard to pay attention to, but the symbolic weight was crucial to the eyeballs watching remotely.

Mbete began, Barnaby began, Kinch began, pontificating. Jacob could not look at him, or at anyone, for long, as all of their different skins, all the persons he'd known each of them to be, fought for presence, each person was a thousand persons, a thousand haircuts, childhood scars, swatches of makeup. The table alone remained unchanging, the carvings on it beckoning to him, soothing him.

"João Sandoval!" The flag popped, and Jacob knew they were applauding him. He squinted and waved, letting the flickering skins wash over him just as he'd let the memories wash over him the might before. Tick, tick, tick.

Anna tapped his thigh, and when he turned to her— a few seconds too late, he was sure, having been unable to stop staring at the table—she pointed at his pocket, where the pig head was, where he felt it, wiggling. He took it out and let it bite down on his thigh. A surge of pink noise blossomed in his mind, and he looked up at the vidscreen. The payload had dropped, and everyone in the room watched as it ate away at the NAS security net, over the infodams, through the breakwalls, emerging first from three interstices, then from a hundred, then from a whole screen full of holes that it opened and re-opened, until the whole net was in tatters. The cheering roared up from the gathered crowed like a diver surfacing from deep water, and João felt himself roaring along with them. Tick. Tick. Tick. The crowd was moving slowly, oozing, a fist upraised took minutes to go a few centimeters, mouths shouting in victory seemed contorted, torn apart, parts of bodies flying everywhere, bloodless, noses and ears and eyes dropping off, floating around the room, smashing into each other and exploding in to tinier particles.

Jacob stared at the table. He could not look elsewhere, saw that it was into the pattern he needed to go, that the carvings were the backdoor, that was where he needed to drop the payload, so he needed to take it with him, the snarling maze of line and half-shape. Anna shouted in his ear, put her hand on his neck, his moment of triumph, the stain seeping across the front of his jumpsuit as he wet himself. Tick. He felt it, felt the piss turning cold, felt Anna crying into his neck, felt Carmine and Mbete pushing his chair off to the side, to the periphery of the scene, running scans, fiddling, but it was no good, he had the pattern there, in front of him, and when they switched off his display and cut him off from the net, is was still there, glowing in front of him, and he dove down inside it and followed the lines, pure and unfettered by memory or knowledge, and he knew he had won, and that he would win again and again, and would it never end, and tick, tick, tick, there was nothing else, the metronome, tick, tick, the white walls, the pattern, swimming the lines like each was a river, the pattern was the kernal, ticking, the master glitch into which he would drop his payload, and if there was nothing after that then his work was done, and if there was something else, he would bend his back to it and work until his angels could work no more.